Jackie e Ken

WALLIS SIMPSON'S DIARY

(1934)

Helen Batting

*with all best wishes
from Helen
– as you have never known him!*

Pen Press Publishers Ltd

First published in Great Britain by
Pen Press Publishers Ltd
39, Chesham Road
Brighton
BN2 1NB

ISBN 1-905621-12-4

Printed and bound in the UK

A catalogue record of this book is available from
the British Library

Cover design by Jacqueline Abromeit
Jacket photographs © Daily Mail & Mail on Sunday

WALLIS SIMPSON'S DIARY

(1934)

INTRODUCTION

The future wife of King Edward VIII was born Bessie Wallis Warfield on 19 June 1895, the child of Teackle Warfield and Alice Montague. Although both parents were from the Confederacy establishment of Baltimore, the union was not looked on with favour by either family since Teackle was already suffering from tuberculosis; worse still, their child was illegitimate and it was not until five months after her birth that they were married.

Teackle duly died only two years later and Alice moved in with her widowed sister, Bessie Merryman; to avoid confusion, her daughter became known as Wallis rather than Bessie. To make ends meet she took in sewing and then some years later rented a boarding house before making an equally unfortunate match with John Rasin, an alcoholic who likewise soon left her a widow. In the meantime Wallis' education was taken in hand by her banker uncle and railroad company chairman Solomon Warfield, who sent her to a fashionable girls' boarding school in the country. It was there that she first developed a crush on Edward, Prince of Wales, heir to the British throne and only a year older than herself, plastering her room with photographs of him and following his every move in the papers.

After coming out as a debutante, she accepted the invitation of a married cousin to join her at an airbase in Florida and quickly won the hand of a naval pilot, Win Spencer from Chicago; she was soon emulated in turn by her best friend from school, Mary Kirk, marrying French military diplomat Jacques Raffray. Wallis then accompanied her husband to San Diego, but he proved to be no more sober than her stepfather, and when the Prince of Wales paid an official visit on the battleship *Renown* with his cousin, Louis Mountbatten, she and Win found themselves excluded from the guest-list at the welcoming banquet.

Wallis now left him to go to Washington where she took up with the Argentinian First Secretary, but when this liaison fell through she rejoined Win at his new posting in Canton, the main port of southern China and near neighbour to the British colony Hong Kong. The reconciliation proved short-lived, however, and she took off for Shanghai and Peking where she enjoyed a number of other affairs, notably with the Italian Naval Attaché, Alberto da Zara, and the 21-year-old Count Galleazzo Ciano, son of one of Italian dictator Mussolini's leading supporters. After falling pregnant and undergoing a backstreet abortion which left her infertile for life, she decided to obtain a divorce from Win and returned to America, where she presently met shipbroker Ernest Simpson, the son of British-born Louis Solomon (whose own father had emigrated from Russia). Wallis soon persuaded him to leave his wife and young daughter in New York for her, and they were married in London in July 1928 shortly after Ernest had been transferred by his father to take over the firm's office there.

Taking the lease on a spacious 3-bedroom flat in Bryanston Court, they were introduced to London society by Ernest's elder sister, Maud Kerr-Smiley, before being taken under the wing of more prominent hostesses such as Lady Sybil Colefax, Syrie Maugham (wife of writer Somerset Maugham and a leading interior designer who helped Wallis redecorate the flat) and the American Emerald Cunard. King George V and Queen Mary stood at its apex, but they rarely ventured into the social whirl (he preferring to spend his evenings with his stamp collection) which instead rotated around the fun-loving Prince of Wales. To the despair of his parents, Edward showed no sign of wanting to marry and settle down, and indeed he would shortly ditch his long-term mistress, Freda Dudley Ward, in favour of Thelma Furness, the estranged wife of shipping magnate Viscount Furness and one of the three famously beautiful Morgan sisters from New York; the other two were Gloria Vanderbilt, whose millionaire but alcoholic husband had died after only two years of marriage, and Consuelo ('Connie') Thaw, whose husband Benny was First Secretary at the US Embassy in London and later Oslo. Edward's brother George (later Duke of Kent) was strongly suspected of being bisexual and led a similarly risqué existence, but the other two, Albert, Duke of York (later to become King George VI and recently married to Lady Elizabeth Bowes-Lyon, the future Queen Mother) and the intellectually-challenged Henry (later Duke of Gloucester) were both models of propriety by contrast. (The youngest, John, had been born epileptic and kept in seclusion until he died at the age of fourteen.)

The Wall Street Crash of 1929 led to massive unemployment in the industrial sector and progressive deterioration in business generally, including Ernest's shipbroking; worse still for Wallis, she was caught in mid-Atlantic on the way home to attend to her dying mother and was thus prevented from cashing the railroad shares which she had recently inherited from her uncle. However, the political situation in Britain remained stable: the coalition National Government formed under Prime Minister Ramsay MacDonald was re-elected with a huge majority in 1930 and the British Empire continued to control a quarter of the globe. The dominant theme of the day was still the fear of another World War (in 1933 the Oxford Union famously voted against 'serving King and Country'), and most people were unperturbed by the rise of Hitler and his 'efficient' Nazis to power in Germany. Sir Oswald 'Tom' Mosley had broken away from the Labour Party to form his own New Party (shortly to become the British Union of Fascists) and enjoyed widespread support, particularly among his fellow aristocrats who were equally happy to ignore his notoriety as a womaniser: married to ex-Viceroy of India Lord Curzon's daughter Cynthia (who would die in 1933), he was conducting simultaneous affairs with Diana Guinness (née Mitford) and his sister-in-law Baba, wife of Edward's faithful equerry, 'Fruity' Metcalfe.

London society thus felt free to continue to concentrate on its traditional round of entertainments, albeit with a reduced number of servants. The Season opened in the spring as usual with the Presentation of debutantes at Court, followed by the Chelsea Flower Show, Royal Ascot, the Eton v Harrow at Lord's and the Regattas at Henley and Cowes, before dispersing to shoot grouse in August and ride to hounds in the autumn. The men met over leisurely lunches at their clubs and the women at the fashionable hotels, before meeting up again in the evening for 'KTs' (cocktails), theatre parties, dinners and dancing the night away at nightclubs like the Embassy and Kit Kat.

Wallis wrote to her aunt Bessie Merryman, 'I've had my mind made up to meet him [Edward] ever since I've been here,' and her moment came in January 1931 at a weekend country house party given by Thelma Furness. She set out with Ernest undeterred by a heavy cold and the prospect of having to carry off a curtsy for the first time, and on the Sunday she seized the opportunity to seat herself next to him at lunch. He was duly impressed by her boldness, but she was unable to capitalise on it immediately as shortly afterwards he departed on a three-months royal tour of South America.

In his absence Wallis rapidly set about planning her next move - her Presentation at Court in June. She wrote off again to her aunt for the notes on her divorce decree which the Lord Chamberlain required as proof of her innocent-party status, adding that in the event of any complications 'If I ever see the Prince of Wales again, I'll ask him to help.' It proved unnecessary, but she did meet him again in May at Thelma's party given for him on his return when he came over to her and said 'How nice to see you again ...' For the Presentation itself she was largely kitted out in clothes borrowed from Thelma and her sister, Connie Thaw; they succeeded in drawing a nod of approval from Edward, and it was Thelma again who

3

asked her and Ernest back for drinks afterwards to meet him at greater length. In accordance with protocol Edward left first, but when Wallis emerged with Ernest she found him waiting outside to offer them a lift back to their flat in Bryanston Court. On their arrival there he declined her invitation to come up for another drink, explaining that he had to make an early start the next day, but he added that he would be delighted to 'if you would be so kind as to invite me again.'

It was not until next January that he took her up on it, but the reward for her patience was an invitation to join one of his regular weekend parties at Fort Belvedere, Edward's country retreat near Sunningdale. Over the next two years these reciprocal visits grew gradually more frequent; at the same time Ernest's shipbroking firm became increasingly hit by the Depression, causing him to spend more and more time abroad in search of business. Wallis too was obliged to economise, reducing her staff to a personal maid, parlour maid and cook, but she was still able to enjoy some excursions abroad of her own: first to the South of France in an all-girl party (which gave rise to some scandal) with Connie Thaw, her other sister Gloria Vanderbilt and Nada, Marchioness of Milford Haven (the sister-in-law of Louis Mountbatten, Edward's cousin and constant companion), and then in March 1933 to New York; just as the liner was casting off a messenger arrived with a telegram from Edward wishing her bon voyage and a speedy return. To celebrate the latter, he threw a birthday party for her at the fashionable restaurant Quaglino's and presented her with a rare orchid, adding 'Feed it regularly and it'll flower within the year.'

To Wallis, a fervent devotee of clairvoyance since her childhood, these words seemed to indicate that one particularly cherished prediction was about to be fulfilled...

Helen Batting

DRAMATIS PERSONAE

Wallis,	formerly married to US Navy pilot Win Spencer and now to Anglo-American shipbroker Ernest Simpson
TLM (The Little Man),	= Edward, Prince of Wales
The Woebegones,	= The Royal Family; Big Chief = the King, Squaw = the Queen, Brer = Edward's brothers
Louis Simpson/ Mr Tightwad,	Ernest's father, born Louis Solomon in London
Cain,	Wallis' personal maid
Beckham,	her temporary replacement
Thelma Furness,	Edward's second mistress, sister of Connie Thaw and Gloria Vanderbilt
Connie Thaw,	sister of Thelma Furness, married to US Embassy official Bennie
Freda Dudley Ward,	Edward's first mistress (1917-31); daughter Angela (Angie)
'Fruity',	Edward's equerry, and Baba Metcalfe, mistress of Fascist leader Oswald Mosley
Osborne,	Edward's butler/valet
Aunt Bessie/ Big Bucks,	= Mrs Merryman, sister of Wallis' mother

Louis and Edwina Mountbatten, Second cousins to Edward

Mary Raffray,   Wallis' schoolfriend (and later to marry Ernest
                          Simpson)

Chuck Spencer,   New York dealer in Royal memorabilia

Emerald Cunard,   formerly Mary Bourke of San Francisco,
                          a leading society hostess

Colin Buist,   ex-Navy friend of Edward, married to Gladys

Brig.-Gen. 'G' Trotter,   Groom-in-Waiting to Edward

Hugh Lloyd Thomas,   Private Secretary to Edward

Conte Galleazzo Ciano,   Mussolini's son-in-law and Wallis' lover in
                          China c1924

Guy Trundle,   ex-RAF pilot and MI5 agent working under cover
                          as a Ford salesman

JANUARY

A False Start

(Editor's note: although Wallis has now been living in London for five years, she retains her American vocabulary and spelling - and occasional misspelling. For the sake of clarity I have italicised quotations, inscriptions, ships' names and publications except for book titles, for which I have used capitals. The pasted press cuttings - with Wallis' occasional comments - have been reproduced as faithfully as possible.)

Monday 1 January

Finances: Simpson, Spence & Whoever still heading for the bow-wows according to Ernest, and his tight-wad Pop is even trying to talk him into putting some of his own cash into it - fat chance, if he saw the state of our books!

Staff: chauffeur + motor gone already - but that needn't be so bad if it makes The Little Man (TLM from now on) more likely to come up with a lift - and the housemaid going on Saturday. That'll bring me down to Cain and the deaf (and dumb) cook, though I still haven't given up on getting that treasure Mrs. Ralph back again from Lady Curzon. Let's pray to God I can, or we'll be on Brown Windsor for ever and a day - TLM's childhood diet, so he told me last time at the Fort [Belvedere], which converted him to all the colors of the rainbow for life.

State of Play in the Major League: Thelma [Furness] still heads the table, Freda [Dudley Ward] apparently hanging in and ditto who knows how many other passing fancies, but no other big hitters that I can see and with a few more good pitches from yours truly, who knows...

Horoscope: I'll forget Madame Claire in Cain's *Daily Sketch* for once and go for what that gipsy dame Evangeline Adams said was in store for me when I went to her feeling down on my luck back in 1926 - heading up for divorce from Win and losing the one and only job I've ever landed in my life. *'You will lead a woman's life, Wallis - marrying, divorcing and marrying again, with several emotional crises. Between the ages of 40 and 50 you will win fame and exercise considerable power of some kind relating to a man.'* Well, I'm 39 this June, so this looks like the year that's going to set it all up, girl!

Court Circ: The Holy Family, inc. Brer Bertie of York and Lizzie, his fat cook of a wife, are still hunkered down in the Sandringham House of Mirth (you've got nothing on that one, Edith Wharton!) except for TLM, who quit yesterday. He was aiming to fly down but the fog knocked that one on the head and Big Chief Woebegone (his name for him, not mine) barred him taking the Royal train, so how he made it to Thelma's on time is anybody's guess - where there's a will, there's a way?

There were 16 of us for dinner - Connie & Benny [Thaw] over from the Oslo Embassy with their South African kike pal Mala Brand, Fruity (and with a face to match) & Baba Metcalfe, Tiger somebody from the Spanish Embassy (theirs, not ours), Julia Diercks minus the two fingers she lost in a motor smash last month, poor girl (though the Chinks would say that's a bonus in bed), Fred & Gebe Bate (he's just come over for Nat. Broadcasting - should be worth keeping sweet), Mrs. Russell (ditto - father's a Hoover), Miss Giantess Frazer (but at least she won't be competing for TLM!) and another couple called Dodero who dropped out en route to the Kit Kat and so I never got to talk to (according to Ernest, the family runs most of the shipping in Argentina and they'd taken TLM by the hand during his tour there a couple of years back - so there's somebody in the shipping business who's off the breadline after all?) Tried to persuade Ernest to do ditto, but he insisted on sticking around even when we went back to Tiger's flat. Finally shook him when we rolled up the mat for a tango - and when who should pass him on the way in but 'the man of the hour', Tom [Oswald] Mosley! Next thing he had us all madly doing the goose-step, TLM getting his leg up as high as the best of them, ie Baba - with a helping hand from Tom under her butt. OK, he's her brother-in-law, but this was something else - I must remember to check those two out with Emerald [Cunard] at our next lunch date.

Back here at 6.30am, just as Ernest was getting up again for the City.

Up about noon and hardly dared look in the mirror - mouth/nose seem bigger/longer than ever, and still can't decide whether to risk having the mole cut out. Granny Warfield used to tell me to look in it every day 'for your conscience, because only you can see it', but it's funny, I've never spotted it yet!

Outside the fog was so bad I couldn't even face diving round the block to check out the start of the M[arshall] & Snelgrove sale, so decided to spend the day resting up from last night and the whole Xmas whoopee. Polished off the last of Mr. Tightwad's Virginia ham, a big deal that was - if he'd taken a leaf out of Aunt Bessie Big Bucks's checkbook and written us another $300 we wouldn't be down to our last cent like we are now. Still, I shouldn't complain I guess about my haul after TLM's antique side-table - especially as he let me pick it myself out of Partridge's window in Bond Street to let me know it wasn't something off the junk-pile that he gets gifted from glad-handers all over the Brit Empire and keeps saying he can't get rid of fast enough.

As for Thelma's ring, I felt I had to wear it last night if I wanted to keep in with her even though she'd probably picked it up for a couple of dimes in one of those little second-hand shops down the back end of the King's Road in Chelsea - and of course TLM just had to say how good it looked on me right there in front of her, darn it.

I won't have it on tonight when they come here, that's for sure. Just the 8 - Thaws, Grants included - for dinner before TLM takes us on to the Chelsea Arts Ball. Fancy dress, of course, and still can't decide whether to go for my Odol toothpaste costume (and maybe get a 'Little' squeeze!) or play safe with Cleopatra. Tried to get out of him what he's going as, but he wouldn't let on. Ernest's sticking to his bottle of Guinness outfit - say no more...

Wednesday 3 January

(Back to Madame Claire) *The quick-witted planet Mercury is moving into your sign, which may lead to a situation where the whys and wherefores of an opportunity for profit are blindingly obvious to you, but not to others. Tempting though it may be, you should be careful about coming out with it, both to protect your own advantage and to avoid causing possible offence.*
Remember: more haste, less speed - especially when you start treading on other people's toes.

Still trying to figure out what the message is when I put *The Times* (nothing on TLM in the Court Circ. today) back on his side-table and then of course it hit me - if he's really serious about offloading his junk-pile, then who's in a better position to help out than yours truly? The folks back home will sign their lives away for anything with a Royal crest on it, if I can still go by that time way back in 1920 when he and Dickie Mountbatten called in on some battleship at San Diego and the whole of California was ready to break the bank to get hold of signed programs for the Mayoral Ball they threw for him (and to think I could have gotten myself on the guest-list and set out my stall if it hadn't been for that skunk Win - then I could have been spared Ernest, but better late than never, I guess). I'd have to find somebody over there to handle them who could be trusted to keep their trap shut (Mary R[affray]?) and they'd have to have their cut too of course, but that would still leave plenty over and boy, could I use it just now. I wouldn't put it past some of that army of flunkies of his to have a racket going already, so you'd better watch out for those toes, Wallis, like the lady says…

Talking of toes, Ernest's lumbering around in his bottle had mine pulped to mincemeat by the time the party broke up. I'd almost fixed on going as Cleopatra when I had a sudden big idea - and just as well I did or I'd have gone snap with Baba! 'I say, I wonder what this is?' TLM cracked, grabbing hold of her boa. 'Oh of course, what a silly asp I am!' Fruit-Face obediently fell about laughing like he was fit to bust, and by the color of his face he might have done just that if Baba hadn't fetched him one with an elbow in the ribs. TLM himself was got up in one of new pal Adolf's brown shirts complete with swanky swastika armband. When Fruit-Face weighed in again with 'Just as well Tom Mosley isn't here or he'd think you were taking the micky out of him, what?' TLM came back with 'Oh. I don't know why he would - it's not black, you know,' which really put him back in his box.

'And who are you supposed to be, Wallis?'

'You should be able to tell, if anyone can.'

'Oh, really? Why's that?'

'Because the lady was a bit of a royal favourite.'

'Ah, I see… I've got it - Nell Gwynne.'

'No, you're a couple of centuries out.'

'Oh, you mean one of Henry's wives, then. Dashed if I can remember any of their names, though.'

'You don't have to, you're getting colder.'

'Colder, you say? Can't have that. All right, tell me, then.'

'Alice Keppel.'

'Grandpapa's bit of fluff, you mean? I say, that's getting warmer, what?'

It was on the tip of my tongue to come back with 'Well, what about it, then?' but then I reckoned that even you, Wallis Warfield, can't have that big a nerve, surely, so I let it go - for the moment, anyhow…

One look at the fog outside is enough to show I won't be missing too much by resting my poor feet up again for the day. Called Mary after lunch - 9AM New York time - which should have been early enough to catch her before she went out, but no reply. Back on the loose again (like someone else I know!) ?

Thursday 4 January

You have the knack of persuading others to take you into their confidence, but beware of giving them the impression that you have nothing of interest in your own life to offer in return. Offering sympathy is one thing, but allowing yourself to be exploited is quite another. Even those you regard as your closest friends may be tempted to take advantage of you to talk you into making commitments which you may later come to regret, and if so you must prepare yourself to make a stand. Remember: once a doormat, always a doormat.

Connie called at 7.30 with Ernest only just out of the door and me still in bed waiting for my breakfast, so I guessed something was up. She was following Bennie back to Oslo on tomorrow's boat and didn't know when she'd be over again, so how about the Ritz for lunch - on her? Well, a meal ticket is a meal ticket whatever Madame Claire might say…

We were almost into the sweets before she came to the point, which was that Sis Gloria was being taken to court by their crazy mother for the custody of Gloria Junior. Apparently they'd been spitting fire at each other practically from the moment the kid was born, and the first time they'd come over to Europe together the old bat threw a fit about her being allowed out on deck. Then when G had set up with her Boche princeling in Paris she began putting it around that they were plotting to put a pillow over the kid's head. That was enough for the guy to see just what kind of a madhouse he was getting into, and so he'd legged it back to Germany with some Greek royal and left them to it.

'And then?'

'Well, they patched things up eventually and got back over to New York again with a Swiss nanny they'd picked up in London. G moved into a separate apartment with Junior and everything seemed just fine till she was half way over the Atlantic again when she got this cable from the nanny saying "Gloria Junior in hospital for serious operation, suggest you turn around at Southampton". So of course she did just that, but what do you reckon she found when she got back? The kid dancing around with nothing more than a plaster on her little finger!'

'So she fired the nanny?'

'She tried, naturally, but the girl was in Mom's pay, of course - along with the butler and chauffeur. G may have married a Vanderbilt, but we weren't born Morgans for nothing either, I don't have to remind you. Then they started working on the kid, making out that G was failing her as a mother dragging her around Europe while she lived it up with the Boche and one or two others.'

'And so? Aren't widows allowed to make a bit of merry?'

13

'Yes, but there's a bit more to it than that. Remember that week the three of us had with Nada [Milford-Haven] in Cannes a couple of years back?'

'Of course. We had a whole load of fun together, didn't we?' (Did we ever!)

'That's just the problem, don't you see? G's gotten wind they're going after the maids in the hotel to give evidence.'

'Is that right?' I saw OK - and what was coming next...

'Yes. Wallis darling, I wanted to ask you if you wouldn't mind doing the two of us a bit of a favor. If the worst comes to the worst and it does go to court, we were wondering if you wouldn't mind very much making a statement that nothing like that happened.' She must have seen my shutters go down, because she went on 'You don't have to give an answer right now, of course, or even before I take off tomorrow. You can always let Thelma know - I guess you'll need time to think it over.'

She was right there. Either way TLM's going to get to hear about it, and what about my chances then? Unless I go over onto the attack and secure my position first, as Win used to quote me from his military training manuals...

Saturday 6 January

For someone as competitive and confident of your own ability as yourself, it is surprising how prone you can be to bouts of self-doubt. This is particularly so when the Moon is moving through that sector of your chart that is concerned with your most deeply held hopes and wishes. During this phase you find it hard to accept seeing others find success, but begrudging it to them won't bring your own success any nearer. Not even you can win all the prizes.

Fog, fog and still more fog - is this hell-hole of a place ever going to see the light of day again? It still doesn't stop Ernest heading off for his morning stint in the office.

'I thought you said business was dropping off by the day,' I reminded him.

'Yes, that's right, it is. According to the Chamber of Shipping's latest figures, the tonnage of the British merchant fleet is now less than what it was before the beginning of the war in 1914. Can you imagine that?'

'Is that so?' In fact, I didn't have a problem with it at all - with the sort of dim-witted saps at the steering wheel that he produces here for business dinners, it'd be more of a surprise if there was a single ship still above surface.

'Yes. There should be a law against selling off our ships to foreigners at knock-down prices, like that oily little Greek Onassis.'

That was rich, coming from the grandson of Louis Solomon not so long out of a Russian ghetto! 'So what's so bad about him?'

'What's good about him, more like it. Half his ships have either mysteriously gone up in smoke or been run aground, but not before he's insured them for twice what he bought them at, of course.'

'Well, I'd have thought that was good news for you. I mean, that way he's cutting down the competition, isn't he?'

'Maybe, but every time it happens Lloyd's puts up insurance rates all round by another ten per cent, so there's even less profit left for everyone else - unless you're running drugs, like most people seem to think he is with the ships he's got left.'

'No kidding?'

'No. Of course his father was one of the biggest dealers in Turkey until they ran the Greeks out of the country, so I suppose South America must have seemed the next best place to set up. They say he's as thick as thieves with that Dodero lot we met the other night, and nobody asks too many questions where they make all their money from either.'

'At least they make it. Maybe we should be getting to know them better too.'

'Well, I don't know that I'd want to be seen associating with them, I'm sure.'

'Oh, come off it, Ernest! They'd say just the same about being seen with a guy who goes into the office on a Saturday, I'd guess.'

Unless the office happened to be on the top floor of the Cumberland Hotel just round the corner here, that is. If Mary wasn't back in NY I might have my suspicions, the way he and she were starting to get fresh with each other the last time she was over...

Thinking of her reminded me of my little business proposition, but what I forgot was the time difference and when I called, the voice that answered wasn't any too pleased at being disturbed - and it wasn't female, either.

'Jesus Christ, can't a guy have his fun in peace? Just get off the line, you nosy bitch!'

'Who is it, Ari darling?' I heard Mary say, then after a few more words from him I won't repeat she took over. 'Wallis, what a surprise! You're calling from London? Oh well, that explains it then. And don't worry about my little Greek friend here - his table manners are just terrible, but when it comes to serving a girl with the main course he sure knows his knife from his fork, if you know what I mean, darling.'

Yes, I know exactly what you mean, darling.

Sunday 7 January

No Cain, no *Daily Sketch*, no Madame Claire, so how's a poor girl meant to know what to do with herself?

I still wasn't going to fall for any of Ernest's ideas of fun, though.

'Why don't we take a little trip up to Oxford? I'd love to take another look at those wonderful flying buttresses at Christchurch Cathedral, and perhaps we could stay on for Evensong if the choir are singing. I think you'd find that an unforgettable experience, honeybunch - quite unforgettable.'

'Maybe, but haven't you forgotten something?'

'What's that?'

'We had to ditch the motor last month. Remember?'

'Yes, of course, but there's an excellent train service there from Paddington, you know.'

'Ernest, I don't care how good the trains are, they're not going to stop me shivering to pieces once we get there.'

'Well, we can always go and rub some brasses in the University Church if you want to warm up.'

'It wouldn't be brasses I'd be rubbing, that's for sure. And if we want to keep warm, why don't we just stay home and do something useful, like giving the kitchen another coat of paint?'

'Repaint the kitchen? But I only did it a couple of months ago.'

'It was all of six months ago, to be precise - before we had the Prince to dinner for the Fourth of July. Just as well you did too, the way he kept popping in to see what was cooking and giving Mrs. Ralph kittens.'

'All right, six months then, but I still can't see why it's really necessary to do it again quite so soon. I mean, it's not as if he'll be coming back again in a hurry, is it?'

'Well, I'm not so sure about that. Something he said the other night made me think that he was pretty much expecting another invitation - and soon.'

'I say, do you really think so? In that case…'

To keep myself from interrupting the good work I took off after lunch to the Curzon for the new Shirley Temple movie. When I got back I found the sap hadn't bothered to do behind the fridge, so of course I had him do the whole wall over again. Not that he kicked up too much, as when it comes to licking Royal toes, Ernest's right up there with the rest - or rather, down there!

Monday 8 January

Money worries may seem to be piling up, but this is not the time to let them get on top of you. Today's New Moon coincides with a happy alignment between the carefree Mercury and the bountiful Neptune, signalling that for once no harm will come from allowing your heart to rule your head and the state of your bank balance. Something which might seem like a wild extravagance could pay for itself handsomely in the long run - and you might never get the same chance again.

First day of the sales and belting with rain, but with a fair wind like that behind her there's no holding our Wallis. Headed straight for Harrods, where there were terrific bargains but terrific scrums too and all I came away with was a pair of leather gloves reduced to five shillings - and even then some hell-cat almost snatched them out of my hands before I could pay for them.

A deal more civilised at Harvey Nicks (as usual), even if the prices weren't so hot. The best were the velvet jackets down from 39/6 to 29/6, and I picked one up in a shade of plum red which I reckoned set off my complexion rather well. They had a new line in half-length knitted wool with fur-trimmed collar and sleeves which weren't in the sale, and I really fell for one in tangerine - I don't usually go for such bright colors, but it seemed a perfect match with TLM's brilliant yellow turtle-neck sweater which he had on the last time at the Fort. It was priced at all of nine guineas, but they said they wouldn't be getting any more in this season and so I had to go for it. Wound up in Shoes with a pair of Delman crocodile-skin low-heels (lower anyhow than TLM's!) reduced to 24/6.

Stopped off at Debenhams on the way back and almost went for broke on a white ermine wrap at forty guineas, until I realized Ernest would hit the ceiling. He came on strong enough as it was at our weekly accounts session - 'Do you realize you've just gone over your entire winter clothes allowance in one? Well, you'll just have to take it out of the food budget, which means no more dinner parties or girls' lunches for the next month.'

He'll change his tune fast enough if TLM drops any more hints, I'll bet my bottom dollar…

Tuesday 9 January

Court Circular: *YORK HOUSE ST. JAMES'S PALACE His Royal Highness The Prince Of Wales received the Ambassador to Italy, His Excellence Count Dino Grandi, this morning. His Royal Highness wishes it to be known that he has decided to postpone his proposed tour of the Bahamas Islands colony indefinitely.*

That's the first I've heard he was even planning on going. For a bit of 'rest and recreation' with Thelma?? And now, dare I hope, there's been a bust-up????

I didn't have to pin my ears back for long - I was just getting into the tub when Emerald called and I fixed for lunch at the Savoy tomorrow. If anyone could throw some light on the matter (plus the Baba-Tom Mosley set-up), she could. 'You don't get higher up the social ladder than her,' I told the Keeper of the Purse when he got in, and of course he OK'd it without so much as a blink.

Wednesday 10 January

Given the air of worldliness which your wide experience of life has given you, you mustn't be surprised when others seek you out in the belief that you know something that they don't. You may tend to find this tiresome, but you should guard against the temptation to brush them off; no one is all-knowing, and one day you might find yourself needing to seek out even the most unlikely source in turn! Remember too that when you do want to keep something to yourself, success in guarding secrets only comes with constant practice.

Dead right, Madame Claire - it was me who ended up being given the Third Degree!

Granted her 'wider experience of life', I should have seen it coming, I guess - what could poor humble Wallis Warfield's marriages to naval pilot Win Spencer and ship-broker Ernest Simpson possibly have over the daughter of the Comstock Silver Mine magnate, wife of the Cunard Steamship Line owner, mistress of leading author George Moore, star conductor Thomas Beecham, etc, etc? She wanted to know every last detail about our Chelsea Arts whoopee, what TLM had said about the Bahamas, why he'd been going there, who he'd been planning on taking and for how long, etc. etc…

I had to tell her that was just as much news to me as it was to her and that if he'd been taking Thelma she'd have let the world know about it for sure. In the end the only thing she could come up with was that he was hoping to have a get-together with his millionaire pal Harry Oakes, who'd then been called away to sort out a strike at one of his mines in Canada. According to her, Big Chief Woebegone had been keeping TLM on a tight rein ever since he accused him of showing up in a boiler suit on some parade in India, and to lead any sort of life since he'd had to rely on the super-rich from wherever - eg, my new pals the Doderos.

'Well, after the Wall Street Crash none of us can afford to be too choosy, can we, darling?'

'That's right' - as if I'd ever had two cents to rub together, let alone stock certificates!

Another stand-off over the bill, she looking at me as if I was paying and me looking right back at her. In the end in we settled on splitting it (though I got away with my half of the tip).

Turned in early with a raw throat (maybe from yelling at Ernest over our lack of funds) - and only then realised I'd forgotten all about picking her brains on the Baba-Tom set-up. Still, that can wait…

Sunday 14 January

Fourth day in bed with a raging flu, and the first I've been able to even sit up and open my eyes properly - all thanks to my soaking at the sales, I guess. Insisted Ernest call the (new) doctor, who then started to get nosy about what I'd got up to in China (or rather, what had got up me). The nerve of it - as if he didn't have it all down in my notes on the botched abortion already, so I soon sent him packing and had Ernest run down to the all-week drugstore in Paddington for some more aspirin.

'So who was that who called?' I croaked when he got back.

'Called?'

'Yes. You know, while the doctor was here.'

'Oh, that. It was only Thelma. I said you were too ill to talk, but you'd ring her back some time in the week when you were better.'

'You did that? Ernest, really!'

'But that's what you told me to say if anyone rang, honeybunch.'

'Maybe, but not to somebody like that, you great sap. And now she'll have gone out for the day, I'll bet.'

But luckily for me (and Ernest) she hadn't.

'Wallis darling, what a surprise! Ernest quite convinced me you had one foot in the grave. How are you, you poor thing?'

'Oh, I'm fine - it's just the usual cold which is doing the rounds.'

'Oh, I see. So I can count you in for next weekend at the Fort, can I? If you're not doing anything better, that is?'

'No, of course not. (that was one stupid question that wasn't going to get a stupid answer!) And that includes Ernest, does it?'

'Why, yes of course, darling.'

'Oh, good.' Well, a girl can't have everything all at once, I guess.

'It's just a little farewell party The Little Man's throwing for me.'

'Farewell party?'

'Yes, I'm off to New York again in a couple of weeks to help out in Gloria's custody case. It's just the craziest thing ever, but I won't spoil the party going on about it, that's a promise, darling.'

Not much danger of that, darling…

Monday 15 January

No Cain, so sent Ernest to investigate and of course she's down with the flu too, or so she says - servants these days seem to take any excuse to dodge work, and if it had been anybody but Cain I'd have sent her cards straight down.

So no Madame Claire either and nothing in the Court Circ, but there on the front page of Cook's *Daily Mail* was

HUNTING GIRL THROWS PRINCE

His Royal Highness, the Prince of Wales, was involved in an accident while out hunting on Saturday with the Belvoir Hunt, but thankfully he escaped with no more than a severe shaking.

He told our reporter that he had been holding

a gate for a young lady, 23-year-old 'Millie'
Boulter, when she suddenly lunged forward into
him, catching him off balance and throwing
him. (photo of Mrs C. Boulter mounted)
Asked if it had spoilt his enjoyment of the day,
he replied with a laugh: 'Good Lord, no! We
had an absolute wizard time, killing three foxes
and a ginger thingie. Simply wizard!'
The latter was found to have been a cat
belonging to a local villager Mr. Andrew
Parkes. When told of this, His Royal Highness
graciously offered to make good the loss with
an inmate of the Battersea Lost Dogs Home.
He then drove back to London to attend a
dinner for 300 unemployed held at the
Kennington Oval Cricket Club, where he was
greeted with a hearty cheer. Apologising for
his late arrival, he joked 'It's usually me who
bowls the maiden over!'
This splendid example of His Royal Highness's
lively sense of humour set the tone for the
evening, which was greatly enjoyed by all those
present.

Let's hope they all enjoy it when I get to the pitcher's mound...

Wednesday 17 January

Still no sign of Cain returning to duty - or worse still of Ernest going sick before Saturday. The next time he says 'Well of course, if you went to bed with a cup of Horlicks every night like me you'd never catch anything' I really think I'll slam him.

Court Circ: *YORK HOUSE ST. JAMES'S PALACE His Royal Highness The Prince Of Wales this afternoon paid his annual visit to the Centre of the National Book Appeal for the Unemployed and graciously made a donation of one hundred books inscribed with his signature. Major Edward Metcalfe was in attendance.*

So there might be a few more for export stacked away some place - at the Fort? I've never had sight of any down there that I can recall, so better pack some Vick and get that big nose of yours back in working order, girl…

I had to be in the tub when Thelma called again of course - and from the Fort, so it cost me long distance to call her back.

All she wanted was to tell me not to dress up as there were only going to be the four of us plus the Metcalfes and Mountbattens. 'You've met Dickie and Edwina before of course, haven't you?'

'No, I don't think so,' I had to admit - all thanks to Win flunking that San Diego Mayoral Ball.

'Oh, you'll love them, they're both divine - especially him. You'll be driving down I guess, won't you?'

I almost said yes before I remembered, then made up some story about not having the motor because Ernest had run it into a lamp post in the fog.

'But he's OK, is he?'

'Yes, yes, he's fine. Just a little cut about the face, that's all.'

'Oh, I'm so glad. Well, I know Fruity and Baba are driving down, so why don't you give them a call? I'm sure they'll be happy to give you a lift.'

Which they were. The only problem was fixing Ernest's cut - I thought about letting him have it with the crockery the next time he picked a row at supper over my dress bills, but then I reckoned it would be simpler (and cheaper) just to sneak into the bathroom and loosen off his razor a turn or two, which did the trick.

Saturday 20 January

It all kicked off so well. Fruit-Face pitched up at half four as arranged and got us to the Fort on the dot of six as Thelma had ordered. Osborne the butler was right there as we pulled up, but no sooner had he got the bags out of the trunk than who should come skipping down the steps but TLM himself and even insisted on taking my vanity case for me! He still had his red hunting jacket on which had a great streak of mud on the back and made me wonder if the eager Beaver hadn't made another lunge at him.

Thelma was in the drawing room playing Lady Muck and handing out tea and cookies to the Mountbattens who'd gotten there ahead of us. Dickie was all action - jumping up, shaking hands, giving me and Baba a king-size

22

smacker on both cheeks - but Edwina just sat there looking down her nose like she was scared of picking up my flu bug.

We'd hardly had time for our first cup when TLM looked at his watch and announced that we'd all better get up to our tubs as he wanted us down again for KTs sharp at seven.

I was on the way out when I noticed a tapestry stretcher in the corner with a nearly-finished pattern of tulips and roses.

'Say, isn't that just beautiful,' I said. 'You are the cleverest girl, Thelma.'

'Oh no, it's not Toots who's the clever girl,' TLM came in, 'It's me!'

'You, sir?'

'Yes, it's my secret vice - and my only one, what? Ha, ha!'

'Well, I'm really impressed, I have to say. But how did you come to pick up such an accomplishment?'

'If I tell you, you must promise not to breathe a word about it to anybody - it would shock the country rigid if it got out. Cross your heart?'

'Cross my heart, sir.' (and how!)

'Well, while we were growing up Mama was always at it while we sat round her at teatime, and as there wasn't much else on she taught all of us to do it too. I'm the only one who still keeps it up, of course, but I find it so much less like hard work than reading, don't you know.'

'So that's why you gave all those books away the other day, is it?'

'Books?'

'You know, to the unemployed.'

'Oh, those. Yes, people will keep sending me them from all over the country. Never read any of them of course, and I have to get rid of them somehow - I always say to everyone who comes here just to help themselves. (Did you hear that, Mary?) Come and look in the library here - it's always full to bursting.'

It was a little room just off the bathroom that I'd never really noticed before. As we went in, he took a book out from the nearest shelf and showed it to me.

'See this one, WITHERING HEIGHTS - damnfool name, if ever there was one, what? Written by some woman called Bront - took me ages not to pronounce her as Brunt, mind you. Freda was on at me for years to read it and I tried the first few pages, but it was the most awful rot.'

The dollar sign flashed up again. 'Are any of them signed, sir?'

'Oh, nearly all of them. Let's take a look… Yes, here we are: *To His Royal Highness, The Prince Of Wales, with our greatest respect. Signed, John Thomas, Secretary of the Keighley and District Society of Undertakers.* Well, no wonder it was a stiff read, ha, ha!'

'Oh, I say, sir, that's a good one!' Fruit-Face roared and of course

Ernest had to take the cue and split his sides ditto, but I had to wait until we got upstairs to our room to find out what the hell the joke was.

Before that TLM insisted on giving us a conducted tour of the other rooms (the only times we'd been before there'd always been a whole houseful and we've never gotten to see most of them) - including even his own bathroom, which he'd had rigged up with a steam bath and was as pleased as all get out with. There was just one thing that seemed to be missing, though.

'Wondering where the loo paper thingie is, are you, Wallis?' he said, reading my mind.

'Well…'

'You needn't worry, that's Osborne's department.'

'You mean every time you need to…'

'That's right, I just ring for Osborne. That's what he's paid for, what?'

So now I know the difference between royalty and the rest of the human race, I guess…

We were given the Orange Room, which I wasn't too happy about as it clashed rather with my new tangerine woollen dress, but at least we had our very own tub and didn't have to walk the best part of half a mile to find one as we usually do in the average English country house. And by even more of a change, the water was hot - so hot in fact that by the time we got down again we only had time for one round of KTs (Manhattans) before we went into dinner.

Nothing fancy - oysters from the Duchy of Cornwall beds, T-bone steaks from the Windsor Royal Farm, blueberry tart from Balmoral and quails in aspic from Sandringham. I was sat between TLM and Fruit-Face, so no prizes for guessing who I gave most time to. Ernest had Thelma and Edwina and didn't seem to make too much mileage either way, and as soon as the coffee came in he grabbed a cigar and lit up without even stopping to take off the brand label - I could have died.

So it was relief all round when Thelma announced she felt like a dance and went over to the gramophone and put a record on. It was a tango that TLM had brought back from S. America, and so the next second he was on his feet too.

'Come on, Major, you're not going to miss out on this one, are you?' I put it to Fruit-Face, but whoever said it takes two to tango must have reckoned without him!

Anyhow, I was soon out of my agony because when it finished and Thelma turned to put another record on, up came TLM with 'Excuse me, Fruity, old bean', and away we went… Even better, the next up was *Tea For Two*, my number one favorite ever since the Shanghai Lotus Hotel on

Bubbling Well Road and my twirl with Galleazzo [Ciano] - or was it his Fascist buddy Alberto?

Ernest was still sitting it out, puffing away like he was giving the signal for the final assault on General Custer.

'I say, that husband of yours must be really hot stuff,' TLM whispered in my ear. 'No smoke without fire, what?'

If only…

Sunday 21 January

TLM had told us we could lie in as late as we liked, so we did just that - it was past ten when we rang for breakfast, and when it came the maid said he'd gotten all the others working overtime outside.

We were still only half dressed when I heard the rain rattling the window and saw them all trooping back in again - even Sailor Dickie looked as if he'd had quite enough of a wetting for one day, thanks very much.

'I say, you two have been taking your time,' TLM greeted us with when we finally made it down. 'Didn't fancy getting your hands dirty, eh, Simpson?'

'Doing what, sir?'

'Clearing away some of those laurels so that I can fit in another nine holes. It's damn tough work, I can tell you, it's such beastly hardy stuff.'

'Oh no, sir, not at all, sir. I can assure you that if -'

'I say, people, did you hear what I just said? Laurel and Hardy! I suppose next time you come down you'll all be saying to Toots "Here's another fine mess you've got us into," what? I've always said I was a bit of a comedian,, eh, Fruity?'

'Oh, rather, sir. That's a real cracker, that is!'

After we'd all been through the splitting-sides routine, TLM turned to me and said, 'There's something over here you two eggheads can help me out on, then.'

He led us over to a table in the bow window. I hadn't noticed it before, but it was covered with jigsaw pieces and on the chair next to it was the box with a picture of Windsor Castle. Only the turrets and flagpole had been put together.

'I've been at it for weeks now and I'm absolutely stuck. I know it's a thousand-piecer, but it really is too sick-making. How do you think I can get going again, Wallis?'

'What do you suggest, Ernest?' I'd never had to tackle one of these in my life, and I wasn't about to admit it!

'Well, sir…'

'Yes?'

'I think, sir…'

'Go on.'

'If I may suggest, sir…'

I'm all for due respect, but this was getting ridiculous. 'Come on, Ernest, let's hear it,' I said.

'Well, I've always found it easiest if you do the edges first.'

'Oh, really?'

'Yes, sir.'

'Why's that, then?'

'Well, sir, one of the sides on an edge piece is straight, you see.'

'And so?'

'And so you can pick them out from the others Then when you've put all the edges together, you can gradually work towards the middle.'

'Good Lord, I'd never thought of that! Of course, that's obviously the way to go about it, I can see that now. I say, you're an absolute genius, do you know that, Simpson? Golly, I wish we had you for a Prime Minister instead of Old Farmer MacDonald.'

We were getting into deep waters here, so I decided to leave the two of them to it and backed off again to the others around the fire.

Osborne had just announced lunch when TLM came up rubbing his hands and grinning like a three-year-old who's just gotten his first treat at Halloween.

'Well, how about that? You'll never believe it, people, but I've got the whole thing finished, right down to Mama's Corgi! And all thanks to Simpson here and his secret method! The man's a genius, an absolute genius, I tell you…'

It was congratulations all round in the dining room too, only this time Thelma was the hero. Dickie was chief cheerleader, saying how she was the sweetest, the prettiest, the gayest, the hostess with the mostest, you name it, followed by a repeat from Fruit-Face and even Ernest chipped in - ugh!

In fact, the only one who didn't go overboard was TLM himself, I couldn't help noticing - because he was saving it for later? Or could it just be that he's going off the boil, I wonder…

Then it was back to the drawing room for coffee. This time the pooches were allowed in, and one of them headed straight over to Ernest and started poking its nose as far as it could get up his pants.

26

'Cora, come here, you naughty girl!' TLM tried, but this was one who wasn't going to jump to his every command.

'Why don't you sit down, Ernest,' I suggested as he stood there like he'd taken root. 'I'm sure it'll go away if you just ignore it.'

'That's right, she does it to everybody she doesn't know very well. Heel, will you, Cora, or you'll catch one on the bottie from Daddy!'

This time it started to back off, but just then the bigger critter began to take an interest.

'Jaggs, come here, boy!' TLM yelled, but it evidently decided it wasn't going to miss out on the chance of a free lunch and helped itself to Ernest's ankle.

Next thing Ernest set off round the room hopping on his good leg until he smacked into the side-table by Edwina. The cup and saucer - not to mention the coffee - went flying and ended up on the floor in as about as many bits as the jigsaw, while Edwina jumped up out her chair like, well, a scalded cat.

Ernest opened and shut his mouth several times without managing to get anything out, then got down on his hands and knees and started scrabbling around for the bits.

'Looking for the edges, are you, old bean?' TLM cracked. 'Well, don't worry, there are plenty more where that came from. Sixty odd, in fact, if I remember rightly - all part of that old Saxe-Coburg-Gotha rubbish, eh, Dickie?'

For once R. von Battenberg didn't seem to see the funny side, while Edwina turned the colour of expresso minus the milk and announced she was going upstairs to get a change of skirt.

She didn't seem any too happier when she got down again and told Dickie the rain looked as if it was really set in, so shouldn't they try and get home before dark...

So that was the end of that. Another fine mess, I'll say - as I let Ernest know when we got back in.

Listened to the news on the radio as Baba told us to and heard Tom Mosley launching his British Fascist Union, black shirts and all - eat your heart out, Galeazzo Ciano! If you've quite finished with mine, that is...

Monday 22 January

(Cain finally back up on deck, just as I was thinking I was booked into steerage class for life) *If you're one of the many feeling the pinch at the moment, you must face up to the situation and use your own initiative to find a way out of it Always relying on others to tide you over will only leave you more in their debt (and not just financially), a position which can only be demoralising to such an independent spirit as yourself. Before you rush into an undertaking, however, make sure that you have all the necessary figures worked out. The last thing you want is making your present hole any deeper.*

Had Cain bring me lunch in bed before I got up and tried Mary again (just to make sure it was past playtime with her Greek)

She was up and about this time - and alone, being just off to take her Mom to hospital.

'I've got just the guy for you, Wallis. Remember my ex-broker pal Chuck Spencer? But of course you do - he was a cousin of Win's, wasn't he? (Sure, but as if I wanted to be reminded! Tact never was one of her strong suits) Well, he set up a little shop when lost his job in the Crash on the corner of Broadway and Houston dealing in autographs, letters, postcards, photos, you name it, and soon he had half the Street turning out their desks for signatures of anyone with half a name.'

'And he's doing good business, is he?'

'You bet he is! He's had to take on four staff to handle it all.'

'And what sort of prices is he fetching?'

'Big, big bucks. Sometimes he tells me he thinks of a figure and then adds a zero on, and they still come running. Like the twenty grand he fetched for one of Joe Kennedy's insider dealing contracts before the Crash - though now his pal Roosevelt's fixed him up as the Securities Commission Chairman the sky could have been the limit, I guess!'

'And he takes things from over this side of the pond, does he?'

'Oh yes, plenty.'

'Like from the Royal Family here?'

'Especially from the Royals. Some people are just crazy for anything of theirs not just letters, but bills, checks, Christmas cards, even locks of hair, would you believe, not to mention all the knick-knacks they've picked up on Royal tours that they've junked. Someone came in the other day with some of your Prince's cufflinks from his old flame Freda - Chuck recognised them because they were engraved with GF and apparently her pet name for him was Goofy, so he called the Palace to check they weren't stolen but nobody wanted to know. One of the servants has to be in on the racket, I'd say.'

'Yes, I guessed that. (that Osborne creep?) How about books? Are they saleable?'

'Oh, sure - just as long as they're signed, of course.'

'Well, in that case I might have struck lucky. I was down at the Fort again for the weekend and the Prince was saying he was gifted more books than he could ever manage and I was welcome to help myself.'

'He did?'

'Yes, any time I fancied some. Not that that's ever going to make me a millionaire, though.'

'You'd be surprised. Chuck's asking six hundred for a LITTLE BLACK SAMBO that belonged to the brother that they locked away out of sight because he had epilepsy or something. John - wasn't that his name?'

'Yes, that's right.' (though it was only the other day that I found out that he'd even ever existed)

'So even after his usual fifty per cent mark-up there'll still be a tidy sum in it for you.'

'Well, I could certainly do with that right now. But of course I'll cut you in on it too, darling.'

'That's very sweet of you, Wallis.'

I was hoping she'd come in with a figure, but when she didn't I suggested fifty-fifty - then realised straight off that was way too generous, but of course she jumped at it.

'OK, that's a deal. I can do with some extra bucks too, I don't mind telling you, now I've finally ditched Jacques.'

'For keeps?'

'For keeps. I'm off to Arizona any day now to seal it.'

'So you've found something better?'

No, not yet. In fact, I'm thinking of giving men a rest for the moment.'

'But how about your little Greek friend? He's pretty keen, isn't he?'

'You can say that again. Between you and me, darling, he's absolutely insatiable! I could never last that pace. If he ever got inside the White House, I reckon even Eleanor would have to watch her butt.'

'You don't say!'

'And anyhow, he's pushed off back to his pals in Sicily to fix a shipment of something or other. Getting back to our little business, how soon do you reckon you'll be able to send something over?'

'Whenever I'm down at the Fort again, which should be any time soon.'

'You certainly seem to be well in there, darling.'

'Oh no, not more than anybody else. He just loves a party, that's all.'

'I see. And how's that lovely man of yours?'

'Ernest? Oh, he's fine.'

'Well, give him some hugs and kisses from me, and tell him I'll be right over to see him again.'

'I sure will, darling.'

Now that really would be a deal…

Thursday 25 January

From the frost on the window it looked like Hell was freezing over outside, so I gave Cain the day off for the sales in return for her coming in on Sunday to help with dinner for a couple more of Ernest's Swedish heavies.

Pictures in *The Times* of trucks in a ditch, icicles on the fountains in Trafalgar Square, a fog-bound football stadium, etc, followed by *ALL SPORT OFF All today's sporting fixtures, including meets of the hounds, have been cancelled due to the frozen state of the ground…*

Court Circ: *YORK HOUSE ST. JAMES'S PALACE His Royal Highness The Prince Of Wales will this afternoon visit the offices of the British Executive of the Employment Society.* Little does he know it, but he's about to help this little girl off the dole!

Emerald called and suggested lunch on Monday, obviously wanting to pump me about the weekend, so I said I was 'otherwise engaged' - and I'll stay that way till it's pay-back time.

Next thing Thelma was on the line, saying she wasn't sailing now till Tuesday (to give herself a final weekend twosome?) and so would I like lunch on Monday at Claridges? 'There's something I want to have a little talk about, darling. It'll be on me, of course' - with a return ticket to NY thrown in if I agreed to take the stand for Gloria, I bet. Thanks, but no thanks, I was going to tell her, but then I realized I needed to know how much time I was going to have to play with while she was gone, so I decided I'd better show willing…

Ernest came in from the office with a bunch of pigeons one of his pals had skidded into on his way into work while they were helping themselves to some corn that a little old lady was putting out for them on the sidewalk, so that's the problem of the menu for Sunday solved - I can't imagine that the Swedes will make too much of a thing of searching for the pellets.

Sunday 28 January

And they didn't.

Monday 29 January

If you have had the feeling that you have been treading water for some time, or even that events have somehow been conspiring against you, you can take heart: this could be the moment when things turn positive. Saturn, the planet of structures, is aligned with Neptune in a way that promises to make even the most far-fetched hopes a reality. Opportunity seldom knocks twice, so when it does come be sure to recognise it for what it is and seize it with both hands.

OK, I'm all eyes, Madame Claire.

Bitterly cold still and another battle with Ernest to keep the heating on all day as well as a coal fire in the drawing room, but at least I got to see the SUN properly for the first time this year. All the way down to Claridges I went through my lines - the doctor says I really ought to have an operation straight away for my sinusitis, Aunt Bessie's talking of coming over next month, Ernest's promised to put up his senior partner in the NY office for a couple of weeks after that...

And all for nothing!

'Oh, it's only the preliminary hearing, so there's no need for you to be there until it goes to the Central Court in the fall sometime, darling. According to the lawyers, it shouldn't take more than a couple of weeks this time round.'

'And then you'll be back?'

'Not straight away - I thought I might stop over in California until this dreadful weather improves here.'

So here was the 'opportunity'...

'But what about The Little Man? Isn't he going to be terribly lonely without you?'

'Well, he said he might try to get over to his little place in Canada.'

'Canada?'

'Yes, didn't you know? He has this ranch in Alberta which he's mad about - just why, I can't think, it's hundreds of miles out in the back of

31

beyond. But if he doesn't, you'll just have to look after him for me, won't you, darling?'

Now that's an invitation a girl can't refuse - not this girl, anyhow!

(Memo: if I ever get to write my memoirs, it's Thelma who says the bit about his being lonely)

Wednesday 31 January

I never got as far as Madame Claire, because there on the gossip page opposite was

> ### A RIGHT ROYAL FAREWELL
> *Southampton. Among the passengers boarding the luxury liner Mauretania for New York today was Lady Thelma Furness, wife of the shipping magnate. Asked why she wasn't travelling on one of her husband's liners, she joked 'I may be married to him, but I'm not part of his fleet!'*
> *Dressed in an ankle-length mink coat, Lady Thelma said she expected to be some time in New York, where she was going to lend support to her sister, the celebrated heiress Gloria Vanderbilt, in the custody case for her daughter, Gloria Junior.*
>
> *Asked to comment, she said 'Our mother claims she only wants the best for the kid, but this doesn't look the best way to me.'*
> *As she mounted the gangway, she waved to a small plane circling the ship, which then dipped its wing. Lady Thelma refused to identify the pilot, but painted on the fuselage were the arms of a Very Royal Person.*

Well, at least he wasn't heading out over the Atlantic...

FEBRUARY
Back To The Starting Line

Saturday 3 February

UNITED STATES RETURNS TO THE GOLD STANDARD is all over the front pages - though I don't know about the *Sketch* as Cain forgot to bring it in with her and I didn't have the will to tell her to go get it. Things might be looking up for the folks back home, but this US citizen is still scraping along on the nickel standard and I couldn't figure how even Madame Claire was going to change that.

For a moment last night I reckoned that our luck had turned when Ernest came in grinning like King Kong with the news that one of the partners had kicked the bucket while on the job (not the one in the office!) which was going to give us all of an extra $100 a month, but then Mr. Tightwad called this morning saying he was going to knock it off Ernest's company loan and so we wouldn't be seeing a cent of it!

Ernest said there was nothing for it now but to sub-let this flat and find somewhere cheaper - 'either that or giving Cain and Cook notice.'

'Oh, so I'm expected to do everything for myself now, am I? All the cooking and shopping, washing the dishes, hoovering the floors, making the beds, dusting the -'

'No, of - '

'I was born into two of the oldest families in the Confederacy, but I'm the one who's supposed to play the slave, is that it?'

' - of course it isn't, honeybunch.'

'Well, that's the way they'd all see it, I'm here to tell you. (Let's hope they weren't looking when I was earning my crust in Peking on the poker tables - and elsewhere!) If you don't want another Warfield seceding from the union, Ernest, I suggest you get down to the agents right now and find out what sort of rent we could be looking at.'

Which he did, but no go - they said so many new apartment blocks had gone up in the area recently that we'd never get more than 12 guineas a week - as against the 15 we're paying.

Which leaves only two ways out that I can see - 1) squeeze another check out of Bessie Big Bucks, or 2) get the business plan with Mary up and running - but that looks like it's on ice right now, so it has to be 1).

Spend the rest of the day on a letter to Bessie filling her in on the Fort weekend (minus only Ernest's tangle with the pooch) and mailed it with a cutting of the Harvey Nicks ad. for their Early Spring Sale, underlining the most expensive dress on offer (39gns). Maybe I should have been sending over my measurements for the number she said she'd have made up for me by her Mrs. Jordan, but the way things are I'd rather have the cash in hand, thanks.

Monday 5 February

Now that you have the chance to realise a long-held ambition, you must remain confident in your ability to do so by means of your usual ingenuity and perseverance. Some people might accuse you of being absurdly over-ambitious, but that's because they don't appreciate the strength of purpose inside you. That's not to say that you're bound to succeed, but at least nobody will be able to say that you're not a trier.

As if I didn't know - they didn't call me Princess Pushy at prep school for nothing! But when's this chance going to happen? That's what I really need to know.

I didn't have long to wait, as it turned out - in fact, I was still in the tub when I heard the phone ring. Cain took it, but I couldn't make out what she was saying through the door and even when I told her to open it she was shaking so much she still couldn't get a word out edgeways.

'Well, if it's the bank manager, you can tell him I'm out for the day.'

'No, Madam, it's - it's - '

'Ditto the landlord.'

' - it's - it's - '

'Oh, for Christ's sake, Cain, spit it out!'

' - it's His, His Royal, His - '

I was out of the tub and across the lobby so fast I didn't even stop to grab a towel.

'Good morning, Sir.' (he'd never called me direct before, so I reckoned I'd better stick to protocol)

'Oh hello, Wallis.'

'I'm so sorry to have kept you.'

'Not at all, not at all. Probably interrupted your beauty sleep, what?'

'Oh no, Sir. I was just on my way out to luncheon, in fact.'

'Oh, really? Mustn't keep you, in that case,' he said, and had me almost wetting myself that he was going to hang up, but he went on (wow, the relief!), 'Just wanted to tell you I've booked a private room at the Dorch next Tuesday for a cosy little dinner with the Bateses and Metcalfes and wondered if you'd care to join us. There'll be a three-piece band, so we'll be able to have a little tango or two, don't you know.'

'I'd say I would, Sir. That includes Ernest, does it?'

'Ernest?'

'My husband.'

'Oh yes, rather. Shall I wait while you check with him that you haven't got anything else on that night?'

'No, no, he's not here at the moment.'

'He's not?'

'No, he's at his office in the City, Sir.'

'Oh, he works, does he?'

'Yes.' (too late I realized I should have said he had an early lunch date at the Guards Club or some place)

'I say, how amusing. Still, there's not much golf to be had in this weather, is there? I mean, when you can hardly see twenty yards off the tee.'

'I guess not, Sir.'

'Bally fog, it's too sick-making. So you'll ring me back when you've spoken to him and let me know, will you?'

'Yes - I mean, I'm sure he's got nothing else on.' (liar - Tuesday's his Masons' night)

'Oh, jolly good. How about meeting up at half seven - would that suit you?'

'Yes, perfectly, Sir.' (as if any time of day or night wouldn't!)

'Okey-dokey. Oh, and Wallis, you can drop the Sir - just make it David from now on, will you?'

'Yes, of course, S - I mean David.'

'Righty-oh. Tootle-loo, then.'

'Bye bye.'

I was still up there on Cloud Nine in my birthday suit when I saw Cook gawping at me from the lobby.

'Cook, how dare you! Shut the door this second, will you!'

'I just wanted to check the shopping list with you, Missus, but please yourself.'

As well as being deaf and dumb, the woman's as insolent as they come and about as much use in the kitchen as a bent can-opener.

Called Baba as soon as I was dressed to see if there was any chance yet of getting Mrs. Ralph back from her Mom. She didn't think so, but I fixed to meet her for a Slimmers Week lunch at Harrods on Wednesday (on me) - with luck I'll get some lowdown on TLM's Canada plans off her.

Ernest was all ears when he got back in and of course agreed to let the Masons go by the board.

Tuesday 6 February

No show from either Cain or Cook, so assumed they must have struck in sympathy, but then remembered I'd given Cain the day off for her sister's wedding (in return for working Sunday) and Cook turns out to be down with food poisoning - and they say there's no justice in this world!

Court Circ: *YORK HOUSE ST. JAMES'S PALACE His Royal Highness The Prince of Wales will visit a soup kitchen for the unemployed at Windsor this morning before returning to London to address the Annual General Meeting of the Council of Social Service as Patron.*

And I thought he said he'd had enough of Brown Windsor for life! This Social Service Council is a new one on me, but if it's anything to do with the servant problem I can soon fill him in on that.

Wednesday 7 February

No one can criticise you for doing all you can to achieve your ambition, but you must be careful not to cause offence by giving the impression of self-centredness by being too openly single-minded. An attitude of 'Me first, and the Devil take the hindmost' is not likely to win you many friends, especially among those who might tend to see your success as a reflection of their own failure. Making enemies won't bring it any nearer - quite the reverse, in fact.

In other words play it long, girl, play it long…

Lunch with Baba went according to plan, except that the bill was anything but slimline - the servings were so mean, Baba helped herself to seconds of everything! Looks like Fruit-Face is going to be back on the bananas and raisins again if they're eating in tonight, poor guy.

I kicked off as casually as I could with the Social Service Council. It turned out that there's a bit more to it than solving the servant problem - eg, finding situations for miners and mill girls that have been laid off, though with the trouble all of our friends still seem to have finding reliable chauffeurs and skivvies (unlike us, whose trouble is finding the cash to keep them, given the enormous wage they all demand - four pounds a month now even for a kitchen maid) it beats me why there's a problem at all. According to Baba, it was something Freda led him into, but then she'd gone off and started some sort of charity of her own (and put him in as the patsy president), so maybe it's not something to be losing sleep over after all...

Anyhow, I then steered the chat away from TLM in case I was getting to sound too interested, and it wasn't until we were on the coffee that I slipped in a question about Canada. She said he'd bought the place during his North American tour after the war as a little hideout to get away from it all and used to hop over there every year or so to begin with, but he hadn't been for some time now and as far as she knew he didn't have any plans to go back.

'Oh? Thelma said something about meeting up with him there, but maybe I got her wrong.'

'She did? I think she must have got her lines crossed in that case. I really can't see her there - Fruity's only been once and that was enough. He said he'd never been so cold in his life.'

'No, it doesn't sound her sort of place.'

'And actually, what we were planning was a couple of weeks skiing in Austria together, but then the Foreign Office stepped in and said the Commies were stirring some sort of trouble there. And did you read about that ghastly riot they put on in Paris in the paper today?'

'No, I just noticed the headline, that's all.'

'Four police horses stabbed to death, poor things, and one or two people killed as well, I think. Can you imagine what sort of brutes they must be to do a thing like that, darling? Tom - you know, Mosley - thinks it's only a matter of time before the same thing happens here, unless we all get together now and nip it in the bud like our splendid friend Benito in Italy. I gather you're a chum of Ciano, his son-in-law.'

Just as well we weren't still on the fruit salad, or she'd have caught a pineapple chunk right between the eyes. As it was, most of the coffee went down the wrong way, and next thing I had the waiter beating the daylights out of my back, but at least it gave me time to put my thoughts together again. How she'd gotten hold of the story I couldn't imagine, but now it was out I reckoned there was nothing for it but to play along with it.

'Yes. Or rather, I was some years back.'

'Before he married Edda, was that?'

'Oh sure, ages before.' (I was hardly going to tell her that if he hadn't insisted on the abortion, Edda would never have made it onto his scene!) 'It was while I was out in China that we crossed paths for a week or two - and then I met Ernest, of course!'

'But you've kept in touch, have you?'

'Jesus, no!' Maybe I shouldn't have been quite so sharp with her, but I didn't like the way her questions were leading. Anyhow, it stopped her in her tracks long enough for me to get on to the other big issue of the moment. 'There really isn't any chance of my getting Mrs. Ralph back any time soon, is there, darling? The present creature I've got is driving me right up the wall.'

'Well, actually you might be in luck there. Mummy was saying only this morning that the husband has just signed up as a steward in a liner on the India run, and he's such a treasure that she thought she'd take the chance to go too and look up her old chums there. Two weeks from now it's sailing, I think she said...'

Baba sweetheart, I wanted to yell out loud, you've just made my day - if that was still possible!

Friday 9 February

Good-natured though you are, there are times when even you feel the need to respond to provocation. Just now you're sorely tempted to give a particular individual a piece of your mind, so it's fortunate that Venus, who always holds such a strong influence over you (you can say that again, Madame!) *is entering your sign. Tongues wag, and however justified you may feel in giving vent to your feelings, it's you who may end up being portrayed as the one in the wrong. By all means do what you feel you have to, but in a way that the world will think the better of you for it.*

Caught Lady Curzon at home at last and yessiree, Mrs. Ralph is free and ready to come back in ten days time!

Gave Cook a week's notice on the spot. With a big, big effort I managed to hold my voice down to the minimum level needed to get the message into her stupid head - which was several levels below what she then worked herself up to in replying that there was no love lost on her side either. 'I've worked for some awkward customers in my time, but you beats the lot, I can tell you, how I've stood it all these weeks I'll never know, I'm sure, you'd think anyone with a sticky beak your size would want to keep it to themselves instead of poking it into my kitchen every ten seconds, and as for…'

On and on she went - Old Man River just wasn't in the same league.

Thinking of noses, I'm still trying to figure out who could have put Baba onto Galleazzo's scent. If there was anyone from London who saw us in Shanghai I still don't know them, and I've never heard of Baba/Fruit-Face ever being further east than India. So it has to be him who's been shooting his mouth off (which isn't too hard to imagine), and from him it must have gone down the wires to Mussolini to Tom Mosley and somehow on to Baba. But why now, ten years down the track? I'm darn'd if I can see it…

Monday 12 February

If you're honest with yourself, you'll have to admit that your attitude is usually a little cavalier when it comes to controlling your spending habits, but just at this moment you should be able to take a more relaxed view on the matter. Money has recently been the dominant topic of conversation with those closest to you, and it will be a relief to be able to switch to other subjects which hold more interest for you. This is not to say, of course, that you can suddenly afford to throw all caution to the wind, but only that you can enjoy those little treats with an easier conscience.

Right on cue the mail brings a check for $100 from Big Bucks, so I book a wash and set with Thelma's little man Antonio in Bond Street that she swears by.

Look in on the M & Snelgrove sale in the hope of picking up something a bit special for tomorrow night, and bingo! a knockout lacquer lace number in royal blue with a pattern of king-size (well, prince-size, anyhow) roses, fitting me down to the last inch and best of all, knocked down to just seven and a half guineas, would you believe.

Just get into the restaurant for lunch on the cheap before the doors close and find everything on the first course is off bar - you've guessed it - the Brown Windsor. Console myself with the thought that at least the Dorch should save me from another dose. Going out through the shoe department I saw they're having a 'Foot Comfort Week' with free chiropody - just what I'll need if Ernest starts up again at the table about how the Americans lost out when they ditched the Monarchy. (and who's to say they're not going to get it back again?)

Then onto Bond St.

Antonio (the usual wop greaser - as if I hadn't had my share of them already!) 'You like a change this time, Madam?'

'No, I don't think so, Antonio.'

'The parting a little to the side, perhaps?'

'No, just keep it straight down the middle, please.'

'But the new style is for the right. I think it would suit you so much, madam.' (And point up my mole? Great!)

'Thanks, but no thanks, Antonio.'

'Ah (with much sighing, shrugging, snickering of scissors, etc), you ladies never change. Your friend the Lady Furness, she stays always in the middle and you the same.' Then bending down practically into my ear, 'You like to hear a little joke about her Ladyship I was hearing myself this morning?'

'Yes - go right ahead.'

'OK. If the Lord saved Daniel from the lion's den, who will save David from the fiery Furness?'

Who indeed? There you are, Wallis - you've even got Jehovah rooting for you!

Tuesday 13 February

Gave Madame Claire a miss for once - I wasn't going to leave anything to chance or the stars for tonight (especially it being the 13th)

Rested up at home all day and got Cain to do my nails (my manicure sessions having gone down the pan anyhow along with the rest of Ernest's economies) 5.30 bathed and left the water for him (another of ditto), but it was well after 6 when he got in.

'You're leaving it a bit late, aren't you?' I said as I gave the mole a final dab of powder.

'Yes, awfully, sorry, honeybunch, but -'

'You know we're due at half seven, don't you?'

'Yes, I know, but -'

'Well, you'd better get a move on.'

'But I actually had rather a busy day at the office for once. I know the figures out today showed another 120,000-ton drop in the British merchant fleet over 1933, but America going back on the Gold Standard looks like giving us a real shot in the arm. Grain contracts on the River Plate in particular are -'

'OK, OK, I'll take your word for it. So that means you'll be getting a rise, does it?'

'Oh no, I can't see that happening in a hurry. The New York partners were only saying yesterday that -'

'So why are you telling me all this? The bath water must be cold by now, by the way, so you'll have to run another.'

'Oh, I don't think I'll bother.'

'But I'm not having you coming along stinking like a skunk!'

'It's all right, I'll just give my hair an extra drop or two of Mister Thomas's Royal Yacht. I won't possibly have time if we're walking.'

'Walking?' I yelled. I knew I was walking with Destiny tonight, but not that literally.

'Yes. You know what we said about cutting out taxis when we did the accounts last night, and the Dorchester's only half a mile down the road.'

'Well, that's half a mile too far in my book. You can walk if you want to, but I'm taking a cab, OK?'

'Oh no, it's all right, honeybunch, I'll ring and order one now.'

In fact, the fog was so darn'd thick we could have done better on foot.

So you win some, you lose some - but if it's the big one you win, what the hell...

Sunday 18 February

Did I say Cloud Nine? Well, you can make that Ninety-Nine now! Which is why it's taken me all this time to climb down and put pen to paper again.

Not that it looked as if the evening was going to shape up that way. I was only reckoning on the seven of us, but who should blow in but Connie - 'just thought I'd stop off for the sales and pick up something for little Gloria on the way over, darling.' More likely Thelma's told her to take a check on TLM, but two can play at that game - I'll call Mary and tell her to keep her eyes peeled over there.

Over dinner (Scotch haggis, Irish stew, Bakewell tart, Welsh rabbit - TLM explained he'd ordered a 'Best of British' menu in the Bates's honor, though I can't say they looked all that flattered) all of the talk was on the Gold Standard and the cut in the gold content of the dollar, which didn't leave me with too many openings.

'And who's the best person to ask what it all means? You don't know? Why, a gold-digger, of course!' TLM cracked. 'What's wrong, Wallis, don't you get the joke? You'd better give us one of your own, then.'

'Me? I really can't say that I know any.'

'Oh come on, you Yanks are always full of gags. I bet you've heard a few in your time from her, eh, Simpson?'

'Oh rather, sir,' Ernest came back before I could get my foot into him. 'And some rather juicy ones, actually.'

'There you go, Wallis. And the juicier, the better.'

'Well, there's the one about Coney Island. But maybe Fred knows it.'

'Coney Island?'

'You know, the sunbathing one.'

'Nope, not guilty.'

'Oh, OK, then. What's the difference between sunbathing on Coney Island and Hollywood Beach? Answer: on Coney Island the girls lie on the sand looking into the stars, and in Hollywood the stars lie on the girls looking into the sand.'

'Hot diggety-dog, that's a good one! Eh, Fruity? Come on, raise a laugh, old bean, or I'll be forced to tell the one about how you came by your nickname.'

'Oh yes, do, David!' Connie came in. 'I've always wondered.'

'Well, I can't disappoint a lady, so here goes. We first met on my Indian tour in twenty-two when Fruity was in charge of my polo ponies. Well, one day I was feeling rather peckish after a particularly stiff chukkah, so I asked him to send off one of his men for something to eat. I was still taking off my boots when the wallah came back with a great pile of curry and those poppa thingies, so I told him to put it down on the ground for the moment and the next thing I knew my pony had scoffed the lot! I thought it had better have some water pronto, so I told Fruity to get the bucket standing by its rear end. Then just as he bent down to pick it up, the animal let rip a tremendous blast all over him. "My God, Metcalfe," I said, "that'll turn you fruity for life" - and it has!'

TLM was still falling about when the band came in and started up. Fruit-Face beat it to the floor with Baba, followed by the Bates and (after I'd given him the nod) Ernest and Connie so then there were two...

'Tell me about your good works at Windsor last week, David,' I kicked off with. 'I'd love to hear all about it.'

'At Windsor? What was I doing there?'

'You know - helping with the unemployed.'

'Oh, that. Well, there's not much to tell, actually, just standing there watching soup being ladled out to all these layabouts and telling them to get it down while it was still hot, don't you know. One's got to do one's bit for the poor, what?'

'That's right - I used to be one of them!'

'You don't say? But at least it was all over in time for me to get in a round at the Berkshire on the way back. There's nothing like a round of golf for clearing one's head of all this wretched Monarchy business and getting down to the important things in life. Do you play, by the way, Wallis?'

'Sure, I used to be real keen back in the States before I came over,' I lied. (Win took me out once or twice on the station course at Pensacola before we both realised I was a total no-hoper - though I did get to be quite an ace at finding balls!). 'But there aren't too many courses around Bryanston Square, I'm afraid.'

'No, there wouldn't be, but I can get you into one of my clubs.'

'Well, that's very -'

'And I can fix you some lessons at Coombe Hill with Archie Crampston, he's the best pro around. I'm taking Angie - you know, Freda's eldest - to him at the moment.'

'You are?' (Like mother, like daughter???) 'Tell me some more.'

'Yes, just once a month. Anyway, to get back to the Berkshire, the Red's my favorite, but I thought I'd give the Blue a go this time. The first is a bit of a tough one - I know it's supposed to be only a short hole, but it's still the best part of two hundred yards and if you go for the flag it's all carry over some really frightful heather perched on the side of a hill. Of course, you can play safe with a niblick out to the left, but even then you've still got...'

By Hole Five my eyes must have been glazing over because I heard him say, 'I'm so sorry, I must be boring you rigid.'

'Oh no, not in the least, I couldn't be more interested. Do go on, David, please.'

'Okey dokey, then. Well, the sixth is a pretty long hole...'

Just then the band stopped, thank my lucky stars, and the others came back to the table. When it started up again Ernest was shaping up to ask me, but TLM got in first.

'Do you know, Wallis,' he suddenly said in my ear when we were on the floor, 'you're the only woman who's ever been interested in my game.'

You don't say?

'Yes. All the others can say is "How sick-making!" whenever I tell them how I foozled into a bunker or missed a short putt and try to change the subject, but I can see you really feel for me. Would you mind awfully if I dropped into your flat for a KT now and then after a round?'

'But of course, David, I'd be only too honored.'

'And how about your husband?'

'Oh, I'm sure that goes for him too.'

'Good, that's OK then.'

I'll say it was - only I didn't expect him to pitch up the very next night when I was hardly out of the tub!! I didn't have time for more than a quick lipstick and when the conversation never got past a blow-by-blow account of his afternoon's round I reckoned I must have blown it, but then his parting shot was 'I'd love it if you could come down to the Fort again next weekend. And you'd better bring your wellies, Simpson, because I'll be taking another crack at the laurel and hardy, what? Ha, ha...'

And you, girl, had better pack your skates - it sounds like Canada might be off the menu now and there's no telling if Thelma mightn't cut short her supporting act and head back over the pond.

Monday 19 February

There's no denying your happiness at the return of somebody in your life who could be an important ally in the fulfilment of your ambitions. You should guard against making it too obvious, however, which could result in the person taking your support for them too much for granted and so becoming more of a hindrance than a help. The Moon is pointing up a rather high-flown area of your chart, and if you pitch your hopes too high you could end up heading for a fall.

Keep your feet on the ground in other words, Wallis. But if I'm not allowed to give Mrs. Ralph too much of a hello, there was nothing against giving the deaf and dumb one a big goodbye. The sweet she served up for Sunday lunch had to be the most revolting bit of food I've ever set eyes on - a roll of solid suet dotted all over with raisins.

'And it ain't the first one of these you'll have had inside you, I'll be bound, missus,' she said as if that was the biggest payback of all time, but I soon wiped the smile off her fat face by refusing to write her a reference.

Glad as I was to get Mrs R back, I was still wondering whether Madame Claire wasn't maybe rating her a bit high ('important ally', etc) when the mail arrived with a letter from Italy - or rather what looked like a letter, but what should I find when I opened it up but a Valentine card signed *'Con mi'amore per sempre e molti, molti baci, Galleazzo'*!!! And then on the back he'd written 'Hello again, my dear Wallis, after so many years! But still I remember all our times together like yesterday, you must believe me even if I am now a married man! And not only married, but to the most beautiful daughter of our great Leader, so I must be very careful what I do, capito? Perhaps you have heard that I am holding a position molto importante in the Foreign Ministry here, and I expect to come to London soon to speak with your Anthony Eden. I say 'your' because I know that you have married now an Englishman. I would like very much to meet with you also and practice my English again, but this time I will be the perfect gentleman, please believe me!'

I was still trying to figure it all out when I took a look at the envelope again and saw that it was mailed in Rome on the 4th. Friend Benito may have his trains running on time, but he still hasn't got round to sorting out the Italian Post Office, I guess!

Just what can he be playing at? Whatever it is, I won't be taking any chances this time round, that's for sure. Then Emerald called and made a date for lunch at Fortnum's on Thursday - maybe she can come up with an answer as she seems to have so much on him.

I'd just decided that was as many people coming back into my life as I was going to get in one day when sharp at six the doorbell rang and who should be standing there but The Big One of them all, TLM himself! He'd just got back from a weekend's golf at Sandwich in Kent and so of course we had to hear about every stroke (air shots included) he'd taken over all four rounds, but after three in the same bunker the second time around even Ernest had the guts to draw a line.

'I'm awfully sorry to cut you short, sir, but Wallis and I always do our household accounts on Monday evenings, and as I'm having to make an early -'

'Household accounts, eh? Quite right, quite right. Pop is always on at me about them - "Otherwise you never know what all the servants might be getting up to," he says - and I mustn't keep you, but that bunker on the fourth is the very devil. If only I could learn to play up short, we'd all be happy, what? Anyhow, I won't be taking up any more of your time this week as I'm off to Belgium tomorrow for the King's funeral. Killed himself mountaineering, poor chap - you may have read about it.'

Well, nobody would accuse him of breaking his neck social-climbing, I guess.

Thursday 22 February

Because you lead a more interesting life than most, you will always be confronted by people who have a strong appetite for news of all your most intimate affairs. It may be, of course, that they simply wish to share their own experiences with you in return and genuinely have your welfare at heart, but others will sadly have their own agenda and will seek to turn any confidences to their own advantage. The only answer is to hold back until you're quite sure which category you're dealing with. If you think that this may risk causing offence to the former, you can rest assured that they will respect your motives and think all the better of you for it. As for the others, this tactic may provoke them into imparting news of their own which could be to your advantage!

There can't be much doubt which bag Emerald falls into, so mum's the word, Wallis…

Arrived at Fortnum's a few minutes early and was filling in with a spot of window-shopping when I heard glass being stove in further down Duke Street followed by some yelling and the sound of a cab racing its engine. Getting closer, I saw there'd been a smash-and-grab at Ogden's the jewelers, but apparently the cabdriver wasn't the getaway man at all but had actually chased the hoodlums and cornered them. Then the cops showed up and arrested them, which makes a nice change.

Then for the Inquisition on the Dorch party - or so I thought, but Emerald seemed to know almost more about it than I did, so there was nothing left worth telling her even if I'd wanted to. Trying to figure it out where she'd got it all from, Connie'd told me she was heading on again to NY the very next morning, while the Bates had only been in the country a couple of weeks and as far as I knew weren't even on speaking terms with her yet, so it looked like it had to be Baba.

'So when did it break up, darling?'

'Oh, I don't know - I never looked at the time, to be honest.'

'Well, you made quite a night of it, according to Tom.'

'Tom Mosley?'

'Yes, of course - if you can believe the pillow talk with Baba.'

'You mean …?'

'Sure, didn't you know?'

'But she's his sister-in-law!'

'Well, that's our girl for you. And that's only when she's taking time off from fun and games with our pal Grandi.'

'What, the new Italian Ambassador?'

'Yes, that's the guy.'

So that's it! It all figures now - Baba sees me hitting it off with TLM and tips off Grandi, who tips off Musso, who lines up Galleazzo to cosy up to me again as their best way into the whole set-up here.

Spot on again, Madame Claire. OK, a girl likes to know when she's being used, but just as long as the price is right this girl will never say no to playing ball…

Sunday 25 February

Hitched a ride down with the Bates to the Fort, only to have Osborne announce that TLM had had another tumble out hunting with the Beavers and had taken to his bed, which didn't exactly make for a fun evening - especially as Ernest had his eyes fixed the whole time on the two pooches in case they took another fancy to his ankles.

Woke up at 9AM wondering if the whole weekend was going to be a washout, but just then there was a hammering on the door and TLM yelling 'Come on, Simpson, get those wellies on! Fred and I are all ready to go.'

Before I could blink Ernest was out of bed like his pajamas were on fire, threw his clothes on, shot down the stairs, took a spoonful of kedgeree on the run and that was him gone for the morning.

Three hours later he was back again in such a state he could have just gone the full fifteen rounds at Madison Square until TLM pushed a double-strength White Lady into his hands.

'Jolly good show, Ernest, that's the short hole just about cleared. Only two more to go now.'

'Thanks very much, Sir.'

'Oh, do call me David - now that you're a fully paid-up member of the Hackers Club, what?'

Anyone who saw the effect that had on Ernest wouldn't needed to have gone to church that morning to believe in a power to rise from the dead and ascend into heaven! I haven't been so short on the Davids myself, but now - to borrow again from the Good Book - he couldn't open his mouth without firing them off fast enough to knock over any Goliath.

The talk at lunch got round to the heist at Ogdens, and Ernest came in with news of another one at some wine merchants in the City.

'Yes, you don't have to remind me about that,' TLM said. 'I had six pipes of Taylors '99 laid down there to keep me in port for life, and now the blighters have swiped the lot, dash it! It's all this wretched unemployment that's behind it, of course - you never read about this sort of thing happening in Italy or Germany. This country could do with a dictator, I don't mind telling you - look how this new chap Hitler has got them all off the dole building those marvelous roads.'

Fred: 'So that's what you'd put them onto here, is it?'

'No, no, not roads - we've got plenty enough of those already. Shall I tell you what this country desperately needs more of? Golf courses.'

'Golf courses?'

'Yes, golf courses. Do you realize how many courses there are in this country per one hundred thousand head of population compared with your country, Fred?'

'Nope, I can't say I do.'

'Well, I'll tell you: one point two, compared with over three in America. And if you ask me how I know that, I read it in this month's *Readers Digest*. Just think how many unemployed it would take to build another thousand courses.'

'Okay, but what would they do once the courses were built?'

'Why, play on them, of course! Then we might have a chance of beating you Yanks again at our own game. Do you know how long it is since one of our own men won the Open? Ten years! I tell you, something must be done! I've tried to set an example myself, but if it takes a dictator to finish the job, then that's the way it has to be and all those useless pollies can go hang, what? You only have to see how much our chum Benito is getting done without them…' - and so on and so on, even after we'd moved back into the drawing-room for the coffee. (Sounds like your trip over here is going to be a push-over, Galleazzo)

Just when I was packing up again in the bedroom and thinking that the whole thing really had been a washout, I found a copy of LITTLE LORD FAUNTLEROY stuck away in a bottom drawer. It didn't give me any hot flushes at first glance, but then I opened it and saw the first page had written on it *'To my dear boy Edward, With fondest love from your affectionate Mama on the occasion of your 18th birthday.'*

That has to be worth a dime or two to us, doesn't it, Mary?

MARCH
Get Set

Saturday 3 March

Tried calling Mary all week, but no go. I guess she must still be in Reno fixing her divorce - let's hope it all went through OK.

That's not to say the phone's been dead - anything but. TLM comes on two or three times a day and asks himself for KTs. Began to worry that someone might be noticing, so got a few others in too last night, but the net result was the same - he outstayed the lot! By then it was way past dinner time, so I had to ask him if he'd care to take pot luck with the beef casserole Mrs. Ralph had left in the oven.

Luckily there was just about enough to go round for the three of us, but even then he still hung on, and it was past midnight before he was finally out of the door - not that I was pushing him too hard!

Monday 5 March

With your sharp mind, you're never likely to let slip an opportunity, especially one which promises a useful financial return. However, with the Sun about to enter the money-related area of your chart you must guard against looking at it purely in terms of profit, especially if it is a project involving friends. Their needs may not be as pressing as yours, and they may be more interested in the pleasure of working with you and getting to know you still better. Friendships bring benefits which are not to be calculated in pounds, shillings and pence, and by exploiting them you could end up losing everything.

Well, I've always thought of Mary as just as much a go-getter as I am, but I guess people can change - especially if she's managed to take Jacques to the cleaners.

TLM called first thing to say that he wouldn't be able to drop in this week as every night he was going to be lumbered with some official dinner, but he'd be down at the Fort for the weekend if we'd care to join him, and while we were about it why not bring down some of my Yankee pals to liven the place up? Why not indeed - though you didn't have to be from over the pond to make more sparks fly than Baba and Fruit-Face, I might have added.

Spent the rest of the morning ringing round and got a good crowd together, even if I did have to make up the numbers with some of the new people at the Embassy.

Tried Mary after lunch once more and finally caught her. Yes, Jacques hadn't raised a peep, and she'd stopped off on the way back to lay some her winnings on the tables at Las Vegas and had cleaned up there too!

I asked about 1) her Mom, and she said they'd definitely diagnosed cancer now and were giving her only a matter of weeks, so she herself should be free to come over here for the summer - and find Ernest waiting on the dockside and ready to pounce if all goes according to plan! 2) the Vanderbilt case: it's just been adjourned to the fall - not such good news if it means Thelma's heading straight back. 3) the spring fashions: she says the Garbo look is all the rage, silk and slinky - I'll call Big Bucks and have Mrs. Jordan knock up something for me on the hoof, in case Thelma can bring it back for me. 4) the big freeze over there (the coldest for 30 years, according to the papers) - even in Times Square it was down practically to zero and it was all she could do to haul herself out of bed in the morning. Does that mean her little Greek beau is still around?? Let's hope not - Ernest may be in shipping, but he's not competing in that league, that's for sure.

Then finally down to business. She didn't know LITTLE LORD FAUNTLEROY, but the inscription from the Squaw would be a big plus. She couldn't put a figure on it until she'd seen it, of course, but it sure sounded like it was worth the price of an airmail stamp if I wanted a quick sale.

'Oh no, there's no rush,' I lied, 'but it just happens that the Prince has asked us down to the Fort again this weekend, so I'll clear it with him and give you a call back. Oh, and Ernest told me to send you his best love when I said I was going to be talking to you.'

'And give him mine too .'

'I'll do that, darling...' And how!

Called Big Bucks and checked Mrs. Jordan still had my measurements, then gave her an order for a slimline number in navy blue shot silk and said to bill me for $40 maximum to avoid the import duty and I'd make up the difference later. Told her to call Thelma when it was ready and ask if she could bring it with her on her way back - and give me a clue when that was going to be.

Thursday 8 March

Yet another pea-souper outside and Cain down with her 'bronchials', so stayed in and caught up with this week's *Times*.

Monday's had a big story on TLM's 'rapid tour' (he'd told me he had booked the afternoon for golf) of the Brit Industry Fair at Olympia, pausing only to look at some film projectors, a king-size fishing rod and some model planes and test a pop-gun on the toy stand before stopping off in the fashion section to watch a parade of mannequins in tennis shorts on the Gorringe's stand. *'There's no reason why women shouldn't wear shorts,' His Royal Highness observed. 'They're quite the most practical for the game, and I don't think that those who do lose anything in looks.'* Don't try and kid me he still hasn't got an eye for a bit of skirt!

Then in today's Court Circ: *YORK HOUSE ST. JAMES'S PALACE His Royal Highness The Prince of Wales gave a dinner last night in honour of the Greek Foreign Minister. The guests included... Sir Farquar and Lady Buzzard.* (just as well I wasn't there to be picked to pieces)

Her Royal Highness, The Duchess of York, attended a meeting in the afternoon in aid of the Cripples Training College Fund. (teaching them how to cook and/or put on weight??)

Not much else of interest bar the sales ads - a knee-length coat and skirt with crepe de chine lining in beige or lobelia at Jay's for only 6 ½ guineas looks like a great buy, but no doubt the Keeper of the Purse will have other ideas.

Sunday 11 March

There were 12 of us Yanks altogether (including Ernest, that is - however hard he might try to make out as a true Brit), and TLM insisted on us all meeting up at the Embassy Club on Friday night first 'to get to know you all' - though when it came to taking the floor it seemed like the only person he wanted to know was me! (not that the competition was too hot - I'd seen to that OK)

Motored down to the Fort in convoy the next morning in pouring rain, but it fined up after lunch so of course TLM had all the men in a chain gang on jungle clearance again.

That left us girls to knock up some balls on the tennis court for couple of hours, until that little critter Jaggs ran off with the last of them into the house. I managed to get it back off him in the lobby, but when I slammed him one for good measure he set up such a hollering that the next second Osborne came belting out from behind the green baize.

'I hardly think His Royal Highness would have approved,' he huffed when I explained what had happened.

'Oh, I'm sure he'll understand,' I replied. 'He'd hate to have our little game spoilt.'

He wouldn't answer that, but picked up the pooch and started muttering to it, 'What, spoil the lady's little game? Oh no, we can't have that now, Jaggs, can we? Oh no, no, no...' and headed back to his lair.

'Oh, Osborne...'

'Yes, madam?'

'It's such a nice afternoon, I think we'll have tea out on the terrace.'

'I'm sorry, madam, but His Royal Highness specifically told me to serve it in the drawing room.'

'Well, that was a couple of hours ago before the sun came out. Just do as I say, will you?'

'I repeat, I'm very sorry, madam, but I cannot. I only take my orders from His Royal Highness, I'm afraid, so that's that.'

We were still standing there toe to toe when TLM himself came bouncing in.

'Tea-time, Osborne! Chop, chop! We're all absolutely dying of thirst, I can tell you.'

'Yes, Your Royal Highness, I was just about to take it into the drawing room.'

'But I was saying, David, why don't we have it out on the terrace? It's so gorgeous out there now.'

'Oh, what a splendid idea, Wallis! Yes, let's make use of the sun while it's there - I mean, it's not as if we see it too often at this time of year, what?'

'But Your Royal Highness, you said -'

'Oh, come on, Osborne, do as Mrs. Simpson says.'

'Very good, Your Royal Highness...'

If looks could kill, I was as good as out for the count. Somehow I had the feeling that this was going to be just the first of a full fifteen-rounder...

After all the fresh air even TLM was pretty well pooped, and he'd only had a couple of jazz records on the gramophone after dinner before he led us all up to bed.

By next morning it was back to the usual rain, so we stayed in and helped out with his new jigsaw, a 2000-piecer of a picture headed 'Hounds In Full Cry'. Ernest had a star role again, but his real big moment came over lunch when somehow the talk got on to the demonstration in Trafalgar Square by the so-called Hunger Marchers.

'Can't understand why they'd want to walk all the way from Glasgow when there's a perfectly good train service,' TLM said. 'Just think how many rounds of golf they could have been playing over that distance.'

'You mean on the courses along the way, Dave?'

'No, no, I meant if you laid them end-to-end. If you take the average course as being six thousand yards and add a bit for the distance between tees, that means you're walking about four miles a round - provided you hit the ball straight down the middle every time like I do, what?'

'You do?'

'No, no, only joking, old bean, ha, ha. Now the distance between London and Glasgow is 392 miles - and you can take that from me, because my nanny always said that if I was going to rule the country the first thing I'd need to know was the distance between all the principal cities - so what does that make it? Come on, Ernest, you're the boffin.'

'Oh, that's easy - ninety-eight courses.'

'Good Lord! However did you work that out so fast?'

'Well, it's pretty simple, really. 392 is eight short of 400, so divide that by four and you get a hundred, then divide the eight by four and you get two and take that away and there's your answer.'

'Jeez! OK, if that's so easy, tell me how many holes they'd have played, then.'

'Same thing again. A hundred times eighteen is eighteen hundred, then take away two times eighteen which is thirty-six and you get 1764.'

'Hot diggety dog! What did I tell you, the man's a genius! You ought to be on the Brains Trust with that professor chappy on the wireless. Not that I ever listen to it, mind you.'

Ernest's face lit up like a Christmas tree and he puffed so hard on his cigar that the ash dropped off into his fruit salad. The poor sap thought he'd try and hide it by mashing it in with the rest, then swallowed the lot - talk about sour grapes and ashes!

After the coffee TLM suggested setting up a poker school, which took up the rest of the day - me keeping very quiet about the sort of tricks I used to pull in Peking. So quiet in fact that I quite forgot about asking him about taking LITTLE LORD FAUNTLEROY away with me until we were all packed up and ready to go.

'Oh, good heavens, yes, and any others you fancy, Wallis. I told you, just help yourself - the more, the better, in fact, and then I might have room to breathe in this house.'

It was just my luck that Osborne happened to be standing by and overheard, and I could see he was already figuring out how to put a block on it.

'Beg pardon, Your Royal Highness, but when can we expect the Lady Furness back again?'

'Oh, some time before the end of the month. I spoke to her a couple of days ago and she said she's hoping to get a suite on the *Bremen* which sails on the 20th or thereabouts, I believe.'

'Very good, Your Royal Highness' - this with a sideways snicker at me, but little did he know he'd just done me one great big favour! Now I've got a firm date to work on, and if Mrs. Jordan does her stuff the dress should get to Thelma in time for her to bring it over - even if that's the last thing she ever does for me.

So that's about quits on Round One with the Ogre, I guess…

Monday 12 March

Down to the post office with the book - over two pounds to airmail, so let's hope it earns its passage.

Cain still down with the bronchials - once more and I might really have to start thinking of giving her her cards.

Ernest came in from work looking so chipper I figured he must have been lunching out all over the City on his star turn as a ready-reckoner - but no, he said it was all down to 'a decided improvement in the rates for Romanian maize.'

Anyhow, he OK'd the coat at Jay's.

Tuesday 13 March

Ernest back down in the dumps again because one of his Norwegian pal's steamers had been sunk by pirates in the South China Sea (another sensation by the crew of The Good Ship Venus??), so just as well that I made it down to Jay's this morning - and that they still had one with the lobelia lining in my size.

58

No show from TLM - according to the Court Circ he was hosting one of his Boche cousins (and one of Hitler's biggest fans, so they say), the Duke of Brunswick. No doubt Baba/Fruit-Face were right in there too.

Thursday 15 March

(Cain back at last) *With the Sun and Jupiter in conjunction, you are probably itching to confide your high hopes of a current project to a close friend or relative, but for the time being you should bite your tongue. Given its exciting nature, even those you trust most may have difficulty in doing likewise, and any premature publication could render those hopes stillborn. All might seem set fair at the moment, but there will inevitably come a time when you begin to harbour some doubts or misgivings and it's then that you will need to call on others for their moral support* - or immoral support, more like it!

Big Bucks called to say the dress was ready, so I told her she needed to get it to Thelma in the next week.

'So you're still on speaking terms together, are you, Wallis?'

'Yes, of course, darling. Why ever should you think we weren't?'

'Well, there was a report in the *Baltimore Post News* two days back saying you'd been seen with the Prince several times just recently and wondering if you weren't, well, you know -'

'Aunt Bessie, you're surely not going to believe everything you read in the papers, are you? Especially at this time of year when nothing much is going on and they have to fill them with every little scrap of gossip they can dream up.'

'No, but -'

'He just loves to dance and takes anyone who's available for a partner, that's all. You don't really believe that I go round stealing my girl friends' beaux, do you? I thought you knew me better than that, I must say.'

'Yes, of -'

'Especially when I've got Ernest hanging around my neck the whole time. You don't seriously think I'm going to risk losing him, do you? Really and truly.'

'I'm so sorry, darling. Forget I ever mentioned it.'

'OK, I will this time. I can't help it if people want to write that sort of trash, but in future I'd just ask you to spare me having to hear about it, that's all.'

'Yes, of course I will. Now about the dress…'

Sorry, Bessie, but I was only obeying the lady's orders.

So who's been blabbing this time? If it had been Fred it would be all over America by now, and none of the others at the weekend have any ties that I know of with Baltimore. Emerald? Her mouth is big enough, that's for sure, and if she's as hard up as she makes out I wouldn't put it past her playing stringer for one of the East Coast agencies.

Called her to fix a date for lunch and test her out, but was told she's in Paris. Checking if that daughter of hers is still hitched up with her nigger there, I'll bet - no wonder she never told me she was going.

TLM dropped in again for KTs and stayed on for supper as usual - Mrs. Ralph must be wondering why Ernest and I aren't balloons by now! Said the weekend's out as he has to be in Liverpool for some unemployed 'jolly' as he called it (with Freda?), though he was hoping to get in a couple of rounds of golf on the course at Hoylake (ditto?).

Monday 19 March

Given your forthright approach to life in general, people involved with you in any enterprise or organisation will probably look to you for a lead. If so, their confidence likely to be justified; indeed, with Mars about to enter your chart, you may well bring them more success than they bargained for. This makes it all the more important that your respective roles are clearly defined from the outset, especially if money is involved. However well you know the others, you may be required to take a firm stand; failure to do so can result in even the closest of friendships ending in tears.

Tried Emerald again and found she'd just got back, so fixed lunch on Thursday at Harrods (on me this time) - aside from their sale, they're doing a demo of the latest Electrolux hoovers, which I'll need if it ever comes down to firing Cain.

Just on my way out for a snack lunch and the afternoon show (Harold Lloyd) at the Curzon with Gebe when Mary called - right on cue.

'I got the book in Saturday's mail OK, darling, and took it over to lunch at the Spencers yesterday with me.'

'And was Chuck interested?'

'Interested? I'll say he was!'

'So what sort of figure did he put on it?'

'Well, hold your hat on - he said it would make two and a half grand, minimum!'

'No, really?'

'Yes, really. You know that LITTLE BLACK SAMBO I told you he sold for six hundred? Well, apparently that was only signed by someone outside of the family - some godfather or other - and to the little idiot prince, whereas as this one being to the Prince of Wales would make it worth double that, and then being signed by the Queen herself doubles it up again.'

'And so how soon does he reckon he can sell it?'

'Oh, he says it'd fly out of the shop tomorrow, no trouble, but of course he's going to advertise it a bit first. And the other good news is that he'll cut the mark-up to thirty per cent, so that make our share even better. We're still going fifty-fifty, aren't we?'

'Well, I was wondering about that, darling. I know that was the deal, but I've been thinking I'll really have to give the Prince something out of my share, so that won't leave me with all that much.'

'No, I suppose not.'

'Especially as I thought the whole thing up.'

'Yes, perhaps that isn't very fair, I agree. Also I have to say that I'm not exactly on the breadline at the moment, what with Jacques' loot and my attentive little Greek friend.'

'So he's still around, is he?'

'I'll say he is, whenever he's not heading off to Sicily or New Orleans or some place. He took me to lunch the other day to meet one of his pals here and insisted on introducing me as his 'moll', would you believe. Meyer Lansky, I think his name was. Typical little Jew-boy, not my type at all, but Ari said he had a big, big deal going with him. (I'd better not have her digging too deep into Ernest's origins, then!) Anyhow, let's not go into that just now, darling. Getting back to our own little deal, what sort of figure have you got in mind?'

'Well, maybe something more like sixty-forty to me, I was thinking.'

'Oh, OK then. So if it does make two and a half grand, what will that leave us both with?'

'Search me - you know how hopeless I was at school with figures, darling. I'll have to get Ernest to work it out.'

One and a half to me, he made it - call that the best part of £350 (I'm not so slow when it comes to figuring dollars into pounds!). I kept quiet, of course, about letting TLM in on it, until Ernest suddenly got the same idea into his head.

'You think that? And what difference do you reckon is a few pounds going to make to him?'

'Well, I know, not very much, but it's the principle of the thing. It's not quite cricket, that's all, honeybunch.'

'Cricket? And what the hell do I know about cricket? All I know is that that's enough to keep us in this flat for the next four months.'

'Yes, I appreciate that, but -'

'And if we're talking games, how much is your playing ships bringing in? Just tell me that.'

'Not a lot at the moment, I admit, but the market's bound to turn up sooner or later. We'll just have to be patient.'

'And so how long do we wait? Four months? Four years? Ten years?'

'Well, it won't happen overnight. I know there was a bit of a spurt in Romanian maize the other day, but overall tramp rates are still at their lowest since -'

'Don't talk to me about tramp rates, please. The only tramp rate I know is working the streets finding somewhere to lay my head for the night, and if you want us out of this door, then I'll take one street and you can take another. OK?'

That brought him to his senses soon enough.

Wednesday 21 March

Court Circ: *YORK HOUSE ST. JAMES'S PALACE His Royal Highness The Prince of Wales will attend the final of the Unemployed Men's Association Football Club Competition on Clapham Common this afternoon. Brigadier-General Gerald Trotter and Mrs. Freda Dudley Ward, the Honorary Adjudicator of The Competition, will also be in attendance.*

Let's hope that's the only game he gets up to...

Thursday 22 March

You have a strong suspicion that something is going on behind your back between people who are important to you. Whatever the likelihood might be that this is in fact the case, you should tell yourself that you have no evidence that this will turn out one way or the other; in other words, if it does eventuate, it could just as well work in your favour as against you! By all means keep your ear to the ground, but until you have that evidence you should avoid all temptation to jump to conclusions and thereby risk making an exhibition of yourself.

So easy does it, girl…

And as it turned out, it was Emerald who set the ball rolling.

'Did you see the shot of David and Freda in the paper today, darling?'

'No, I don't think so,' I lied.

'They were at some football match or other. He was doing the handshakes and she was dishing out the medals. They looked so sweet together, it was just like old times.'

'Oh?'

'Yes, but of course all that's old hat now. Some people are trying to make out that he's after the daughter now, but course that's ridiculous.'

'It is?'

'Quite ridiculous. I know he's had a name as a bit of a cradle-snatcher in his time, but the girl hasn't even been presented yet!'

'And then of course there's Thelma…'

'Yes, but for how much longer? That's the question.'

'Oh, really?'

'Yes. Strictly between you and me, darling, a little dickie-bird's been chirping in my ear. You know our darkie friend Aly Khan, don't you?'

'Well, not personally.'

'No, no, but you know who I mean. Well, I gather that he and Toots have been having a bit of a fling together over the other side.'

'You don't say. Are you quite sure?'

'Oh, yes. From what I've heard, they've been as good as living in each other's pockets for weeks now.'

'Well, I suppose anybody can have a fling.'

'Maybe, but what's Our Mutual Friend going to make of it when he gets to hear? Not very much, I'd guess.'

'Possibly.'

'So here's your chance, don't you see, Wallis.'

'MY chance?'

'Yes. You don't have to pretend to me that you're not in the hunt there, darling.'

'No, really, I wouldn't know anything about that, I'm sure…'

Luckily, we were on the coffee by now and the Electrolux demo finished at three, so I was able to cut her short and make my getaway. If I'm ever going to keep the American press off my back you can say goodbye to any more lunches off me, Emerald darling…

Called Mary as soon as I got back in to check out the New York papers, but she hadn't seen anything.

'But there's a little bit about your friend Thelma Furness in the *Post*'s gossip column, if you'd like to hear it.'

'Yes, please.'

'Well, pin your ears back. It's headed 'The Tale of Two Princes', and goes on: *Thelma Furness, youngest of the three celebrated Morgan sisters and estranged wife of British shipping magnate Lord Furness, sailed over last month to help elder sis Gloria Vanderbilt battle her claim for custody of her daughter Gloria Junior. The case was quickly adjourned to the fall, but Thelma has found good reason to stay on. Most nights since she has been seen at the Twenty-One Club on the arm of the young millionaire playboy Prince Aly Khan, son and heir of the fabulously wealthy Indian potentate, Aga Khan. She finally sailed for Britain on the liner Bremen yesterday after a tearful farewell, and boarded to find her cabin lined with roses. Aly called her up and invited her to dinner, and she replied 'Sure, next time I'm in Palm Beach.' Imagine her surprise when he told her, 'No, here in the First Class Dining-Room,' and discovered that he had taken the next-door suite! All eyes are now on the dockside at Southampton, where her long-standing beau, England's Prince Edward of Wales, is expected to welcome her ashore. Are we in for a battle royal?'*

So the press has its uses after all - assuming that TLM gets to see a copy…

Tuesday 27 March

For some time now you have had the feeling that your life is building towards some sort of crux, but for one reason or another you have been able to postpone the moment of decision. With Mars now in the most sensitive area of your chart you may be inclined to exaggerate the possibility of an unfavourable outcome and be tempted to take refuge in the smallest pretexts to procrastinate, but in doing so you could well be letting slip an opportunity which will never recur. 'He who hesitates is lost', so now is the time to take the bull by the horns and remind yourself that it's the big issues in life that matter.

The *Bremen* was due in on Sunday and so of course that ruled out the weekend at the Fort, but in fact it didn't dock till yesterday - held up by bad weather, according to Ernest.

That meant sitting by the phone all today too waiting for the showdown call - I'd just about given up on it when it finally came through.

'Hello Wallis, is that you? It's Thelma here.'

'Thelma, darling! How lovely to hear from you again. How are you?'

'I'm fine, thanks.'

'That's great. And how's Gloria?'

'Yes, she's fine too.'

'Oh, good. I gathered from Connie that the case has been put off to the fall. Apparently the judge said that -'

'OK, I'll leave that for another time, if you don't mind. It's really The Little Man. I'm calling about.'

'Oh yes?'

'Yes. He's been behaving rather oddly towards me since I got back, you see. There's something which seems to have come between us, and I can't put my finger on what it could be at the moment. You wouldn't have any idea, would you?'

'No, I wouldn't. Of course he's been quite lost without you, darling, but he still absolutely adores you, I can promise you that.'

'That's just what I'd like to be sure about. I thought maybe if you and Ernest weren't doing anything for Easter, you'd like to come down to the Fort on Saturday and we could talk about it.'

'Oh yes, we'd love to. We hadn't gotten anything planned at all.'

'Good. There'll be some others there of course, but I'm sure we won't have a problem finding a bit of time to ourselves.'

'No, I'm sure we won't. Oh, and did my aunt manage to get the dress to you OK?'

'Yes. I'll have it with me ready for you to collect.'

'It's so sweet of you to go to all that trouble, it really is. I just don't know how I - '

'Bye for now, then.'

'Bye bye, darling.'

Looks like it's all set for the shoot-out at OK Corral, then. Wallis get your gun, girl...

APRIL

Go, Go, Go!

Sunday 1 April

I'd called Baba on Thursday in the hope of a lift down, but they and the rest (all the usuals) had been asked for Friday and so it was the train or nothing.

Being the Bank Holiday, Third Class (Ernest of course still refusing to go First) was bursting at the seams, but he just about managed to keep the Woodbines at bay with his cigar.

When we got to Virginia Water there wasn't a single cab to be seen, so I had him call the Fort to send a motor - and of course I had to get the Ogre himself on the other end.

'I'm very sorry, madam, but the party has just gone into luncheon and the staff will be fully occupied with the serving until they have finished. Would you care for Cook to prepare you a cold collation from the left-overs?'

'No, it's OK, thanks, we'll get something in the buffet here.'

I wasn't to know that the only thing on offer was a steak-and-kidney which looked like it had been given up for Lent, it had been there so long - talk about humble pie... I was just telling Ernest we should try the next station down the track when a cab finally showed, but even so it was past 3 before we made it to the Fort.

As I could have bet, Osborne had made himself scarce and Ernest had to carry the bags in himself. No such luck with Thelma - she was waiting to pounce the moment we got inside the door and gave Ernest his marching orders to join the chain gang in the shrubbery.

So this was it, death at five paces - or so I thought. I tried to play for time by checking that she had the dress with her and insisting that I wanted pay her for it there and then, but she wasn't having any.

'No, really, that can wait. Like I said, it's David that I want to talk to you about. Have you heard him mention the name Aly Khan recently at all? You know, the Aga Khan's son.'

'No, not that I recall, darling.'

'He's an old friend from Paris and we just happened to bump into each other on board last week. I was just asking because David somehow got hold of the story and seems to be reading all sorts of things into it. "You're not jealous, are you, darling?" I said jokingly, but he seemed to take it dead seriously and has pretty much given me the cold shoulder ever since. It's so ridiculous, Aly's hardly out of his short pants, but I can't think of any other reason for David wanting to act like that. Can you?'

'No, I can't imagine.'

'I mean, there's no one else he's been playing around with, I suppose?'

'Not that I've heard of, no.'

'You're quite sure on that?'

'Yes - but then I'd hardly be the first to know, would I, darling?'

'No, I guess not. It's just that something gave me the idea that Freda was back on the scene. Could that be right?'

'Well, I read they were up at some meeting in Liverpool together for the unemployed last month.'

'Really?'

'Yes, and he still takes the daughter golfing now and then, I gather.'

'I see. Tell me more.'

You bet I did - and then some on top, till a thunderstorm broke outside and the chain gang came racing back in, ditto the wives from the terrace.

Thelma had us in the Orange Room as usual and the dress laid out ready on the bed, but when I tried it on it was a good two sizes too big in the waist - thanks to TLM taking his share of all Mrs. Ralph's casseroles for two since I sent Big Bucks my measurements? Just as well I'd brought a couple of reserves along.

I was hanging them in the wardrobe when I saw there was a box of books in the bottom. It had a note on it saying *'Wallis, do me a favour and get rid of these for me, will you? I'd be ever so grateful. Happy reading! David'*

The one on top was called THE WATER BABIES and had written inside *'Dear Edward, from your affectionate Great Aunt Louise, on your joining the Royal Naval College 20.IX. 1906'*, but none of the others seemed to be signed.

I couldn't make up my mind between the tartan woollen and the blue lace lacquer, but eventually went for the first which proved to be just the ticket, as when we went down TLM was all gotten up in his Scotch skirt and bonnet. It was Scotches all round too instead of the usual Manhattans and Sidecars, and even the menu was an all Scotch affair - Cockie-leakie soup, poached salmon, raspberry soufflé (from my recipe, if Thelma had but known) and Highland cheese.

TLM had Thelma and me beside him at one end, so the conversation didn't go with too much of a swing - especially as she'd now come out with a streaming cold - but on our other side they were going at it hammer and tongs over the government's crazy idea of bringing in a drivers test.

'It looks as if we're the high handicappers here Wallis, what?' TLM cracked. 'Be a darling and pass the salad, will you?'

He picked out a bit of lettuce and began eating it in his fingers, so I grabbed his other hand and gave it a little slap. 'Naughty boy!' I said. 'I'm sure Nanny never let you do that.'

Thelma glared right back at me with a sort of 'How dare you be so familiar with the future King of England' look. I hadn't exactly meant it that way, but she must have taken it as a signal that he was my baby now because she hardly uttered another word for the rest of the meal, and as soon as TLM began to warm up on the bagpipes she made a run for it upstairs.

After the rest of us had sat there being blasted out of our skulls for half an hour that looked like a pretty smart move, but then she came belting back down again and hollered at him, 'David, can't a girl get some sleep for her cold without having to put up with that filthy racket?'

'Oh, awfully sorry, Toots old girl, I didn't think you could hear it up there. Okey dokey, I'll - ' but by that time she'd swung on her heel and was off up the stairs again. 'I don't know, some people are never satisfied, ha, ha. I say, how about a record or two? That'll get the party going again, what?'

But it didn't, and after another half hour or so we broke up.

Ernest set up his usual foghorn of a snore as soon as he hit the sack and so I had to put my ear to the door to catch anything going on outside, but I didn't have to wait too long before I heard TLM knock on Thelma's and ask if he could have anything sent up for her. I couldn't make out what followed, but the next minute the door slammed shut again and he trailed off back to his room, so I guessed there wasn't too much for me to lose sleep over.

Woke up to the sound of crunching on the gravel outside and a motor ticking over, which was strange as it was only showing just after seven on the clock. I went over to the window to see what was going on - and darn me, there was Thelma all dressed to go and piling her bags into a cab. There was no sign of TLM, and a minute later she'd vamoosed, never to return!

So that looks like one down, two (Freda and daughter) to go, playing it on the safe side - whatever Emerald says.

Friday 6 April

As a naturally outgoing personality, you are always interested to find out as much as you can about the people you're involved with. Occasionally your curiosity can get the better of you, especially when it relates to someone that you care for, and you should guard against appearing over-inquisitive. By the same token, you are usually happy to present an open book when you yourself are the object of interest, but there may be times when you should remind yourself that others may be tempted to exploit your good nature for their own advantage.

Well, it didn't take long for the message to get around - the phone's been red hot all week with invitations from all the grand dames in town from Edith Londonderry down to the all-time trier from Denver, Colorado, Laura Corrigan. (she of 'Do you know the Dardanelles, Laura?' 'Oh, rather. Loved him, hated her.')

Emerald of course wouldn't take no for another lunch, but she seemed to know the whole story anyhow (as usual). Apparently Thelma had had her chauffeur meet her at Southampton when she docked and hadn't counted on TLM showing too, so when he told her to stop off at the Fort she had to say she couldn't because she'd offered Aly a lift up to town. He still wasn't going to take no for an answer, however, and as soon as she'd dropped Aly off he went in and had it out with her. She tried to say it was just a coincidence they were on board together, but then he produced the chapter and verse from the *Post* and she had to come clean - and according to Emerald, that's it, period. Whoopee!

Also got some more lowdown on Baba. Apparently she doesn't have Tom Mosley all to herself, but has to take turns with Diana Guinness, one of the crazy Mitford girls. That was OK while her Ambassador was on hand to plug the gaps, but he had to be back to Italy on family duty over Easter and so she called in Jock Whitney to take her to Dublin for the races (leaving poor old Fruit-Face literally holding the babies, plus the Mosley and the Guinness kids on top.)

Jock might not be much of an oil painting, but looks aren't everything - or even worth noticing - when you're talking about a bank balance the size his is. This girl Baba seems like she needs watching…

Going back to Mary, she called yesterday that Chuck had gotten so much interest running in LITTLE LORD FAUNTLEROY that he's going to auction it. The other good news was that her Mom had died at last and so I needn't mail the new lot of books as she'd be free now to come over and collect them for herself any time soon.

TLM had our usual gang to dinner at the Embassy and on to the Kit Kat as he was having to be on hand over the weekend to greet Brer George back from his African jaunt. Half wondered if Freda was going to show in place of Thelma, but she didn't - relief!

Sunday 8 April

Torrents of rain again outside, so put my feet up and settled down with the mags for another boring old Sunday - but at least I had the place to myself, Ernest having taken off to Canterbury to rub brasses or whatever.

But then

1) Mary called - LITTLE LORD F had made over three thousand dollars! That's £400+ for me - which should make tomorrow's accounts session a ball for once. Against that, she'd seen another pair of TLM's cufflinks listed in the catalogue for Park Burnet's next sale, so who's the competition at this end? I'll have to keep my eyes peeled...

2) Emerald ditto - 'Darling, my little birdie's been tooting again, if you catch who I mean.'

'Thelma?'

'Yes. She's just flown her nest with her black prince to another one in Paris - and she'll be there some time if he's up to form. He may only be just out of short pants, but his old man's had him trained up in Imsak by a Cairo pro.'

'Imsak? What's that?'

'You know, the trick of keeping himself on hold and a girl on heat at one and the same time.'

'Oh, Fang Chung, you mean. Same thing.'

'Is that right? Anyhow, she'll find it a big change from Our Mutual Friend's performance, by all accounts - which puts time on your side there, doesn't it, darling?'

And a lot more than time, I could have added...

I'd hardly put the phone down and the kettle on for some tea when the doorbell went and there was this charmer in a trilby and Services jacket with brass buttons on the mat. I don't say he was a spit image of Win, but there was something about him that screamed 'ex-flier' at me - in the nicest possible way!

'Mrs. Simpson? I'm awfully sorry to disturb you, but I was wondering if I might have a word with your husband if he's in.'

'No, I'm afraid he's out for the day. Can you tell me what it's about?'

'Yes, rather. I'm representing the Ford garage round the corner in the Edgeware Road, you see. We've just taken delivery of the new Aristo model, and I was wondering if I could interest you in a trial spin. The name's Trundle by the way, Guy Trundle - here's my card, if you'd like to have a dekko at it.'

'Yes, thanks. Oh, Squadron Leader - is that Royal Air Force?'

'Well, the Royal Flying Corps as it then was, actually.'

'That's funny, my first husband was a US Navy flier, though I don't suppose you ever came across him. Look, I've got the kettle boiling for some tea - you wouldn't fancy a cup, would you? It's China, of course.'

'Oh, that's terribly kind of you - that's my favorite too. I know I shouldn't be barging in on you on a Sunday like this, but a good salesman never misses the chance of a sale, don't they say?'

Talk about a good salesman, he had my hand going through the gear changes in no time, and was just getting into the business of inserting the starting handle when of course Ernest had to show up and put an end to it all. Even worse, he ruined my story of my maybe looking for a little run-about-town model for myself by saying we were right down to our uppers and couldn't afford to run one motor between us, let alone two.

'Well, if you fancy a trial spin, just give me a buzz - no obligation, of course,' the poor guy - Guy! - was just able to manage before he was rushed out of the door.

Still, if that was a boring old Sunday, the next one can't come fast enough!

Thursday 12 April

TLM only had time to throw down a couple of KTs before he had to dash off for the night train to Glasgow and a tour tomorrow of the big new liner being named after the Squaw.

He was still going to be back down again in time for our weekend at the Fort, he said, 'though I'm aiming to squeeze in a round at Troon, don't you know. There's that hole there called The Postage Stamp which is only 110 yards, so it has to be my best ever chance of getting on the green in one. Besides, I need to get some practice in on a championship course before my week at St. Andrew's at the end of the month.'

What's up - a five-day conference on Unemployed Scotch Green-keepers and Caddy-boys, chaired by Mrs. Freda Dudley Ward? I'll need to check this one out, pronto.

Sunday 15 April

Arrived in style this time, TLM having sent his chauffeur Ladbrook round with the Rolls to drive us down - only to find the whole place upside down and TLM flying around like a headless chicken all because that little critter Jaggs had gone off limits. He was apparently last seen Thursday night near the main road - maybe he'd gotten a sniff of Thelma and was heading for Paris? That wouldn't be too hard to believe if Emerald has the black prince's form right.

TLM had a map of Windsor Great Park laid out on the dining table and covered with little flags where he'd sent out search parties. He wanted us to cover the corner up towards Englefield Green with him, and we'd barely had time to get down a couple of mouthfuls of salmon salad before he was handing us a pair of whistles and marching us out again.

It was just our luck, of course, that it had to be the hottest day of the year so far - right up into the mid 70s, would you believe - so what that and the new broges did to my poor feet was nobody's business. Then to cap it all was the din from the darn'd whistles - every time TLM gave a blast, Ernest felt duty bound to let rip with an even longer and louder one, which went right through my head and out the other side.

After a couple of hours of this carry-on I'd had more than I could take and said I was going to have to chuck it in, and luckily we were almost back where we'd started from. Ernest looked at me as if I was committing high treason, but TLM said that was fine by him and he'd get Osborne to rustle up some tea while he checked with the police to see if they've had any luck.

I flopped into the nearest chaise long feeling like a shot of something a bit stronger than tea, so I told the Ogre he could get me a king-size Manhattan.

'A Manhattan, madam?' said he from a great height (even allowing for me being horizontal)

'Yes, and I'll have it with bourbon, not Scotch.'

'I'm sorry, madam, we don't serve cocktails here before seven o'clock. It's His Royal Highness's rule.'

'Well, if he made it, I guess he can unmake it. Ernest, go and have a word with David, will you?'

'All right, honeybunch.'

'I'm afraid that won't be possible, sir. His Royal Highness has just driven over to the Castle, you see.'

I had to admit he'd landed one on me there, but after the best-ever soak in the tub I was ready to come out swinging again by seven - and this time I had TLM in my corner.

'And with plenty of ice.'

'With ice, madam? At this time of year?'

'Yes, it's an American thingie, Osborne,' TLM came in with. 'Just put it in the shaker and I'll do the honours myself.'

That caught him in the solar plexus OK, and boy, did he show it!

The KTs came and went, but TLM was none the happier. He couldn't understand it, the whole of the Park had been covered and there hadn't been a sign of him, he'd never done anything like this before except for the day he'd got lost in Buck House as a puppy and ended up in The Lady of The Wardrobe's laundry basket. Then there was the time Corah had fallen into the pool, the time Jaggs had swallowed a golf ball, the time Corah had taken a chunk out of Angie Dudley Ward's pet rabbit, the time Jaggs had been caught on the job with one of The Fat Cook's corgis…

'So why don't you go for cats, then?' I cut in when I saw Ernest's head about to pitch into his sweet. 'They're a whole lot less hassle than dogs.'

'Cats? Good Lord, no, we've never ever had a cat in the family.'

'Why not? They're so much smarter up top.'

'Well, that's the problem, don't you see? We Royals are all so thick.'

Ernest reckoned that was a great gag and creased himself laughing.

'Oh, it's no laughing matter, I assure you, Ernest. How would you like to spend your life reading out speeches which you've never written a word of yourself? For instance, I'm in a terrible hole just now about one I've got to give on Friday to some Master Mariners dinner or other. I know I was a cadet at Osborne once upon a time, but I haven't the first clue about merchant ships, don't you know?'

'Well, what about Fruity?' I suggested. 'He's a bit of an old salt, isn't he?'

'Fruity? Oh no, no, he's got even less of an idea than I have. Put him on the back of a horse and you're away, but put him on a deck and he wouldn't know his barnacle from his binnacle. I say, hang on a sec - you've got something to do with shipping, Ernest, haven't you? How would you like to have a go at it?'

That wiped the laugh off his face pretty darn'd quick!

'Well, of course usually I'd be only too honoured to, David, but the trouble is I've got a particularly busy week coming up in the office, unfortunately. There's an important delegation over from the River Plate Mercantile Association which I'm having to look after, and then there's -'

'Oh that's OK, I'll come round some evening and talk you through it. There's going to be a presentation of a picture by some artist chappy so you'll have to kick off with that, but otherwise I'll leave it up to you to decide what'll go down with the assembled burghers. So it's deal, is it?'

'Well, all right, then.'

'Ernest, you're a real brick! That's one big blot off my horizon, I can tell you. And now if you don't mind, I think I'm going to turn in as I want to get the search going again for Jaggs first thing in the morning, the little wretch…'

7.AM. As if poor old Ernest hadn't lost enough sleep already over what he'd just let himself in for, there was such a hammering on the door that I thought it had to be the bailiffs back at the flat, but of course it was only TLM all gotten up and ready to go.

'I say, come on, you two layabouts, or you'll be missing out on breakfast. Get your skates on!'

I was still trying to force down my first mouthful of kedgeree when I heard the phone ring, and TLM came bouncing in like he'd just broken the bank at Monte Carlo.

'He's been found! He's been found!'

'Where?'

'In Southampton, of all places!'

So I wasn't so far out, was I?! 'What, on the dockside?'

'I don't know where exactly, but they've got him safely under lock and key in the police station there. I'm afraid I'm going to have to love you and leave you, if you don't mind. I don't know when I'll be back, it rather depends on what sort of state the poor little chap's in, so just tell Osborne what you fancy for lunch. Tootle-ooh, then.'

That sounded like the bell for Round Three…

I gave it an hour and then cornered him in the pantry while he was giving the silver the once-over.

'Oh, Osborne, His Roy -'

'Mister Osborne to you, if you don't mind, madam.'

'OK, Mister Osborne, if that's the way you want it. His Royal Highness told me to tell you to fix some lunch for us. It looks like it's shaping up pretty warm again outside, so I think we'll go for something cold like the salmon salad we had yesterday, but this time I want -'

'The salmon is finished, I fear, madam.'

'Oh, come on, there was still a whole side left yesterday.'

'Indeed so, but I have to report that the cat consumed the other, most unfortunately.'

Now I had him where I wanted him, I reckoned. 'The cat? You're sure you're right on that, Mister Osborne?'

'Perfectly, madam.'

'But His Royal Highness distinctly told me just last night that he'd never owned a cat in his life.'

'Speaking for himself, I believe that is the case, but the animal in question happens to belong to Cook. Passes by the name of Falconer, and lightning on his feet he once was too when he was on the take. Run to fat rather now, mind you, but that's not surprising, the number of hot dinners he's helped himself to. Gray all over, he is, just excepting his white paws and -'

'OK, OK, Mister Osborne, you can cut the small print, thanks. So if the salmon's gone the way you say it has, what else have you got on offer?'

'Well, we could make up a collation of luncheon meat and Scotch eggs, if that would be agreeable to you.'

'Luncheon meat? Isn't that out of a can?'

'Out of a tin, yes, madam.'

'You're kidding! I think I'll go and have a look around for myself in the kitchen.'

'No, I am afraid that will not be possible, madam. Guests are not permitted in the kitchen under any circumstances, with the sole exception of Lady Furness.'

'So what's she got that I haven't?'

'That, madam, is something that I'm hardly in a position to judge, am I?'

As soon as I said I realised I'd let myself in for a sucker punch, but I wasn't going to hang around for the knock-out and so I told Ernest to get the bags packed - Wallis Warfield hadn't come all the way from Baltimore, Maryland to be fed out of a tin can by some snot-nosed Limey butler.

It was only when we got back home that I remembered that I hadn't gotten what I wanted from TLM on what sort of game he was going to be playing at St. Andrew's.

Still, that had saved us from hearing out whether he'd managed to lick The Postage Stamp, I guess.

Monday 16 April

Daily Sketch

JAGGS FOUND - BY JAGGS!

(photo of TLM holding Jaggs and shaking hands with J. Jaggs, inset of Miss S. Boot)

Southampton. 48 hours of heartache for the nation's doglovers ended this morning when Jaggs was found alive and well. The Prince of Wales' beloved six-year-old Cairn terrier went missing from His Royal Highness's Virginia Water mansion, Fort Belvedere, on Thursday night shortly after he had left for his tour of the John Brown shipyard in Glasgow.

On his return he organised a huge search of the area with the help of the Windsor police and a company of the Welsh Guards at nearby Pirbright, but without success.

Then on Sunday morning a dog was brought into a vet's surgery in Foster Street in Southampton's dock-area by the local police. 21-year-old assistant Sherry Boot said, 'As soon as I saw him, I felt sure it was Jaggs from the photo in the Daily Sketch. Then when I called him by his name and his little ears pricked up, I knew for certain.'

The police were also able to trace his rescuer, a foppish 58-year-old Blue Funnel Line steward named none other than Jeremy Jaggs! Taking up the story, he stated that 'I was negotiating the A30 Thursday night in my Baby Austin when my headlamps observed a small dog imposing on the kerb. He appeared disoriented, so I reversed backwards and requisitioned him.

'Having no means of identification and me not being cognizant with the location, so I resoluted to accompany him to my domicile in Eastleigh.

'I was minding to expatriate him to the police custody in the morning, but not seeming fully rehabilited I retained him until conveying there via reporting for duty last night.'

After driving down to be reunited with his pet, His Royal Highness sought out his rescuer on the liner Thersites in order to thank him in person (pictured).

Mr. Jaggs told our reporter, 'I've been privileged to serve any number of kings and queens in my 30 years at sea, but this has to be the proudest moment of my life.'

Saturday 21 April

The Times - Dinners column

MERCHANT NAVY OFFICERS

His Royal Highness, The Prince of Wales, as Master of the Honourable Company of Master Mariners, presided at a dinner held by the Company at the Mansion House last night. There were nearly 500 present, including the Lord Mayor and Sheriffs, together with the Masters and Wardens of many City Guilds.

The occasion was marked by the formal presentation by Lord Wakefield of the picture, painted by Sir John Lavery, R.A., depicting the ceremony at the Mansion House in November, 1932 when the Prince received from the Lord Mayor the grant of Livery to the Company, of which he is the first Master.

The PRINCE of WALES, on rising to the accompanying toasts, was warmly greeted. "The gift of Sir John Lavatory's picture is," he said, " on a par, if I may

borrow an expression from the golf course, with the great-hearted generosity with which Lord Wankfield — WAKE *treats everything he touches, and I am very much looking forward to the day when I'll be able to see it hanging from the balls of the Master Mariners' Hall."*
(Applause.)

"Of even greater value than the gift itself is the hand of friendship which the oldest companies have stretched out to the members of the youngest. These sinners mean that at long last the Merchant Navy - the industry of the sea - is taking its proper place in the conviviality on which the City of London's reputation rests. Who knows, but one day the Company might procure a Lord Mayor of London."
(Renewed applause.)

"These occasions give them an opportunity for making known to all the aspirations of the members of the company to sip at the highest tables in the land. Two years ago I introduced a member of the younger generation of shipowners to one of your sinners, and, speaking from the chair, I emphasised the importance of training young semen from the general copulation in the finer details of manners and etiquette."
(Prolonged applause.)

"Tonight," the Prince continued, "I am concerned with the education of the officers of the Merchant Navy, and I say with all sincerity that if we are to maintain our reputation as the gentlemen of the high teas, one of the conditions must be that the men in positions of command in our merchant ships, both on the bridge and in the engine-room, shall be the best that we can possibly elevate to the highest standards of ejaculation and the other social graces."
(Cheers.)

"Things are looking up just a little both in sipping and commerce, and it will not need me to remind you who are here tonight of the recent most encouraging rise in the rates for Romanian maize. Though I agree it is just as bad to be too much of an optimist as too much of a pessimist, it was a great thrill for me exactly a week ago today to be a visitor to the world-famous shipyard

of John Blair on the Clyde and see the workers hard at it on the hull of the biggest ship that has ever been built and the champagne already in position for its launch."
(Redoubled cheers.)

"I repeat, that as a nation we must pay more attention to the selection and training of our officers and semen as ambassadors to the rest of the world, both for the well-being of our sipping industry and for the social success of the boys of this country, who will always, please God, have the call of the sea in their blood. This cannot be accomplished simply by singing 'Pull Britannia': it is only if the words are ejaculated according to the rules of the King's English that the desired effect will be achieved.

That is my conception of the high duty which is ours as officers and gentlemen."

(All stood, a five-minute ovation, a chorus of "Encore" and a hearty rendering of "What Shall We Do With The Drunken Sailor?").

Sunday 22 April

Lunch at the Fort with the usuals, with TLM still playing the Master Mariner knocking off the toasts.

'And to our friend Herr Hitler, the saviour of the unemployed in Germany, with our best wishes on this, his birthday.'

Baba (holding out her glass in a Fascist salute) 'Heil Hitler!'

'And finally, to that all-round genius and saviour of the illiterate, my chum Ernest here. To the importance of being Ernest, what!'

'Hear, hear! Ha, ha!'

Me (holding out my glass to catch his eye) 'And?'

He (caught) 'Oh yes, and of course to Wallis, the woman behind his success. To the importance of being Wallis!'

That was more like it.

Afterwards the chain gang was excused work because of the weather outside - gales, rain, lightning, you name it - and so we all headed upstairs for a lie-down.

I wandered down again about half four to see if there was any tea on the way, but there was no sign of life anywhere until suddenly I heard a shout of 'Get in the hole, baby!' from the direction of the study, and there was TLM all rigged up in some yellow plus-fours hitting golf balls at a trash basket in the middle of the carpet.

'Oh I say, I'm most awfully sorry, Wallis, I never saw you there. You must think I'm bananas.'

'Well…'

'The thing is, I've got this awfully important week coming up at St. Andrew's and I just wanted to make sure my putting was tickety-boo, don't you know. Then I'm having a lesson with Archie to check over my long game tomorrow before I fly up.'

'And are the Dudley Wards going along too?'

'Oh no, no such luck. Actually, Angie's flat on her back in hospital right now, poor girl. Freda says it's quite serious, one of those itis thingies. She could be in there for a couple of months, apparently.'

'Oh, I see. So this trip's got nothing to do with the unemployed then, has it?'

'Good Lord, no, I haven't got time for any of that. Look here, do you mind awfully if I carry on with this a bit longer? I was just getting the hang of a new technique I'd thought up.'

'No, go right ahead.'

After a good minute of suspended animation he took a sudden jab at the ball, which hit the basket well off center and rolled into the corner.

'Attaboy! If you'll excuse my Turkish.'

'OK, but isn't that a bit easy, David? I mean, shouldn't you be using something a bit more to size?'

'Yes, I should perhaps, really. I suppose I could always make a hole in the carpet, what?'

'No, you don't have that. Why don't you pull that Pembroke table out from under the window and go for one of its legs? I've always reckoned it'd look better for being more in the middle, anyhow.'

'Oh no, we'd have to move it back again or Osborne will have a fit.'

'OK, so he has a fit - he'll get over it.'

'No really, I can't.'

'Say, who's the boss around here? I'll soon put him straight on that if you won't.'

'No, no, it's all right, Wallis, I'll see to that - just leave it to me.'

'That's a promise, is it?'

'Oh, rather.'

As luck would have it, we'd just got it into place when guess who showed and announced tea was up in the drawing room.

We were heading out when the Ogre picked the Pembroke up to take it back where it had come from.

'No, no, Osborne, just leave it where it is, if you don't mind,' TLM told him. 'It's staying there from now on.'

'Staying there?'

'Yes, that's right.'

'But Mrs. Maugham bought it for you particularly to fit with the window, if you remember, Your Royal Highness.'

'Yes, I do, Osborne, but Mrs. Simpson thinks it looks better where it is now.'

'Mrs. Simpson does, does she?'

'Yes.'

The guy followed us out without another sound, but when he got back into the kitchen he brought the tray down with such a crack that it came right through the green baize like a blast from a Smith & Wesson.

Round Four to me - and that without even having to lay a glove on him! But it doesn't need Madame Claire to tell me the fight's not over yet…

Thursday 26 April

The Gospel according to The Times

> *In the first round of the Army Golf Championships at St. Andrew's, the Grenadier Guards beat the Welsh Guards by an aggregate score of eighteen holes to three. Playing at Number Three for the Welsh Guards, His Royal Highness the Prince of Wales opened with a splendid par four at the first, but eventually went down to the high-class play of his opponent, Lt. R. Bushman, by two holes.*

Sunday 29 April

And according to TLM's New Testament

'Well, the first was a bit of a fluke, I have to admit. I had quite a decent drive off the tee, but then I forgot to keep my head down and did a complete foozle. My third wasn't much better and looked as if it was heading straight into the Swilcan Burn, but then at the last minute it got this amazing kick to the right on to the bridge and ended up two feet from the pin! I don't know what it was - head up again, I suppose - but it didn't do me any good and I lost the next five in a row. It looked as if I was going to lose the next too as Bushman was on the green while I was bunkered, but then he suddenly got the yips. I was just getting out of the bunker when I saw his Colonel come up and give him a word of advice, but somehow it must have put him off his game because the poor chap simply couldn't get the ball in the hole from then on and it was me who won the next four to get back to level. After that it was nip and tuck all the way until the Road Hole when I got into that stinker of a bunker beside the green and had to concede, of course. Then at the last I was just at the top of my swing on the tee when some idiot in the crowd shouted 'You're doomed to the Valley of Sin, laddie! You're doomed, I tell you!' And, well, that was that…'

And I'm going to call that amen on the golf.

MAY
Making The Running

Tuesday 1 May

Court Circ: *We are requested to state that applications for tickets for the Royal Enclosure at Ascot should be sent in before May 31st, after which date no applications can be considered. Applications should be addressed to The Master of the Horse, Ascot Office, St. James's Palace, S.W.1.*

So you'd better start upping the pace, Wallis…

Wednesday 2 May

… which I did, while I was clearing away the first casserole of the week, and TLM and Ernest were having their usual political pow-wow.

'And look at Tom Mosley's performance at the Albert Hall the other night. Mind you, Ernest, I don't usually go for a fellow who's ratted to Labor, but then he didn't stay with them too long, did he? There were five thousand people there apparently, and according to Baba and Fruity he had every man jack of them eating out of his hand. Of course he owes it all to his pal Mussolini - I know he's not everybody's cup of tea, but you have to take your hat off to anyone who can make the trains run on time in Italy. Marvellous chap - just the sort of person we could do with here, I don't mind telling you.'

'You've met him then, have you?'

'No, not Musso himself, but we had his son-in-law in our Ascot party last year - you know, Count, Count - oh, what's his name?'

Me, before I could stop myself, 'Ciano.'

'Ah, yes, that's the fellow. Ciano the Charmer, I called him, ha, ha! Delightful chap - spoke the most perfect English and knew his way all round China. Well, the interesting bits, anyway, what? Life and soul of the party, he was.'

Me again, 'And so how many of you were there?'

'Oh, the usual dozen or so, I suppose. Asked him again this year, but he had to cry off. Some business in Austria about bagging a few socialists apparently, according to Baba - didn't understand what it was all about myself.'

And again, 'So you're going to be short, are you?'

'Yes, at the moment, but I haven't got round to organising it yet, what with Toots not being around. I say, how would you two like to come along? Assuming you're not fixed already, that is.'

'Oh, that's awfully kind of you, David, but we'd really decided that we couldn't aff- '

As luck would have it, I was just on my way out past Ernest with the remains of the casserole at that precise moment, so it was a cinch to let one end slip and tip the whole lot into his lap, sending him a couple of feet into the air and racing out of the room for a change of pants.

'I think what Ernest was saying was that we couldn't have considered applying for tickets because of my being divorced, you see - even if I was the innocent party.'

'Oh, Good Lord, you needn't worry about that, old girl - I'll have a quiet word in the Lord Chamberlain's ear and that'll fix it. He'll just need to see the legal bumf, that's all.'

He was hardly out of the door before I was making out a telegram to Big Bucks to send over the papers just as fast as she could - plus a shopping list of the dresses, hats, shoes, accessories, etc I was going to need. Adding them all up, I reckoned they were going to come to $400 minimum, so I went for broke and called it $500. (Mary told me when I called last night that Chuck Spencer said he couldn't let her have the check until the end of the month, so she'd bring it over with her)

Thursday 10 May

A week later and nothing's arrived yet, so I called her and she swore blind that she'd sent everything off the very next day by Express. You'd better be telling the truth, Bessie Merryman...

Monday 14 May

You may have a feeling that recently you haven't being paying as much attention to a loved one as you should have done. With the Sun about to move into the most high-minded area of your chart your conscience will be pricked, but you should guard against appearing insincere by going to the opposite extreme. Your plate has been rather full elsewhere of late, as can happen to the best of us at times, and it would be unreasonable of the other person not to accept that; so by all means make amends, but not at the cost of making commitments which you may not be in a position to keep.

Just when I'd given up on it and reckoned it must be sitting somewhere on the bottom of the Atlantic, a package turns up with

1) The divorce papers, signed and sealed by the Court of Virginia in 1927. Reading them through again I suddenly noticed that Win's letter which the lawyers told him to write as from China in 1924 to prove his 'desertion' actually had a US stamp on it - thank my lucky stars the judge never picked up on that! Just as well too my Lord Chamberlain isn't calling for my birth certificate - if he's picky about divorcees, the chances of an illegit getting past him wouldn't be too hot, I'd guess.

2) The check for $500. I did the rounds of the shops last week ahead of its arrival, but then TLM said we'll only be going on the Tuesday and Wednesday, so that's cut my list down a bit. Harvey Nicks had a new range of Vionnet model dresses in cyclamen pink or malmaison red which I really went for, and there was a smart little Chanel number in black marocain and white piqué with a bib bolero - but maybe that would be better for KTs? To go on top they had an Edwardian-style black silk wrap with a collar in sable-dyed squirrel, but this darn'd English weather is so dodgy I'm wondering whether I shouldn't go for a full length coat. Bradley's had a parade in Somali leopard skins which I could have died for and M & Snelgrove's sale had some in pony or foal skin with fox fur collars reduced from 79 to 39 guineas, but I guess I should wait till nearer the time and see what the temperature's going to be. As back-ups I've still got the pale blue and brown number from last year and Debenhams had a nice range in floral silk blouses in fancy crepe de chine, while Fenwicks definitely had the pick of the hats - I tried one with a double brim in black tulle and trimmed with a cluster of old-fashioned roses which was just divine - and which should keep the nosey-parkers at bay!

3) The sting in the tail - a long sermon on what sort of game was I playing with TLM, how lucky I was to capture Ernest after my previous record, how she'd hate to think that I was two-timing him, and how she was planning to come over and see for herself what was going on. Obviously the press over there has been blabbing again and so maybe it wouldn't be such a bad idea to get her away from it, but the last thing I want is having her tipping up here in the middle of Ascot and pooping the party, so I'll have to try and hold her off until July. TLM muttered something last time about taking a place in France for the summer - maybe I can work her in on that.

Tuesday 15 May

Court Circ: *YORK HOUSE ST. JAMES'S PALACE His Royal Highness, The Prince of Wales, will be leaving Euston at 8.30pm by the Royal Train for an overnight journey to Harlech and a 3-day tour of unemployment centres in North Wales.*

6.30 to Syrie Maugham's party with TLM on my own - Ernest being tied up (literally) with his Freemasons. TLM wondered whether we'd be there long enough to be worth it because he'd have to leave for his train, but I said if we arrived on time we'd have a good hour together and he agreed - whoopee!

As it turned out, we could hardly get one word across to each other, there was such a crush (Syrie only has the next level over her shop), and he was just about to pack it in when who should I see heading our way but Thelma! Luckily I was wearing my highest heels, so had a good few inches over TLM and was able to pull him into the nearest bedroom before he spotted her.

This was the very first time we'd had just the two of us to ourselves, and it didn't take him long to get weaving.

'Hold on a minute, David, there's something I want to clear up with you first.'

'Um?'

'What's this Welsh jaunt consisting of, exactly?'

'Well, I'm aiming to get in a couple of rounds at Harlech to kick off with - I'm the Club President there, don't you know.'

'No, I didn't.'

'Yes. Wizard course it is, absolutely wizard.'

'And then?'

'Um?' - working his way back into my mouth again.

'What after that?'

'Well, I'm hoping to squeeze in a round at Hoylake on the last day with a bit of luck.'

'No, I meant in between. The unemployed centres.'

'Oh, those.'

'You're not taking Freda with you by any chance, are you?'

'Freda? Good Lord no.'

'You're quite sure?'

'Oh, absolutely. I'm not seeing her again until the Feathers Club thingie - that's at the end of the month some -'

'The Feathers Club? What's that, exactly?'

I never did get the answer because I suddenly heard Thelma outside squealing 'Where's David? Has anybody see David?', then the next second the door swung open and there she was.

'I see, so that's how it is. I should have guessed, I suppose.'

'Oh, good heavens, Toots, just let me explain, it's -'

'You can save your breath, David - I've got all the explanation I need, thanks. So long then, it's been nice knowing you.'

'Please Toots, just -'

But she was gone.

He tried to catch up with her, but he still had me holding on to his hand - well, I wasn't going to let go of him now, was I?! - and she was out of the door and down the stairs before he could blink.

He stood there mopping his face with his handkerchief saying 'Oh, Good Lord' over and over, until he suddenly caught sight of the clock in lobby.

'Hot diggety dog, my train! I've got to go!'

'What's the panic? It'll wait for you, won't it?'

'Yes, but if it's late starting it might have to wait for all the others and I'm due on the first tee at nine in the morning, don't you know.'

'I see. First things first, eh?'

'Yes, that's right. I say, I'm awfully sorry, Wally, about, well, you know…'

'Don't worry, David, everything's just fine between us.'

'Are, you sure?'

'Yes, just fine.'

Just fine…

'What's the Feathers Club when it's at home?' I tried again with Ernest when I got back in.

'I can't think… Oh, unless you means Ma Feathers' place.'

'And who might she be?'

'Mrs. Featherstonehaugh, pronounced Fanshaw - she runs the classiest whorehouse in town. There's always this story about how Lord somebody-or-other knocked on the door once and found his sister there.'

So that's how Freda picked him up! Still, it's about time he put her down again, I'd say…

Monday 21 May

Things may seem to be moving your way, and with your sunny nature you could be tempted to think that you can just lie back and let everything take care of itself. However, life is seldom as easy as that and it's still up to you to make the most of your opportunities. Sometimes it may be necessary to impress your determination on others: you know inside yourself that you have the necessary strength of will, so there's no need to be shy in showing it. Sounds like crunch time, Wallis…

An extra day at the Fort because of the Whitsun holiday, but the downside was that he had an even bigger crowd there than usual and so I didn't have TLM to myself for one single second. He'd asked me to come up with some ideas for redoing the Pink Room, the one right at the end which Syrie had never got round to finishing (there'd been a showdown with Thelma over the colors, I gathered), but then he just left me to it and went out to join the chain gang. Then when the rain came on again, he had them all down in the basement testing out the golf net which he'd rigged up there.

I'd been digging around in the cupboards looking for some more I could pass on to Mary when I hit gold - a teddy bear with a tag on it reading 'I am Benny and I belong to Prince John'. After I'd brushed it down a bit it came up almost as good as new, so I put it out on the bed all ready to go.

We were all taking tea together before packing up when the Ogre came in with a refill and a grin all over his face the size of a slice of watermelon.

'Beg pardon, Your Royal Highness.'

'Yes, Osborne?'

'I have some good news for you, sir. Benny has been found.'

'Benny? Who's that?'

'You know, the Italian bear you were looking for last month.'

'Oh yes, of course, John's teddy. I was wanting to give it to some godchild or other - I forget who now.'

Me, all innocent: 'But you're not seriously going to give it away, are you, David? I mean, wasn't it rather precious to him?'

'Oh no, it wouldn't have meant anything to John - he was just an animal, you know. So where did you find it, Osborne?'

'In the Pink Room, Your Royal Highness, on the bed. I would deduce that Mrs. Simpson discovered it during whatever she might have been doing there.'

'Yes, that's right, it was in the bottom of a cupboard sitting under a pile of empty Cartier boxes.'

'Well, how would you like to keep it then, Wally? Finders keepers, what?'

Me (after a double take): 'Oh no, I couldn't, David.'

'Why not? I'm sure Ernest there wouldn't mind you taking somebody else to bed for a change, would you, Ernest? Ha, ha!'

That had to be one of all TLM's worst gags ever, but it was still enough to set Osborne off on his watermelon routine again. Your round then, buster...

Twenty minutes later we were all fareweling and I still hadn't managed to catch TLM on his own, so I grabbed one of the pooches which was sniffing around the bottom step and called him over.

'David, come and look at this. Cora looks as if she's gotten a tick in her ear.' And then when his ear was close enough, 'You're still seeing Freda this week, are you?'

'Yes. No, wait a minute, I'm off up to Prestwick on Wednesday to watch the last rounds of the British Amateur, so it must be next Wednesday.'

'But still at the Feathers Club?'

'That's right. Pretty yawn-making it'll be too, but one has to show willing once in a while, what?'

'You'll be showing more than willing, if I know anything about it.'

'Oh? How do you mean, exactly?'

'Look, David, it's none of my business what you get up to there, but just don't try and kid me I don't know what goes on in that sort of joint.'

'But Wally -'

'I'm giving it to you straight: any more messing around with Freda and you can count me out. OK?'

'What?'

'You heard.'

'But just let me explain -'

'I don't want explanations, I want a commitment, and if you can't give me that right now I'm going to wave you goodbye and walk clean out of your life for keeps. Got that?'

'No Wallis, don't! You can't do this to me! You can't!'

'Care to bet on it? Here, take this,' I said, pushing the pooch back at him and hustling off to the Metcalfes who were giving us a lift to town again. Ernest had just finished loading the bags into the trunk, so I yelled, 'Hey, Fruity, let's go! And you can step on it this time!'

If there's one thing I've learnt in life, it's that a girl's surest way of catching her man is by playing hard to get. OK, it may mean losing the odd bit of sweat, but if they're keen they'll be sweating a whole lot more and this one doesn't look any different from the rest of them. Anything but, in fact...

Wednesday 30 May

Court Circ: *YORK HOUSE ST. JAMES'S PALACE His Royal Highness, The Prince of Wales, returned from Scotland yesterday evening, but he is indisposed and unable to fulfil his engagement to attend the Annual Dinner of the Three Feathers Club in Shepherd's Bush tonight.*

Three feathers - what's this? A Josephine Baker floor show? And since when has the action been down in Shepherd's Bush (rather than Market)? Maybe I should have let it rest there now that he'd eaten his crow, but I felt I just had to get to the bottom of it once and for all.

'Josephine Baker? What's she got to do with it?' he said when I called.

'You tell me, David - you know the sort of tricks she gets up to with feathers as well as I do.'

'Of course I do, yes, but haven't you got the wrong end of the stick here, old girl?'

'Have I?'

'Yes. I mean, this isn't that sort of place at all, you know - it's just a club for the local unemployed which Freda set up some years back and roped me in as president.'

'And so where do the feathers come into it?'

'Oh, that's just my crest - the three feathers of the Heir Apparent, don't you see.'

I can't recall feeling I wanted the ground to open up and swallow me ever since the prep school play when I trod on the hem of my skirt and brought the whole thing down around my ankles, but boy, did I now!

'Oh I say, Wally, what a card you are! Fancy you thinking the Feathers was a sort of pick-up joint, what? Wait till Freda hears that one, ha, ha…'

'Oh, so you're still talking to her, are you?'

'No, no, I didn't mean from me - I meant if she gets it from someone else.'

'Are you quite sure about that, David?'

'Yes, of course I am.'

'Because if not…'

'But I told her straight that it was all over between us. You've got to believe that, Wally.'

'You did?'

'Yes, Scout's honor. You're the only woman that's ever going to matter to me, I know that now.'

But how was I to know it? That was the problem…

A half hour later and I had cracked it.

'This is Mrs. Dudley Ward speaking,' I told the girl on the switchboard in my best cut-glass when I called back. 'May I speak to his Royal Highness, please.'

'I'm terribly sorry, madam, but His Royal Highness has given me strict instructions not to put you through to him from now on.'

So that's it - it really is curtains for Freda. Going back to my preppy acting days again, we did a Shakespeare title called *The Comedy of Errors* - or was it *All's Well That Ends Well* ? Whichever, I had the lead part and it was a mighty fine performance!

JUNE
Grandstanding

Sunday 3 June

No Fort this weekend as TLM has to be on parade for Big Chief's birthday lunch today, and again tomorrow - literally - for the Trooping of the Color. After that he's got prize-giving at the National Cadet Association and the Grenadier Guards dinner on Tuesday, a get-together with the rest of the Family at the Derby Race on Wednesday, the King Edward's Hospital Fund AGM, a reception for British Empire Service League of South Africa Pilgrimage to the Battlefields of France and Flanders (no less) and the Welsh Guards dinner on Thursday, winding up at Kettering for the Northamptonshire Agricultural Show on Friday - so there'll be no taking pot luck here for the rest of the week either.

'At least you won't be going hungry!' he told me - oh no?

Monday 4 June

You have a habit of letting problems nag at you until it gets to the point where you begin to believe that you actually need something to worry about. Tell yourself that you were never meant to adopt this treadmill mentality, which is threatening to rob you of your ability to relax. Give yourself a little treat of some kind, which will clear your mind and enable you to see the way ahead. Sometimes the answer will be staring you in the face: it's just a matter of knowing where to look.

Thanks, Madame Claire, but I know exactly where to look. Before Simpson, Spence & Young hit the rocks, I used to have a weekly colonic irrigation session with Denise just off Wigmore Street and never came away feeling less than a million dollars - and all for a guinea. Luckily I still had her name in the address book, and better still she had a cancelation at 4 this afternoon.

I'd just about blown Big Bucks's check by now on my Ascot outfits and so I was pretty much relying on Mary, but when I called her there was more bad news - she was having problems with the lawyers winding up her Mom's estate and she didn't reckon she'd be able to get over now until mid-July. That was just the time I had earmarked for Big Bucks, so I suggested they got together and came over on the same boat - that way at least they'd be able to keep watch on each other's checkbooks!

I told her about the near miss with Benny the Bear, and she said that was another line that went down big with the fans - there'd been a golliwog up at auction last year belonging to Brer Henry of Gloucester (Woodentops to the rest of us) which had made nearly $400 even though it was minus an eye and half the stuffing from its head.

'Then there was a big silver presentation tankard of your pal's which came up last month.'

'Of David's, you mean?'

'Yes. It was inscribed to him by some army regiment or other.'

'By the Welsh Guards?'

'Maybe, I forget. Would he have sent it over himself?'

'No, I doubt it.'

'So who else would have?'

'I can't think, right now. Was there anything else to say where it had come from?'

'Well, it was made by Cartier, as I recall.'

'You don't say? Maybe that's just the clue I need...'

I knew me and Osborne were slugging it out together, but I didn't realize we were splitting the purse! Just don't be surprised if my next punch comes in below the belt, buster...

Well, Denise worked her usual magic, the only pain coming with the bill - now up to 25/- a time, which naturally didn't go down too well with the Keeper of the Purse at the weekly audit.

'Read that, woman, if you've still got the brains to read!' he yelled as he unrolled his *Financial Times* on the table and stabbed at the headline *"Shipping subsidized for 13 years, owners' reserves exhausted"* - *Chamber of Shipping President.* 'How many more times do I have to tell you that you'd better get any idea of Ascot out of your tiny -'

'OK, OK, I've got the message' - ie, that it wasn't in that direction that I should be looking.

Tuesday 5 June

I was still trying to figure out where to turn next when TLM called to ask who I was backing for the Derby, and I had to tell him that I hadn't even taken it in that today was the day, let alone getting around to picking a winner for the big race.

'Well, when you do, I hope it won't take you too long.'

'Why's that?'

'Haven't you had a look at the runners?'

'No, not yet. Hang on, I'll just go get the paper.'

I called to Cain to bring me *The Times*, and there it was - Windsor Lad!

'Do you know anything about it?'

'I should say so - it's owned by my chum the Maharaja of Rajpipla. (I'm not kidding!) Remember me telling you the story of how Fruity made his name in India? Well, that's where it all happened!'

'And is it worth backing?'

'Oh, rather. You can still get on it at six to one, I'm told.'

'Where?'

'Don't you have your own hole-in-the-wall bookie?'

'No.'

'Well, I'll look after it for you, then. How much do you want to put on?'

'I'd better just stick to a pound, I reckon,' I said, without going into last night's scene of domestic bliss.

'One pound? Well really, Wally, I thought I meant more to you than that, I must say.'

Put like that, how could a girl refuse? 'OK, make it a tenner, then.'

'I don't know, that still makes me feel like something out of the bottom drawer. Why don't you go for a pony?'

'But I thought this was horse race.'

'Oh, I say, what a card you are, old girl! Fancy thinking the Derby's a pony race! Wait till I tell Fruity that one, he'll go pop like a ripe peach, what? Ha, ha, ha...'

Well, whatever it is, Lover Boy had better come home...

Wednesday 6 June

Decided to pass on Madame Claire for today as I'd committed myself now, but what I did need to know was exactly how much I was kissing goodbye to. Mrs. Ralph couldn't help, so it was down to Cain and guess what - pony is Cockney slang for £25! I guess TLM picked it up along with the accent he always puts on for the hobos. According to *The Times*, Windsor Lad's odds are down to 9-2 - I'd need Ernest to work out what I was standing to clean up, if only I dared tell him…

Looked in on the M & Snelgrove sale on the way to lunch with Baba at the Connaught. They had quite a range of Ascot frocks including a really smart number in black faille with a white organdie trimming and reversible cape (which could be useful if the weather turns lousy) - £55 with matching shoes, and as I was still short on those, I really fell for it. The only problem was having Sweet Fanny Adams in the bank to pay for it, so I had to tell them to hold it a couple of days for me and just pray Windsor Lad would do the rest.

Baba seemed a bit on edge even before she spilled half of her first KT all over the table, and I soon found out why - Tom Mosley was going to be holding his rally to end all rallies at Olympia tomorrow night, and there were stories doing the rounds that the Commies were coming up in force from the East End all set on breaking it up. She was going to be there too of course, but she also had Fruity to worry about as he'd signed up to lend a hand supervizing the stewards (TLM having given him the go-ahead without a second thought)

As we were on the subject of keeping tabs on things, I managed to get her onto Osborne and had they ever reckoned he was up to anything? Yes, they had - there'd been some hideous wooden figure gifted TLM by the Mowries on his New Zealand tour which he'd told the Ogre to chuck on the bonfire during a clear-out last year, and a few months later they'd seen a spit image of it in an auction at Parke Burnet while they were over there. They'd told TLM about it, but the only answer they'd gotten out of him was 'Good Lord no, the fellow's as straight as a die! Just like the toothpaste he puts out for me every day, what? Ha, ha.' Then there'd been some funny business over orders being switched from the butcher in Sunningdale to a branch of Dewhursts and their grant of a Royal Warrant, even though their meat wasn't a patch on the local man's. Certainly sounds like it's all beginning to stack up…

I had to cut it short there before Baba started ordering liqueurs (we were going Dutch), but also I was running out of time to get back and hear the race commentary on the radio. Cain already had the set warmed up, and when she and Mrs. Ralph started hollering every time Windsor Lad got a mention I began to wonder if they hadn't been listening in on TLM's calls. Anyhow he still didn't seem to be in with much of a chance until the favorite was blocked coming out of the final bend and left him clear in the lead. 'Come on, Lover Boy, go go, go!' I found myself yelling, until I caught sight of Cain looking like a fly had just gone down her throat. Anyhow it did the trick, because he came home with a length to spare!

When Cain finally got her vocals back, she had to admit that she'd 'had a little flutter on my (!) prince'. I told her she'd better keep quiet about it when the master got home or he'd dock her for the candy biscuits I knew she was helping herself to - and more to the point, grab my jackpot for the Mutual Poverty Fund if she blabbed.

Luckily TLM called up just before Ernest got back in to give me the full score - all of £112-10-0!! Even my maths could figure out that would cover two of those frocks - but if I just go for the one, then I can keep the rest for something really decent for his birthday in two weeks time on top of the folding stand (called a butler's tray over here) Mrs. Ralph had brought over from Lady Curzon which I was planning on - a silver hip flask, say? He said He'd get his bank to pay the dough direct into my account, so I'll be right round to M & S tomorrow.

He said he'd only just got back from the track because the crowd had gone wild after Windsor Lad had been led in and started singing 'For He's A Jolly Good Fellow' in front of the Royal Box, but Big Chief had gotten it into his head that they were meaning him and started waving back too, then all the rest of the Woebegones had decided to get in on the act! He'd be bringing plenty of fizz with him for his next pot luck (in a week's time), when he just might have some even better news for me - like he'd given Osborne his cards?

Friday 8 June

The Times

SIR O. MOSLEY AT OLYMPIA

INTERRUPTIONS AND EJECTIONS

The Fascist meeting at Olympia last night suffered from continuous interruptions, and the interrupters were roughly dealt with by the blackshirted stewards, both male and female. The meeting began 40 minutes late because of demonstrations outside which, Sir Oswald Mosley said, had attempted to intimidated those entering.

The entire audience then rose and he walked the length of the hall between two lines of his supporters, who saluted him in the Fascist manner and cheered him heartily. The rays of four powerful floodlights were concentrated on him as he made his way to the platform accompanied by some of the principal officers of the movement. On reaching it he turned with military precision and gave the Fascist salute before beginning his speech (which is reported on page 16).

It proceeded peacefully for the first 10 minutes before the Socialists made their first move. After that clashes broke out in different parts of the hall in a well co-ordinated plan and it was countered with a similar thoroughness. Stewards at once made for the offenders and if they resisted they were made the target of fisticuffs; if they still remained standing, they were then seized in ju-jitsu fashion and dragged out. Somewere women, who were often dealt with by women blackshirts and slaps were occasionally exchanged.

The most difficult of all the disturbers to deal with were some who had climbed up into the roof girders, from where they hurled their insults and such light missiles as they were carrying. A posse of stewards eventually followed them into the roof and with the aid of searchlights located and ejected them. The trouble continued right to the end of the meeting, and several stewards departed nursing facial injuries. One of them in particular sported an enormous black eye, which caused a sympathetic onlooker to remark, 'Blimey, you collected a ripe peach there, guv'nor!'

I didn't need Madame Claire to tell me who that was!

Sunday 10 June

Fort B. No show from Fruity and Baba - surprise, surprise - and as his stand-in, General Trotter, only sports one arm we were condemned to the train (Third, as ever) again. Officially named Gerald, TLM always calls him Gee-Gee - I don't think his second name begins with a G, but apparently he's still a riding fanatic even without his arm, which if he told me once, he must have told me a dozen times he'd lost in the Bore War (he must have cleaned up every other way there!)

'I say, have you seen this, Wally?' TLM greeted us with, waving around *The Times* with a shot of him handing a prize cup to some dame holding a gigantic bull (with balls just one inch off the ground), underneath it had *His Royal Highness The Prince of Wales at the Royal Northamptonshire Agricultural Show at Kettering, presenting Lady Robinson with the Aberdeen-Angus Champion Trophy for her Prince Ben of Boghead.* 'I don't know what the beast does to you, but it sure as hell scared the shit out of me, ha ha! Just as well Fruity wasn't there or he'd have copped it, what? Ha, ha...'

The rest of the day (when he wasn't splitting himself over his own gags) he had us helping him figure out his new jigsaw, a 3000-piecer of a hunting scene called 'In Hot Pursuit' (my memory might have been playing tricks, but the girl coming right up behind the red-coated dude in the center looked the spit image of that Millie Boulter - wasn't that her name? - who got herself into the papers a while back by tipping TLM out of the saddle) Maybe he was feeling so chipper because he didn't have The Ogre breathing down his neck - he'd given him the weekend off, he said, seeing as there were just the four of us.

After dinner he got out the cards for a game of Red Dog. In my time in Peking I'd got this one (and one or two other tricks!) down to a fine art and so naturally I made out that I'd never played it before, but of course just when I didn't want it I had all the luck in the world.

'I say, Wally, just as well we're not playing for money or you'd be taking me to the cleaners, what? Ha, ha...'

Many a true word spoken in jest, as they say...

Sunday started fine, so there was no saving poor old Ernest - or even the One-Armed-One - from the chain gang.

TLM blew me a kiss as they started out. 'Awfully sorry to leave you on your own like this, Wally, but first things first, what? And I bet you'll have finished the puzzle by the time we get back, you're such a clever girl.'

'No, it's OK, I think I'll pass on that just now.'

'Oh. Hang on, I know - now that Osborne's not here, how about taking the dogs walkies? I know there's nothing more I'd fancy myself than a little jaunt with you in the woods.'

Put like that, what was I to say? It only had to be for quarter of an hour and I could keep them on the lead the whole time, so it didn't seem like any big deal.

I should have guessed better. I took them up to the nearest Park boundary and was just turning for home again when there was a sudden rumpus on the other side and out shot a rabbit with a Labrador-type pooch right on its tail. Before you could say Jack Robinson my two had slipped their collars and joined in the fun, but as soon as the Lab-type got a whiff of Cora (TLM hadn't let on she was on heat) it gave up on the rabbit and made after her. I needn't go into the details of what happened next - let's just say that before I could get the lead back on, Nature had taken its course.

As for Jaggs, all he was interested in was the rabbit even though he didn't have a hope in hell of catching it and he wasn't going to take a blind bit of notice of me, however hard I yelled. After a few circuits out in the open, he doubled back and headed into the vegetable garden, where I eventually ran him down digging like crazy at a hole in the middle of what looked like a strawberry plant bed (or did before he'd pulled it apart) Before I could get to him, however, Murdoch the gardener came up and managed to haul him out by his back legs.

'Thanks a million, Murdoch - you've just about saved my life there,' I said to him, but he just stood there hands on hips glaring right back at me. Somehow I got the feeling that we weren't exactly going to be pals for life - but then I never did go for the strong silent type!

Anyhow I got my own back on the two little critters when we were inside again and (with no Ogre around to put his spoke in) I really let them both have it with the chain end of the lead.

For the next hour they didn't dare move a muscle, but then the moment TLM put his head round the door all my good work went down the pan - they were jumping on him and licking him all over like he was covered in aniseed.

'Oh, what fun you must all have had together, you little monsters!' he told them when he'd managed to get them off his face 'And think how lonely poor Wally's going to be when she goes back to London tonight without you!'

Just as well I wasn't in on the conversation or he'd have heard differently...

After lunch and another session on the jigsaw TLM said he wanted my advice on some new furniture for the Pink Room and sent the others off to play tennis (Gee-Gee apparently has worked out a trick of placing the ball on his racket and then flipping it up in the air to serve)

There wasn't too much trouble persuading him that the whole lot should go, except maybe the bed (which isn't there for its looks!) The two chests of drawers weren't even antique - in fact they looked like they'd been knocked up by some cowboy carpenter of Syrie's.

'Shall we go and see what they've got in Partridge's then, old girl?'

'Sure, if you want to pay twice over the odds for the Bond Street on the label - and maybe more when they see you coming.'

'Is that right? So where else do you suggest we go?'

'Well, there's a little man called Fossitt down by South Ken Tube where I've bought most of my bits and pieces. All his stuff is hundred per cent genuine and half the price of anything in the West End.'

'Really?'

'Yes, and the last time I was in there he'd just got in a couple of Georgian bow-fronted chests of drawers which would look perfect in here, I reckon.'

'Well, that sounds just the place, what?'

'And you'll have to dump that hideous great cupboard. It could hold half an army inside, by the size of it.'

'The wardrobe, you mean?'

'Yes, if you prefer.'

'But that's just what I like about it, don't you see? Whenever we play Sardines, I come straight up here and it always win hands down.'

'You don't say.'

'Yes. Look, why don't you step inside a minute and I'll show you how.'

He sure showed me how all right! Except that it felt more like being packed in with a sperm whale than a sardine, he came on so heavy and fast.

'Oh Wally, I've been wanting this for so long, I can't tell you,' he spouted when he finally came up for air.

'Me too.'

'You're just the sweetest, cutest, most gorgeous thingie I've ever met, my darling.'

'So I'm not just old girl any longer?'

'How d'you mean?'

'Well, that's what you've been calling me up to now.'

'I say, really? Oh my goodness, how awful, I never realised. Will you ever forgive me, my darling?'

'In time, I guess I might.'

'No, now! Now! Now!'

He was just about to push me under again when Cook's voice came through from the corridor calling for him - the silly sap had jumped in after me so fast he hadn't even shut the door behind him! And now he jumped out again even faster - and still didn't shut the door, but at least it meant I could hear what it was all about.

'Some Italian gentleman for you. Your Royal Highness. Said you was expecting him.'

'Did he give his name, Cook?'

'Some grand count, it sounded like.'

For a moment my heart missed yet another beat or two - I knew Galeazzo had written me that he was due in London soon, but what in hell's name was he doing pitching up here? 'From the Embassy, he said he was.'

'Not Conte Grandi, was it?'

'Yes, that's it.'

'Oh Good Lord, I clean forgot - I had to cancel his audience last week because it clashed with President's Day at the Berkshire, so I told him to call in today if he was passing. Tell him I'll be down in a jiffy, Cook - I'd better spruce myself up a bit first. Oh, and rustle up some tea and sandwiches, will you?'

'Very good, Your Royal Highness.'

It took me a sight longer to spruce myself up before I went down. In fact, I wondered whether I should show at all in case my knowing Galleazzo came up, but when I eventually did I found all they wanted to talk about was some meeting Musso had just had with Hitler in which they'd agreed on the need for 'a virile peace'. Sounds like a meeting of opposites to me - if I know anything about Italians, you'll get plenty of virility, Adolf, but as for peace, you can forget it.

The next moment he was back on his feet saying his addios - I guess what he'd really been hoping for was some more time with Baba. Seeing us without a motor he offered us a lift back to town and of course Ernest leapt at it (he'd only bought singles on the way down), but at least we made it home without a mention of Galleazo still.

So that was that for the weekend - that's cupboard love for you, I guess.

Wednesday 13 June

The feeling of excitement at the prospect of entering a new and hitherto closed world of experience is always an intense one, as is the temptation to disclose all your hopes for it to a loved one or close friend. However, you should guard against being carried away and being drawn into displaying more confidence about the outcome than your present position warrants, in which case the whole project could backfire. Geminis are adventurous by nature, but the current configuration of your chart is calling for caution. Biding your time will bring its own reward.

Spent the morning in the Kings Road and picked up an 'antique' hip flask for 10/-, then took it to Aspreys to have it inscribed *'To David on your birthday, with my greatest admiration and love, Wallis'* - plus their own stamp.

    Met TLM (in the Lagonda) at Fossitt's at 2, the only time he had free all week, he said - and then he only had an hour before he had to do the honours at some stupefying Old Soldiers tea-party. I'd called F yesterday to fix my commission rate - I couldn't shift him from the usual 10% for the introduction, but he's going to double that if I can finagle a Royal Warrant for him.

    The two chests of drawers just had to have gone, of course, but he said he had another two coming in which were more or less identical and TLM said he was happy to take them unseen at the same price. He also fell for a cute little Queen Ann knee-hole desk in walnut which was pretty much a steal at 45gns (making my cut just about enough to cover Mrs. Ralph's wages for a week). He also had some bad and good news for me on the ride back before he dropped me off at B. Ct. - the bad being that he'd had to scrap the Ascot house party because Big Chief was insisting on his being at the Castle to squire some visiting Dutch princess (but at least I didn't have to worry - she was as big and round and plain as an Edam cheese, he said), and the good being that he reckoned he'd found a chateau to rent near Biarritz for the summer which had everything he was looking for, so if I could tell him as soon as I knew for sure when Ernest was going to be otherwise engaged…

    And he had a surprise something for my birthday next week which he promised would remind me of him like nothing else would.

    'I'll give you three guesses, darling.'

    'No, no, I'd hate to spoil the surprise. I'll just wait for the day.'

    A ruby ring? Or a sapphire?? Or a diamond???

    Roll on, Tuesday…

Tuesday 19 June - Birthday/Ascot

You may have high ambitions yourself, but you have to face the fact that not everyone else is aiming quite so high and that even members of your own family may not necessarily support you in them. In this case you would be best advised not to make them quite so obvious, but that's not to say that you should lower your sights. The path to happiness has to lie in being true to yourself, even if it does sometimes lead to a parting of the ways with your nearest and dearest.

I'd just finished arranging all my cards when the bell went, and I was at the door so fast my feet never touched the ground - until I heard this yapping on the other side. That's strange, I thought, he's never brought the poochs here before, but then I guessed he was calling in on his way to the Castle for lunch with Princess Edam. Even stranger when I let him in was seeing that he had them in a wicker picnic-type basket with a Harrods label on it, and then when he put it down and opened it that there was only one of them there and that seemed to have shrunk a couple of sizes.

'So is this Cora or Jaggs?' I asked when he picked it up and handed it to me.

'Neither, sweetheart!'

'Neither?'

'No. This is Slipper, and he's yours!'

'Mine?'

'Yes. It's your surprise, don't you see? Happy Birthday, darling!'

'It's awfully kind of you, David, but -'

'Isn't he just the sweetest, cutest, most gorgeous thingie you've ever met?'

' - but -'

'And you needn't worry about how to look after him, all the instructions are in the basket. And now I must fly or I'll be late for my Brown Windsor with the Big Cheese. See you later on the course - tootle-loo.'

You're right, Madame Claire, I'm in a whole new world of experience - though Ernest had a few other words for it when he got in from buying his floral button-hole in the Edgeware Road and found it had made a meal of his new Guards tie which Cain had laid out for him.

The forecast - 'Not as warm as we have enjoyed of late, with the possibility of thundery showers in the afternoon' - rather put the kibosh on the frock, so I fixed on the Vionnet in red and the Fenwicks hat with the roses which matched just perfectly, and for a bit of fun - and TLM's benefit

- I added some of the ostrich feathers that Thelma had lent me for my presentation and somehow I'd never gotten back to her.

I gave Cain the instructions on the pooch and told her to keep it topped up with food as I didn't want it chewing its way through anything else while we were gone. Also in the basket I found the day's race card from the *Times* which TLM had marked up for me. He was going for Guest of Honour in the big race, and if I was feeling nervous before the first I had a choice between Spend A Penny and Call Of Duty, or Fleetfoot if I was really desperate!

By 11 we were ready to roll - but minus the Rolls which Ernest had refused point-blank to hire for the day from the people in Berkley Square like everybody else - 'A girl in the office has a boyfriend who runs a little garage in Slough and can do us a de luxe tourer for a tenth of the price'- so it was the hike down to Paddington once again. Third was packed out, of course, and the only free seats we could see were in a compartment already pretty well filled by two scrubber women and their kids. We'd just gotten the door open when I heard one say to the other, 'Lord love a duck, Mavis, if it ain't the Queen of Sheba in person!' which set them all hooting at us. This time I really put my foot down and told Ernest we were either going First or not at all, and for once he caved right in - he must have reckoned it was just as much his Big Day as mine.

Well, we got to Slough in style OK and tracked down the garage - only to find that the 'de luxe tourer' was nothing but a beaten-up old Buick with a slit in the roof and half the stuffing coming out of the seat leather! When the guy said sorry, he had nothing else on offer, I knew exactly how the seat must have been feeling.

If we hadn't been lumbered with our Fortnums hamper I'd have been all for walking the rest of the way - and as it was that's just how we finished up, because as soon as we got into the queue for the track parking lot what did the darn'd thing have to do but boil over. So we had to take lunch right there by the roadside, with our heads down around our knees so that nobody would spot us. I was reckoning we could at least drown our sorrows with the bottle of Leebfraumilk Ernest had bought at the off-licence in Paddington, but the next thing I knew he'd poured the whole lot down the jalopy's radiator!

When we finally made it into the Enclosure, it was just in time to see the third carriage in the Royal Parade go by with all my favorite people - Brers Woodentops and Bertie plus Fat Cook showing off their cutie-pie kid Lizzie (now I get why TLM calls them Shirley and Mr. & Mrs. Temple). All the girls must have been holding themselves back for it, because as soon as the last one was out of sight they made a frontal assault on the

Ladies, and by the time I got in and out there was no chance of making it down to the bookies and it just had to happen that Spend A Penny came home at 8-1. There was no problem getting my money on Guest of Honour in the big race - except that it was beaten out of third place by a head at 33-1...

I could see TLM tearing his hair out in the Royal Box too. We'd fixed it that this was when he'd come down and meet us, but we'd hardly said hello when there was a king-size flash of lightning and the heavens opened. The whole crowd headed as one for whatever cover there was and if TLM made it, good luck to him, but I never did and ended up soaked to the skin.

By now I'd had as much as I could take, and when I said to Ernest it was time to head home he didn't put up too much of a fight. The Leebfraumilk must have done its job because the motor started first time and we made it back to Slough in one, even if we did have to stick to 20mph all the way. I was all fired up to roast the 'boyfriend' alive, but the whole place was locked up and he was nowhere to be seen - surprise, surprise.

Even that wasn't the end of the story. It was almost 7 the time we got back into B. Ct., when the biggest blue of the whole day was waiting for us - Cain had shut Slipper in the sitting room with a huge plate of food before taking off, and the little shitter had dumped most of it all over the carpet and my best rug. To cap it all, when I told Ernest to do the honors he said it was down to me as it was my present and cleared off to the Guards Club for his dinner.

So much for my Big Day - Madame C had it dead right on 'a parting of the ways'.

Thursday 20 June

Up half the night sneezing myself silly, and by breakfast I was down with a splitting head, pouring nose, soaring temperature, you name it, so that was my Ascot over for the year, Ladies Day or no Ladies Day. I told Ernest I wasn't stopping him going, but he said he didn't fancy being there on his own and anyhow he had some work to catch up on in the office. If only Mary would get her act together and herself over here...

He had just left for the Tube when TLM called.

'Darling, I just wanted you to hear something Pop told me last night: "My boy," he said, "I saw you talking with some pretty disreputable people this afternoon." So I came back with "And I distinctly saw you talking to someone who's just been divorced, Father," to which he replied, "I know, but she was such a damn'd pretty woman!" So you see he's human after all!'

I had to laugh, didn't I?

Sunday 23 June

TLM's birthday, and the Fort filled with Brers George and Woodentops, the Mountbattens, Metcalfes (Fruit-Face still sporting an eye patch), Anthony & Beatrice Eden, Duff & Diana Cooper, GG Trotter & all the rest of the crowd, so I didn't get him to myself to present him with the flask till he was in the pantry fixing the poochs' little treat after lunch.

'Oh Wally, what an absolute angel you are! Now I'll only have to take a little nip from this and I'll never have to worry about those two-footers on the 18th to save the match ever again! That deserves a kiss, doesn't it? (yessiree!) And from Asprey's too! Oh, you are a naughty girl! Let's have another, then, (ditto) And what's this? "To David on your birthday, with my greatest admiration and love, Wallis" Oh, how sweet of you - whatever love means, what?'

Good question, pal!

Handing over the folding stand/butler's tray wasn't such a problem because I'd put it in with all the other presents - until it came to persuading Osborne to use it, that is. TLM stuck to his guns for once, however, and when the Ogre brought it in with the tea he opened the stand with such a jerk that I reckoned the straps were sure to come apart (it still had its Army & Navy Stores label on it addressed to The Viceregal Lodge, Simla and dated June 1898) By the grace of God they didn't, but he must have been reckoning that they would too because he announced, 'Mark my words, Your Royal Highness, this thing won't last 24 hours.'

Well, that's Round Six to me in the meantime, buster, and let's just see who lasts the distance…

Saturday 29 June

Fossitt called to say the chests of drawers were in.

When I asked about getting them delivered to the Fort, he said 'Oh, that's all right, I'll arrange that with Mister Osborne.'

'You will?'

'Yes, you needn't worry - he's a good friend of mine. And thank you again, madam, for the introduction.'

And thank you, buddy, for that little item - it might just be all I need to know...

JULY
Over The First Hurdle

Monday 2 July

You can be forgiven for having felt a little confused recently, mirroring the position of the planets in your chart. With Venus and Neptune in conjunction you have been encouraged to lay plans for an escape from the humdrum existence of your usual stamping ground, but at the same time the retrograde Saturn has been presaging reasons for delay, both real and imaginary. Now, however, it's all change: with the Sun and Mars together in the ascendant indicating that you have a special ally by you side, you can look forward with confidence to realising your dreams. Some might try to tell you that you're aiming too high, but that won't trouble you if you genuinely feel that this is no more than you deserve. In that case, the sky's the limit!

Well, it's certainly beginning to look like it's all panning out -

First and foremost, Mr. Tightwad has ordered Ernest to take over the New York office for the whole of August to cover for the partners on vacation. That hasn't stopped him (Pop) from taking off himself to Japan with his new French fancy - he may be the wrong side of 80, but who am I to bitch about him taking his pleasures while he can? Especially as if they're anything like what they are in China there, they should be the finish of him!

Second, Mary and Big Bucks have OK'd my idea and are coming over together on the *Aquitania*, due in at Southampton on the 14th - Big Bucks bringing with her the two blue linen dresses and pairs of shoes that I left when I was over last year. Better still, that's a Sunday, which means that Ernest will be around to glad-hand Mary ashore. And even better again, the oily little Greek has taken off again to Argentina with the Swedish shipping heiress that she found he'd had on board all along - which of course I lost no time in passing on too to Ernest, so here's hoping...

Third, TLM called to say he's gone ahead and booked the Biarritz chateau for August. It's a couple of miles downtown with its own grounds and right on the ocean, so there'll be no problem about having it to ourselves

- not literally just the two us (sadly!) as there are going to be half a dozen others making up the party, but at least that made it easier to break it to him that I was aiming to bring Big Bucks along for the ride too.

I was half expecting him to raise hell that she'd throw a damper on the whole show, but as it turned out I needn't have worried.

'Nonsense - from what you've told me about her, I'm sure she'll be the life and soul of the party. And besides, she's just the sort of person we'll need as a chaperone, don't you see?'

'As a chaperone? At my age?'

'Well, you may not need one, but I certainly do when it comes to keeping any of the nosey-parkers of the press at bay. They're bound to cotton on to us sooner or later, but if we can say you're just stopping off for a few days with your Aunt Bessie as part of her European tour, that'll really cut the ground from under their feet, what?'

'And put a walking stick in her hand and she'll be cutting more than that off them.'

'Well, there you are! She'll be perfect, just perfect. Oh, and I've asked Posey Guinness to look in while she's waiting down there to join Walter Moyne on his yacht - she's a cousin of his, don't you know. You'll love her, she's a real poppet.'

So that's everything fixed. Cometh the hour, cometh Mrs. Bessie Merryman, as the poet said. But I'll have to check out this Posey doll with Emerald over lunch on Thursday - from the little I've heard of her, she's an A1 man-eater.

Thursday 5 July

'Posey? Oh no, you've got nothing to worry about there, darling - she and Kenelm are still head over heels by all accounts. I thought for a moment you'd gotten the wrong Guinness.'

'You mean Diana?'

'Yes. But now they're saying she's got Tom Mosley pretty much to herself. I know he's booked Baba into a villa with him on the Riviera next month, but it looks like that's just a final pay-off.'

'Is that so? Still, she's always got her ambassador waiting in the wings.'

'Oh, sure. They don't give up in a hurry, these Italians.' You can say that again, darling!

'So where does that leave poor old Fruity?'

'Flat on his back in hospital with pneumonia, right at this moment. But of course it's Baba we should be feeling sorry for - as Nancy Astor said to me, "I do think it's too mean of him spoiling Baba's fun like this, expecting her to come and sit at his bedside every day."'

'Maybe I'll send Ernest to go and hold his hand.'

'Yes, why not? That way they could both bore each other to death and leave you two to get on with your lives! Talking of our mutual friend, I got the low-down on HRH George from Edwina the other day. You know he's a bit suspect there, don't you?'

'Really? He could have fooled me, the way he was working on my leg when I was next to him at dinner.'

'Well, maybe he's both, then. Not so long ago he was supposed to be hooked up with Kiki Whitney Preston - you know who I mean?'

'The Girl with the Silver Syringe?'

'That's the one. But then the word was that David had to pay out a fortune to a rent boy in Paris for some letters he was blackmailing the Palace with. That's why they packed him off to Africa, and David's had to keep him under lock and key since he got back to make sure he keeps straight while they line him up with this Greek princess. Martina, is it? Or maybe Marina - something like that, anyhow.'

So now I know why he went for the Pink Room!

Sunday 8 July

Fort again. TLM pretty well pooped after another non-stop week on duty parade - Monday, two rounds of golf at Sandwich after watching the British Open there ('Well, I just had to stay on and celebrate Henry Cotton being the first British winner for ten years, don't you see?'); Tuesday, an Air Force Display at Hendon Aerodrome ('I am an Air Vice-Marshal after all, don't you know'); Wednesday, a flying visit to Rugby School where he told the boys they needed to develop a sense of humor for bad jokes thrown at them (no need to quote him on that!); Thursday, another farmers show at Ipswich, where Big Chief won two prizes in the butter class ('pity it doesn't melt in his mouth, what?') but failed with his cheese ('must have been hard, ha ha!'); Friday, opened the Alfred Eichkolz Memorial Clinic and Institute of Massages and Physiotherapy for the Blind and attended the Advertisers Association annual dinner at the Grosvenor ('that was the real blinder of the day, I can tell you!')

I agree, you've got to feel sorry for the guy sometimes.

Brer George now fully installed in the Pink Room, along with Fossitt's chests of drawers. 'A pal of yours, I believe, Mister Osborne,' I was itching to catch the Ogre with as soon as I had him on my own, but I never got the chance, darn it.

Had to spend most of the weekend instead listening to George grandstanding us with yarns from his African trip. There was one which went down a treat with TLM and went something like this: 'It was at some big tribal pow-pow in Basutoland - or was it Bechuanaland? One of those places, don't you know - when I had to spend all day faced by this line of floosies with the biggest Bristols (boobs to us) you've ever seen in your life bouncing up and down in front of me like chocolate jellies. The trouble was, the chief was sitting right there beside me on his throne surrounded by a bunch of fearsome brutes with thundering great spears, which rather put the cold water on any ideas I had of pressing the flesh. You can't imagine the sort of torture of it was - talk about the poor old bull pawing at the gate, what? Anyway, when it was all over and I got back to my VIP hut I thought I'd take a little stroll down by the river to cool off, but I'll be jiggered if I hadn't gone a hundred yards before I spotted the pick of them all catching up with her washing on the bank. As soon as she saw me, of course, she scarpered into the long grass and I thought that was that for the day, but guess what? In two ticks she was back out again, minus skirt and pushing her Bristols literally into my face. Well, no prizes for guessing what happened next - I mean, what else was a chap supposed to do?'

TLM: 'Some people have all the luck, what? Reminds me of my shot on the long fourteenth the other day at St. George's, bro - I was just short of the green in five and thinking everything was tickety-boo when I shanked my chip practically off at right angles. It was heading straight for the out of bounds, but then it hit a post, came straight back across the green, hit the teebox on the fifteenth, bounced back again on to the green and ended up in the hole! How's that for a negress?'

'A negress?'

'Yes, you know - highly satisfactory, but not what you boast about in public, what? Ha, ha…'

All jokes aside, maybe TLM really has gotten him back on the straight??

I'd brought Slipper down for the first time to introduce him to Cora and Jaggs, but I'd hardly set him down on the floor before they were ripping him apart. TLM waded in to try and separate them, but only succeeded in getting his hand bitten to the bone for his pains. The doctor came and put in a couple of stitches, so that was TLM pretty much sidelined for the rest of the stay.

I tried again after Sunday lunch, and the little shitter - or Mister Loo, as he's now been christened - promptly excelled himself all over the tiger skin in the hall. Still, it was worth it just to see the Ogre's face when TLM called him in to do the necessary.

I reckoned I had him on the ropes again, but he came back on the rebound almost before I knew it.

'Where's Mrs. Simpson's butler's tray, Osborne?' TLM asked him when he brought the tea.

'Oh, I had to throw it away, Your Royal Highness.'

'Throw it away? What do you mean?'

'Yes, it collapsed like a house of cards just like I said it would, if you remember.'

'But how?'

'Well, it happened somehow to be near the stove when Cook put one of her heavy saucepans on it, and down it went. It gave Falconer such a nasty turn I thought it had caught his tail for a moment, the poor fellow. Gave us all quite a turn, in fact, I don't mind -'

Me: 'But surely it can be mended?'

'Oh no, madam, that's quite out of the question - it was reduced to matchwood.'

'So where is it now?'

'I put it out on the tip with all Murdoch's rubbish.'

'Well, I'm going to have a look for myself, if you don't mind.'

'You won't find anything, madam, I assure you - Murdoch's had another bonfire since with all the laurel cuttings and dead leaves from the garden. All most unfortunate, but there it is.'

OK, another round to you, buster, but you won't know what's hit you with the next punch I'm packing…

Saturday 14 July

Made Virginia Water by 11 all set to come out swinging straight from the bell - and caught him cold. TLM said he'd come and pick us up himself, and while we were waiting I went over to the florist across the road for some red roses and found his prices were a fraction of what Constance Spry was charging for her weekly order. It wasn't to hard to figure out whose pocket some of the mark-up was going into, so as soon as I had the Ogre within earshot I told TLM I'd be putting a stop on it and taking over all the flowers myself from now on. From the look he shot me I guessed I'd hit him right where it hurts, so that makes it Round Eight to me - maybe even a KO!

The papers were full of TLM's tour yesterday of the Ford factory. He'd insisted on driving the first model of their new Prince line off the production track himself, hadn't been able to locate the brake in time and ended up in a pile of paint barrels. The headlines really went to town on that - THE PRINCE OF PAINTERS, PRINCE MAKES A SPLASH, FORD'S NEW ARTIST MODEL etc, plus shots of the NOT added to the FOR SALE AS DRIVEN BY THE PRINCE OF WALES sticker on it. Even the charming Mr. Trundle is going to have his work cut out selling this one now, I'd guess.

TLM still had his hand bandaged up, but he swore that hadn't had anything to do with it and that he was perfectly OK to drive us to Southampton tomorrow morning. I said he could count me out in that case which threw him into a fit, but when he saw I wasn't going to budge he backed off and fixed for Ladbrook to take us down and then back up to London, where he'd meet up with us all again for some KTs.

The ship was due in at 9, so it was a case of early to bed and early to rise for once.

Sunday 15 July

Arrived dockside dead on time - to find TLM there ahead of us in the Lagonda and grinning his head off! 'See, I took you for a ride, Wally, and now I'm going to take you for another one, what?' he cracked.

The way it turned out in fact, I had to admit it was just as well we had the two motors when we saw the amount of baggage Big Bucks and Mary had between them coming down the gangway. I reckoned they'd be in customs for most of the day, and was just settling back again in the Rolls and having a wager with Ladbrook on how long they'd be when out they came again just like they'd walked straight through!

'Oh my, Wallis, what it is to have friends in high places,' Big Bucks explained when we'd gotten through all the reunions. 'When I showed my passport, the guy took one look at it and said, "Oh, Mrs. Merryman, we know all about you." "You do?" I said. '"Why, am I on the Most Wanted list?" "Yes, you could say that, madam," he sort of snickered.'

'Well, it's not me you have to thank, Aunt Bessie,' I replied, pointing to TLM 'It's the guy standing right there behind you!'

'Delighted to meet you, Mrs. Merryman. And you too, Mrs. Raffray.'

Mary did a neat little curtsy, but when Big Bucks tried it she only got a quarter of the way down when she started to tip over and had to grab

TLM by the hand to save herself. Of course it had to be the one with the bandage and I could see him screwing up with the pain, but with all the stars in her eyes she wasn't going to notice that.

'Oh my, oh my, Your Majesty, the pleasure's all mine, I'm sure. From all Wallis has been telling me I reckoned I knew you pretty much already, if you don't mind my saying so, Your Majesty, but I never -'

'But he's not the King yet, Aunt Bessie, you know.'

'What's that you're saying, Wallis?'

'I'm saying only the King gets to be called Your Majesty.'

'Is that right?'

'Yes, Your Royal Highness will do for now, Mrs. Merryman.'

'Oh my, I do beg your pardon, Your Maj - I mean Your Royal Highness.'

'That's quite all right. In fact, why don't you just call me David? That'll make things a whole lot easier for us both, what?'

'If you're sure that's all right, Your Royal - I mean David.'

'Absolutely. And may I call you Bessie?'

'May you call me Bessie? Oh my, oh my, I should just say so. Did you hear that, Wallis? Here's Mrs. Bessie Merryman of Clinton Boulevard, Monica Cunty, Maryland, USA being called just plain Bessie by the future King of England? Oh my, oh my, oh my...'

While she was going through with all this I could see TLM was trying to get his hand away from her, but the harder he tried, the harder she clung on, and when she threw her other hand in they got in such a tangle that they both pulled each other down and ended up in a heap on the deck together.

When we eventually got them sorted out and back up on their feet again, there was a long pow-wow over how we should divide up between the two motors, but I fixed it by saying TLM, Big Bucks and I should go in the Rolls while Ernest could take Mary in the Lagonda and drop her off at the Cumberland where I'd booked her in.

On the way up I ran through the party to France for Big Bucks's benefit.

'... Then there's General Trotter, an ex-Guards war hero and with only one arm to show for it.'

'Oh my, the poor man. Still, that'll be nice for Ernest, having another Guardsman.'

'But Ernest's not coming.'

'Not coming?'

'No, didn't I tell you? He's going to be in New York running the office there.'

'I see. Wallis dear, forgive my asking...'

'Yes?'

'But do you think it's quite right you're going on vacation on your own with a lot of single men?'

'My darling Bessie, you don't imagine that anyone will think I'm up to something with you in tow, do you?'

'No, no, I wasn't suggesting for a minute you would, don't get me wrong, darling. I was only worried about what the press might make of it, that's all.'

'Oh, in that case you can relax, darling - you're not in the States now. Things are different over here and they respect one's privacy, I'm glad to say.'

She'd dropped her voice a note or two, but TLM had still managed to pick it up from the front seat and came in with 'And if it's me they're interested in, they're going to be in for a big disappointment, I'm afraid, Bessie. I'm going over to Paris for some business there [ie, the rent boy, who's now holding Brer George's cufflinks to ransom] on the way and I've no idea how long it's going to take, so I may not even get to Biarritz at all.'

'And then there's the tour of Italy I've got mapped out afterwards just for the two of us,' I threw in again. 'I reckoned we'd head for Milan first, and from there on to Florence, Rome, Venice, Verona, The Lakes...'

Enough to head her off for now, anyhow.

Friday 20 July

The conjunction of the Sun and Mars have given you an easy run of late and may have even encouraged you to think that things are meant go that way for ever, but with Mars now about to enter Taurus there could be trouble ahead. Difficult as it may be for you to appreciate at the time, it may in the long run prove to be to your advantage, if it results in strengthening your determination to achieve your goals; all of us need to be reminded occasionally that life was never meant to be a piece of cake. Don't be disappointed either if a loved one does not give the support which you expect: they may have perfectly good reasons of their own for not doing so. Given your usual single-mindedness, however, there's no reason to think that you can't see your way through on your own. So chin up!

A week of pounding the sidewalks taking Mary and Big Bucks around all of the summer sales. I decided that the two dresses she brought over were really past it now, so I went to town in a big way. M & Snelgrove had a rather chic line in Ascot frocks reduced to 29 gns - I couldn't make up my mind between one in black faille with white organdie trimming and another in wisteria blue with a reversible Spanish-style cape, so in the end I took them both (let's hope I make it into the Enclosure for more than one day next year). Jay's isn't usually my kind of store, but they had a terrific range of evening gowns with French house labels on them all knocked down to 19gns! I went for two again - one in plum velvet with a pink ostrich feather trimming and the other in black organza, plus a chiffon frock in a green print (12gns). Still in frocks, Derry & Toms had some printed casuals at 9gns which will be just perfect for Biarritz in the evening, plus a rather snappy full-stretch bathing suit in black (5gns) and some French beach sandals knocked down to 10/-. As usual, Fenwicks were tops for hats (straw and cotton) and Harvey Nicks for shoes - some white/blue broges and white open-toes with ankle straps and high heels (but not too high, for TLM's sake), and while I was there I also picked up a Raglan coat and wrap-around wool skirt beach outfit in red and white check.

The whole spree came to over £335, which was only just shy of Mary's check after I'd paid the exchange transfer commission. Of course Big Bucks had to ask where all the money was coming from, so I told her Ernest had finally had a rise which made him even more of a hero in her eyes.

At the end of it she was pretty much out on her feet - which was half the object of the exercise as TLM had booked us seats for Dion Titheradge's new show *'Happy Weekend'* starring Louise Brown at The Duke of York's (though it won't make for a happy weekend if we cross with Mr. & Mrs. Temple there!) and I needed someone to Mr. Loo-sit. I sat between TLM and Ernest, and when Louise began her 'Guess what's my motto, Every girl's gotto, Go out and get her man' number I could feel a hand running up and down my skirt - and it wasn't Ernest's! The way I planned it, of course, he (Ernest) would be getting to work the other side on Mary, and when we got onto the floor at the Kit Kat afterwards that's just the way it seemed to be going…

Got back at 3 ready to drop for a big, big sleep - to find Big Bucks doing her nut because Mr. Loo had given her the slip. She thought she'd heard the bell and gone to the door to see, and while she was checking nobody was there he'd got past her and down the stairs before she could lay a hand on him. She'd gone down to the square and spent an hour hollering for him, but of course the little shitter was nowhere to be seen.

That was more than I'd have done and I certainly wasn't going to hold it against her, I tried to tell her, but she wasn't having any and sat on the couch moaning her heart out for 'the little darling'. Still, if that was going overboard, I hadn't reckoned on the real Little Darling's reaction when I called him to warn what had happened - he'd call the Head of Police first thing and have the whole of the London force out searching, and if they drew a blank he'd bring in the Brigade of Guards and have the Air Force to put up 'one of their barrage balloon thingies and a fellow with a pair of high-powered bins. Oh, and I'll put the whole French trip on hold till he's found.'

'What?'

'Well, of course. I mean, you were going to take him, weren't you?'

'No, I wasn't in fact. I have to tell you, David,' (this at 3.30 by now, and looking like I'm never going to hit the sack at all tonight) 'that if you reckon it's my idea of a vacation running round with a shovel after Mr. Loo every time he poops, you've got another think coming.'

'Oh, okey-dokey then, sweetheart, if that's how you feel.'

'So you'll be bringing Cora and Jaggs, will you?'

'Well, no, actually. I mean, it could be a bit tricky with this business I've got in Paris first, don't you see?'

'You mean they don't let dogs into the Moulin Rouge?'

'No, they don't. Well, actually, I don't know, you know, I mean, I've never tried it before, don't you -'

'OK, forget it. You'll be joining in the search party at the crack of dawn too, I take it?'

'Well, no, actually… I mean, what if he's been spotted in Paddington and the press caught me knocking on doors in Praed Street? Pop would have an absolute fit, don't you see?'

'Oh, absolutely, old bean. David, if you don't mind, I'm going to hang up and go get some sleep - I can't keep my eyes open one more minute and Ernest here looks like he's out for the count too. I'll call you in the morning as soon as we've got some news, OK? Good night.'

Spot on again, Madame Claire.

Sunday 22 July

Saturday - across the Edgeware Road, Sussex Gardens and all round Paddington. Ernest knocked up a broad near the station and said could she help, he was looking for Slipper, and got the answer 'Sorry, luv, I don't do dominatrix.'

Speak for yourself, honey!

Sunday - up to Marilebone Road, along to Great Portland Street, down as far as Condit Street, across to Park Lane and back. Some tramp reckoned he'd seen a dead pooch in Grosvenor Chapel Gardens and I was beginning to get hopeful, but it was only a chucked-out mop head.

Called TLM to report no show - he said the Guards would be coming in tomorrow.

Monday 23 July

I'd just got Ernest away to the Tube and Big Bucks into the tub when I heard the bell, followed by some all-too-familiar yapping, so it was no big surprise to find the little shitter there. But what I wasn't prepared for was who had brought him back - none other than Mr. Trundle the Charmer from the garage!

'Delighted to be of service, Mrs. Simpson,' he said, taking off his trilby with one hand and passing the pooch over with the other.

To cut a long story short (after I'd sat him down on the couch with some coffee), he'd gone over to the factory on Friday morning to pick up a Prince demonstration model, and after staying on for lunch in a pub with some pals in the sales department he'd headed back home about 3.

'That should have left me plenty of time, but then I hit this major prang on Eastern Avenue and just sat there in formation for I can't tell you how long, madam, and it was as good as dark before I got back to base. I'd got out to open the showroom doors when I saw this little blighter come up as bold as brass and cock his leg on my front offside. So I got hold of his collar and was giving him a good old Hokey-Cokey before sending him packing when I saw his tag *Mrs. Ernest Simpson*, etc. That gave me a double take, I don't mind saying. My first thought was just to bring him round here soonest and have done with him, but then I reckoned they've probably gone up west for a show and if they haven't they'll have left for a weekend in the country somewhere, so I might as well take him back to my little pad in Bruton Street and pop him back Monday morning. So here I am - or rather, we are.'

'Well, of course I can't thank you enough, Mr. Trundle. But tell me, why didn't you just hand him into the police? That would have saved you a whole deal of trouble, surely.'

'You might think so, madam, but then you don't know them at Paddington Green like I do. If I'm waiting outside on the Edgeware Road no-parking to give a client a demo run and he's late, all I have to do is slip them a quid and Bob's your uncle. So I said to myself, "If you turn him in, Guy, all that's going to happen is that they'll sell him on to the highest bidder and Mrs. Simpson can kiss him goodbye." Get the picture?'

Yes, I did - or I thought I did...

Tuesday 24 July

But on second thoughts - if the cops were into taking kickbacks, wouldn't they have cut a percentage deal with pal Trundle if he'd handed the pooch in? Or even, could they have had it handed in by someone else and sold it on to him? Interesting...

Sunday 29 July

The Fort for a get-together with the other members of The Great Expedition, plus Ernest and Mary - he leaves for the States tonight on the *Mauretania*, and so does she! She wasn't going to tell me so herself - I had to go to the Cunard office and make out I was her wanting to check the passenger list - but that makes it all the better, surely?

Fruit-Face was still out of action, poor guy, so TLM had roped in his Private Secretary, Hugh Lloyd-Thomas - an ex-Foreign Office staffer, all of six feet three in his drawers and as bald as a Great White Eagle with a beak to match, as well as being a dyed-in-the-wool bachelor (as I pointed out for Big Bucks's benefit) and a dab hand with the KTs (which didn't go down so well - 'But darling, you know I'm teetotal')

Then there were the Buists (pronounced 'Beasts'), Colin and Gladys, but not such a fright as they sounded. He was an ex-Naval College pal of TLM's and a typical old salt with it - the strong, silent type, always scanning the horizon trying to find something to say, and when he did it came out so slowly you'd forget how it started by the time he'd gotten to the end. Gladys was a ball of fire by comparison, but with about as much style and dress sense as The Fat Cook herself - nothing but shirt and skirt, apart from a couple of print dresses that looked like they'd come out of a charity shop. TLM told me he'd asked them along because he'd cut a deal with Lord Moyne to take over his yacht for a trip round Spain into the Mediterranean at the end of the month and he'd need someone else to navigate it with (though it was going to be announced as a big surprise which he'd been talked into by Posey when she arrived at the chateau), and Colin was the only person he could think of who fitted the bill - he'd asked the Mountbattens to join the party, but apparently Edwina had cut up rough (because there weren't going to be any blacks for her?)

Ladbrook took the two lovebirds down to Southampton, which saved me all the fond farewells on the dockside (Mary still making out that she was booked on a different ship sailing tomorrow) I'd managed to sneak her into the library yesterday to take her pick, and she'd packed half a dozen in her case. The one she really went for was a Hulton Library *The World's 50 Greatest Pictures* inscribed *'Presented to His Royal Highness by his fellow Trustees of The National Gallery'* -TLM once told me how he'd been to his first meeting there and they were discussing whether to buy this or that picture, but when he said 'Do tell me, gentlemen, how much does a picture cost?' they'd all cracked up laughing.

TLM was flying to Paris and taking the train on down from there. The Beasts only had a two-seater Alvis, so that left me and Big Bucks with Hairy Hughie, who took us back up to town in his swanky Foreign Office Bentley and fixed to pick us up at 6am on Wednesday - TLM had booked us on the first Newhaven-Dieppe boat across the Channel because he'd reckoned that was our best chance of giving the press the slip.

So it's Biarritz or bust - or is it going to be Biarritz and bust?

August
The Water Jump

Saturday 4 August

(No *Daily Sketch* = no Madame Claire)

Chateau Meretmont - at last. Got in at 7 yesterday evening, to find TLM on the terrace downing KTs with Gee-Gee and looking like the cat with the cream - or rather sun cream, having been sunning himself for the best part of the two days it had taken us to get here - and making a start on his new jigsaw, a close-up of the Folies Bergeres floor show.

'Good Lord, where on earth have you lot been hanging around?' he greeted us with. Where hadn't we been would have been the shorter story...

I'd set the alarm for 4.30 to make sure we were up and ready for Hughie at 6, but I didn't even get that much sleep as I had Big Bucks knocking on my door every half hour saying she was so excited about the trip she couldn't keep her eyes shut, and then when she did finally manage it was all Cain and I could do to get her out of the sack again. Still, I reckoned we'd be able to put our feet up again in his motor - until we saw what it was.

'Awfully sorry to disappoint you, ladies, but David said there was no question of my taking the FO car or any of his as the press knew all their number plates off by heart. I know it's only a Standard Twelve, but it's quite a sporty little number when it gets going.'

Well, 'only' turned out to be the operative word - there was no way Big Bucks was going to fit her great big butt into the front seat without overflowing onto the gears, so it was down to me to sit up there like a preppy girl at table while she spread herself around the back.

Hughie reckoned it was a seventy-mile run to Newhaven, but even that wasn't long enough for the wagon to 'get going' because the speedo never got above forty all the way and we only made it there with less than ten minutes to spare. To get it on the boat we had to drive onto a net laid out on the dockside like some sort of elephant trap, and Hughie and I only just had time to get clear before a crane hoisted it into the air and swung it on board - with Big Bucks still hollering her head off in the back!

That really made her day, as anyone could imagine. By the time she hit the deck she was more or less past it and even Gladys Beast's Eau de Cologne couldn't bring her round - though maybe that was just as well, as the crossing was no picnic on the Potomac and even had Colin The Old Salt reaching for his sickbag.

When we finally made it to the other side it was fixed that we'd travel in convoy, but if we lost one another we'd meet up again for the night half way at a place called Chatellerault. Hughie said he'd discovered a gem of a hotel there during his time at the embassy in Paris called the Grand where they did a venison dish which he said 'You'll be ready to die for, people, I promise you.' He offered to let Colin take over the map seeing as he knew France like the back of his hand, but Colin said it was as near as dammit due south on the main road and he had his Navy compass with him alongside the AA Guide for the Continent, so there'd be no problem.

We were just getting into the first big city when Big Bucks suddenly rose from the dead and yelled 'Wallis, it's ruin! It's ruin!' My first thought was that she'd gotten into one of her Prohibitionist rants on the evils of alcohol, but then I saw another sign saying Rouen and recalled her carrying on about how she just had to stop off at the museum there and see all the Monet pictures of the cathedral in her guide book of France. We were sitting at some lights at the time, but by the time we'd figured out how to get to it, they'd gone green again and the Alvis was out of sight. Hughie said there was no way of catching it again at the speed Colin drove, so we might as well stop off if it was going to keep her sweet and have a bite of lunch at the same time.

He pulled into the cathedral yard and went off to find some sort of eating house while we two looked around for a signpost to the museum. No such luck, so I went into the newsagent to ask, but the dumb clucks just stood and looked at me as if I'd just wandered in off Mars - I know my French isn't exactly par excellence, but I've never had any problem in Cannes making out what I want.

When I came out again, Big Bucks was standing there acting like she'd taken root on the sidewalk, while an old guy in a beret walked past me splitting his sides and muttering over and over 'Incroyable, incroyable...'

'What's been going on, Bessie?'

'Wallis darling, you wouldn't believe. You see that man there with the beret?'

'Yes.'

'Well, I reckoned he looked like he knew the place, so I went up and asked him where the Monet was, and what do you think he came back with? 'You are the most beautiful, Madame, but for me no thanks,' and kissed me on both cheeks.'

'He did that?'

'Yes, and gave me a smack on my behind for good measure.'

'Wow.'

'The darn'd nerve of it. Or is that the way all of the men over here behave?'

'No, not as a rule, they don't.' Then it clicked. 'Did you speak to him in English or French, darling?'

'French. "Monsieur, ou est le" I can just about manage. And then "Monet" I knew from the guide, so what's the problem?"'

'Just that - I mean, the way you pronounced him means money, I have to tell you, so he probably reckoned you were propositioning him.'

'Is that right? And so he was taking me for a, a -'

'A hooker.'

'Oh, the Good Lord save me! Wallis, you'll keep this just between you and me, won't you? Or else I'll never be able to show my face again, ever.'

'Oh come on, darling, David'll laugh fit to bust when he hears it. Didn't I tell you he said you'd be the life and soul of the party?'

'Now Wallis, don't you -'

Just then Hughie showed again, and of course I cracked up and had to explain the whole story. Diplomat that he was, he just about managed to keep a straight face before taking her by the arm and leading her off to a 'super little place with some smashing scoff' he'd found a couple of streets away.

He wasn't far wrong on that. We kicked off with a divine lobster risotto, then went on to the day's special of roast wild boar hash and wound up with a raspberry soufflé which I had to say topped even my recipe - and all washed down with two bottles of wine which Hughie opened before Big Bucks got back from the bathroom - though even she broke the pledge with a glass 'for my nerves'.

After that little lot we never heard another squeak from her on Monet, and I have to say that I didn't remember too much about the rest of the day either.

We eventually hit Chatellerault just before 8, and then came the real bad news - 1) the Grand Hotel was all hung around with scaffolding and a FERME POUR LES TRAVAUX notice pinned to the door, and 2) there was not a sign anywhere of the Alvis and its crew.

Hughie got out his torch - it was pretty much dark by the time we'd finished looking for them - and had another go at the map.

'Ah, I think I can see what's happened - Colin's probably made for Chateauroux over here which is also more or less due south from Dieppe, even though it's over to the east a bit. So it's all aboard again, ladies, I'm afraid.'

'Just how far is a bit?' I wanted to know.

'Let's see… it's rather cross-country, unfortunately… twenty-three… thirty-five… forty-seven… fifty-nine… ninety-nine kils altogether.'

'And how much is that in our lingo?' Big Bucks came in.

'Well, call it a hundred and you get sixty-one miles.'

'Sixty-one miles! You can't be serious.'

'Well, if you multiply by five and divide by -'

'Young man, I want to make three things clear to you: I'm not moving one more yard until A, I've had another square meal; B, I've found somewhere to rest my head for the night; and C, I've had eight hours' sleep minimum. Is that understood?'

'Well, if you insist, Mrs. Merryman…'

'You're too right, I do.'

Bully for you, Bessie, I nearly said out loud.

So we took off again on a tour of the town - at one stage we found ourselves crossing some river and had the Devil's own job finding a way back over it again - but there wasn't one other hotel to be seen in the whole place. There was nothing for it but to head on to the next town, even BB agreed, but we were just hitting open country again when we saw this little café packing up for the night, so Hughie went in to see what magic he could work with the madame.

We knew we wouldn't be getting a night at the Ritz, so when he reported back that she was offering to knock us up an omelette apiece and a couple of rooms for 500 francs all in, we jumped at them - 'And make mine a double portion of French fries on the side,' BB added. In fact, we were so starving hungry by then that we took the omelettes straight off the stove, and it was only when we then got upstairs that we realised that BB and me were booked not only into the same room, but into the same bed as well!

Going by the dip in the middle and the size of Madame, I guessed it was the one she usually hunkered down in, and when BB climbed aboard she rolled into it like a log in a trestle and left me right on the outer - or rather, the upper. Not that she did any better for sleep than I did, as there must have been a regular army of bed bugs waiting there to take off on their night exercises.

I gave up on it quite early on in the piece and sat out the rest of the night in the bathroom - that is, until Hughie came racing in and squatted down on top me! Luckily, it wasn't the omelette that had him on the run, he said, but Madame herself who'd taken a fancy to him, though I could have told her he wasn't a player (and if he had been, I'd have beaten her to it!) He shifted to the bidet, but even so I decided that this wasn't really the scene for polite conversation and went back to take my chances with BB. As it turned out, she'd either flattened all the bugs or they'd run up the white flag and quit, so I was able to get in some sleep after all.

Whether or not Hughie had sat it out all night in there I couldn't say, and when we got down to breakfast there was no sign of Madame except a jug of coffee and a baton of bread laid out on the table. Anyhow, he wasn't taking any chances - he had us both out of the door and ready to go in another 20 minutes flat, leaving the 500 francs out for her in an envelope (he wanted to add 50 as a tip, but I persuaded him that would only be giving her the wrong idea and anyhow it wasn't as if he was ever going to be coming back again)

We checked out the 'Grand' again, but still no sign of the Beasts. Hughie was all for heading over to that other town with the look-alike name to check that out too, but I said what was the point - a) it would add another couple of hours minimum to the trip, and b) we would all be meeting up again tonight at Biarritz anyhow. He began to argue that maybe they'd be sitting there waiting for us, but then BB weighed in with the news that she could feel the bugs stirring again and if he didn't want them jumping over to him he'd better head south just as fast as ever he could go, which clinched it.

If she couldn't make up for lost sleep, she did her darndest to make sure I wasn't going to either. 'Wallis, did you see that man opening his pants right by the side of the road there? What sort of a country is this?' she'd yell from the back every time we hit open country, and every town we got into she'd pipe up 'Do look at that pooch there, Wallis - isn't he just the cutest thing? I do wish we could have brought Slipper the little darling with us.' You certainly wouldn't after having him with you in a motor for two days, girl, I wanted to tell her (I'd left him at the Fort of course to the tender mercies of the Ogre - I'd love to know who was going to survive the longest)

Even she though couldn't keep Hughie from nodding off, and when he crashed clean out sitting at some lights after we'd stopped off for lunch in Bordeaux, we both of us said there was no way we were going on unless he handed over the wheel to me. He wasn't going to argue the toss this time - in fact, he was so pooped he was about to climb into the back seat with BB (bugs and all) when he saw she'd already spread herself out on the seat lengthways.

'Just remember to keep to the right and give way to anything on that side, even if it's only a horse and cart coming out of a field,' he said, which seemed like something of a cinch.

I'd just gotten clear of the city when I had to pull up for a whole crowd of people blocking the road. Half of them seemed to be trying to heave a motorbike out of the ditch, while the rest were milling around a car on the other side hollering the hell out of the driver.

Hughie got out to try and figure what it was all about.

'Oh, my God, it's Colin!' he yelled. 'You two stay where you are while I go and sort it out.'

He waded in waving his arms around with the best of them and eventually made it through to Colin, who was being bawled out by a guy with a cut over his eye who presumably was the biker. However, he changed his tune soon enough when Hughie got out his wallet and flashed a few bills, and in another minute it was handshakes all round and we were on our way again.

'That cost me a pretty packet, I don't mind telling you,' he said when we pulled in for some strong coffee at the next town. 'Or rather David,' he added, explaining that TLM had handed him a 'contingency fund' for hushing anything up that could put the press on our tail.

Colin then told the story of how they'd lost us. They'd hit some place called Chateau-Renault mid-afternoon which sounded right and the compass said was less than one minute latitude off due south from Dieppe, and Gladys agreed that had to be it. They couldn't find any Grand Hotel, but there was a pretty decent one called the Lion d'Or and they thought maybe Hughie had only meant grand with a small g, and what's more they'd had a meal at the two-star restaurant right next door which they reckoned sure enough we'd have died for (they got that right, at least) - even if there wasn't any venison on the menu. Then they'd been on the road again in the morning for a couple of hours when they came to Chatellerault, saw the Grand and realised their mistake. They were feeling a bit peckish, so they'd topped up on breakfast at a little café run by a delightful woman who told them she'd just been short-changed out of 450 francs by a dreadful Englishman with his American wife and mother-in-law in tow, but she was sure there was no connection because they said they were heading off east to Chateauroux…

By this time I'd had enough chateaus to last a life time and the only one I ever wanted to see was Chateau Meretmont, so as soon as I was back behind the wheel I put my foot to the floor and kept it there until we finally made it.

TLM was obviously well ahead of us on the KTs too, and when he'd heard our story he launched into 'a simply killing yarn' he'd just been told about a couple who'd been driving across France with her mother when she'd pegged out on them and then had the car stolen with the body still on board - which I'd heard anyhow a couple of years ago from one of Ernest's Swedes.

Then as if that wasn't hard enough to take, he said the letting people had pulled the wool over his eyes by not telling him there'd been a leak in the roof over the winter and three of the bedrooms still had their ceilings down. He was awfully sorry, but as a result there was nothing for it but for me to share one with Bessie.

Not half as sorry as you would be if you knew what you could be missing, Lover Boy...

(This was written while BB was still sleeping off the trip down here - it could be the first and last chance I'll have to put pen to paper in private till I'm back home.)

Thursday 23 August

We were in the lobby at the Palais in Biarritz to pick up Posey when I noticed an old *Daily Mail* on one of the chairs with the headline *THE HERO PRINCE* on the front page, so naturally I went over and took a look at it. Here it is -

HRH IN SEA RESCUE DRAMA

Biarritz, Monday. His Royal Highness, The Prince of Wales, was the hero of a dramatic rescue at sea while on holiday at this fashionable resort on the French Atlantic coast today.

4-year-old Jacques Chirac was paddling in his rubber ring on one of the resort's many picturesque beaches when he was swamped by a freak wave and swept out to sea.

The Prince, who is staying at the luxury Castle Meretmont two miles to the north, happened to be nearby relaxing with his party at a bar on the promenade.

Hearing little Jacques' pitiful cries for help, he immediately sprang to his feet and raced to the rescue.

*Plunging still fully clothed into the water, he struck
out manfully and managed to catch hold of the ring
just as the strong undercurrent was threatening to
carry it out into the Atlantic.*

*A large crowd had now gathered and applauded the
Prince as he brought the boy ashore and reunited him
with his mother. (photo)*

*Among them was the local Mayor, who proposed that
this heroic action should be marked by the award of
The Life-savers Society Medal of Honour.*

*The Prince turned down the offer, however, claiming
modestly that it was pure chance that he had been
first on the scene. When his rescuer's identity was made
known to Jacques, he thought for a moment and
replied, 'I prefer to have been saved by Marshal Petain.'*

And the French label us perfidious!!

As usual, the press had it all wrong. It had been our first day into town for
lunch at the Café de Paris before we moved on to Bar Basque right on the
beach for coffee and a liqueur or two. Whether or not it was the wine
being on tap or the sun being at its height or a combination of the two, TLM
had scrapped his usual 'no KTs before 7' rule and he was well over the
eight when he started up again on his dead-mother-in-the-trunk yarn.

I could see Big Bucks was beginning to twitch, so I suggested to him it
might be an idea if he went for a swim to cool off.

'Oh, okey-dokey, if you say so, Wally,' he replied and tottered off
down the beach without even stopping to get into his bathers. Of course
he had to head for right where this kid was messing around in his rubber
ring and stump into the water so flat-footed that he splashed him all over.
The kid tried to paddle to get out of range of him, but TLM kept on going
until he fell on his face and set up such a wave that it carried the kid right out
of his depth. By this time the mother had come racing up and started
carrying on such a treat that the message eventually got through to TLM.
Even when he'd got him back on dry land, however, she wasn't going to let
up, and one of the locals sent off for the Mayor in case this was going to
trigger another Hundred Years War, I guess. When he showed a few minutes
later he had a reporter in tow, and the next thing we knew the story was
being wired worldwide.

So much for TLM's hopes of shaking off the press - every day after
that there were a couple of East Coast agency men camped outside the
front gates, and the only way he could get out for his golf was in the trunk

of the Alvis, which then had to motor ten miles down the road to the course at St. Jean-de-Luz while Hughie took me and Big Bucks separately.

The rest of the papers were taken up with friend Adolf being elected German President by 38 to 4 million votes - Tammany Hall has got nothing on him, that's for sure. TLM saw it as a chance to dodge the headlines and slip the news to the boys at the gate that he'd be heading off over the horizon any day now, so that they might as well pack up their deck chairs and beat it.

Tuesday 28 August

Walter Moyne has finally shown with his 'yacht' the *Rosaura,* and we're to go on board on Friday after he's topped her up. She'd started life as a cross-Channel steamer, he said, and she certainly looked pretty much of a paddle-boat from the outside, but thankfully the inside had most of the mod cons after a refit when she'd caught fire last year. The bad news was that he was adamant that he was staying on board himself - and worse still, with his pet monkey, one of those disgusting creatures with a great shiny red butt.

After putting into Portugal for a day, we were going to hop it round into the Med to Majorca and take a bit of time off there before winding up at Cannes on the 9th in time to see Woodentops off on his four-month tour of Australia (shame it's not Mr. & Mrs. Temple who's going). At least, that was the story he was giving the press, TLM told me…

Friday 31 August

A room of my own - and about time! Even if it does only measure twelve feet by nine, hasn't got its own bathroom and I had to walk a gangplank to get to it, at least I don't have Big Bucks literally breathing down my neck every minute of the day - and (more to the point) night.

Right up to yesterday evening she was insisting on coming along for the trip too, until TLM told her there was some heavy weather heading into the Bay of Biscay which was going to be ten times worse than anything she - or the *Rosaura*, for that matter - might have met with in the English Channel, which did the trick. Hughie came to the party too by lending her his jalopy to take to Italy (Gladys was driving the Alvis back home solo) and giving her a crash course through the gears - crash being the operative word. TLM worked out a route for her on the map, taking in Milan-Bologna-Florence-Rome-Venice (*o caro mio* if she gets anywhere near a gondola) before heading back and meeting up with us again at the Villa D'Este, where he'd booked the top floor suite.

'That's if you haven't run off first and married one of those Italian gigolos, Bessie!' TLM cracked when we waved her off. If she was going to kick the bucket en route, at least there'd be no worry about somebody with a line in mother-in-laws taking off with her as they'd never be able to shift her out of the driving seat!

Talking of husbands, what should the mail bring as we were packing up but a postcard of the Empire State from Ernest.

'Honeybunch - this is to mark the six never-to-be forgotten years of our married bliss. We have built much - pray God we destroy nothing. During those years my love for you has grown till even I do not know the breadth or depth of it, save that it is something vast and seemingly immeasurable. Good night, my Darling One, Ernest.'

Six years on, and he still hasn't figured out what makes me tick. The Empire State is his idea of a phallic symbol, I guess, but he might at least have had the common decency to put an envelope around it - or maybe the treacle on the other side was meant for somebody else's eyes? Or then again, can it being so way over the top mean that he's playing fast and loose with Mary?? You're in deep waters here, Wallis, so maybe you're right to be looking out a lifebelt for yourself...

And literally. While I've been writing this up, the boat has started to take on quite a roll even though I can see through the window that we're still tied up in harbor, but just as I'm reckoning that there's no way we can put out to sea I hear the engines start up. I'd better get upstairs double quick to have my say in case they're serious.

(ten minutes later) Up on the bridge the roll was twice as bad and it was all I could do to get through the door. By now we were just about level with the breakwater, but TLM and Walter Moyne were still arguing the toss (pun intended)

'I don't like it, sir, I don't like it. They're forecasting a Force Eight out in the Bay.'

'Oh, come on, Moyne, the old tub must have seen worse than this in the Channel. At least we're heading straight into the wind.'

'I dare say, sir, but this is Biscay, you know. If it was down to me, I wouldn't risk it, but if you insist...'

'Yes, I do in -'

At that moment we hit the open sea and a king-size wave washed right over the window. I knew TLM well enough to see that he wasn't going to budge, come hell or high water - and it was certainly that. The last thing I wanted was for him to call me in to share the rap, so here I am back down again. If the darn table would only stay still long enough, I'd be making out my last will and testament - such as it is…

SEPTEMBER
And Over

Thursday 6 September

By the grace of God - and you can count me in as a believer again for the first time since Uncle Sol's Santa Claus beard came away in my hand - we're back on dry (and level) land in Majorca, though even now I've hardly got the strength in me to hold pen to paper.

The further we got out to sea - though at times it felt like we were being blown right back in again - the bigger and bigger the waves got until they must have been coming right over the whole ship from tip to ass. I tried to keep myself from looking out of the window, but whenever I did all I could see was water, though whether it was above or below surface was anyone's guess. My bags were having a great game playing at dodgems all around the floor, which was just one more reason for sticking to my bunk - except for my trips to the bathroom, that is.

Even when the gong went for dinner I wasn't going to move until the steward put his head round the door and said the rest had gone up, so I reckoned I'd better show willing.

I found them all sitting there in dead silence like store display dummies, and even Walter M was looking pretty green about the gills. TLM tried to act brave and get to his feet, but his butt got only about level with the table when he pitched back into his chair again. He told us not to worry, it'd all be OK as soon as we got round the corner into Portugal, and began reciting the kids' poem about going to sea in a sieve, but he only got as far as 'Our sieve ain't big, but we don't care a button, we don't care a fig' when he slapped his hand to his mouth and ran for his life. Next thing Posey couldn't even hold it that long and brought up right there into her plate, and with that the rest of us decided there was no point in even trying and headed back down.

I'd just got into my room again when I heard some sort of scrabbling and chattering going on up above in the top bunk. I was still trying to figure out what the hell it was when some horrible furry thing landed on the back of my neck and made a grab for my pearls. I must have let out a scream like the Bride of Frankenstein on her wedding night, because the steward heard it over all the other racket and came racing in - only to take one look and run straight back out again!

If I wasn't already dying of fright, I was surely going to snuff it from strangulation by the time he showed again, but this time he had another of the crew with him who explained it was only (!!) the skipper's monkey.

'Naughty little Willy, what have you been up to now? Come to Dick, there's a good boy, little Willy…' he kept saying to it over and over, but as for getting it off me it looked like he wasn't going to lift a finger.

'Just cut the little Willy and do something before it kills me!' I yelled with as much breath as I still had left in my body.

'Oh, don't worry, madam, Willy won't harm you. He's a real little pussy when he gets to know you, aren't you, Willy?'

He told me to turn round so that he could get a proper grip, but then it was his turn to howl blue murder as King Kong helped itself to a king-size chunk out of his arm before taking off out of the door. He stood for a minute trying to stop the blood before he took off after it too with the other guy - and it didn't sound like they were calling it 'a real little pussy' any more.

Even without all that there was no way I could have gotten to sleep, so there was nothing for it but to lie back and think of England - or Cannes - or Peking - or Shanghai - or Hong Kong - or San Diego…

Around midnight the boat suddenly went from pitching up and down back to rolling from side to side, so I asked the steward what was going on when he came in again to check on me.

'We're doing a runner for Corunna, madam.'

Me, thinking he was having me on, 'A runner for Corunna?'

'That's right - it's the next port along.'

'Oh, OK. Well, I just hope we make it.'

'I'm sure we will, madam, with His Lordship at the helm.'

'His Lordship? I thought the Prince was running the show.'

'Oh no, His Royal Highness hasn't been seen for several hours now since he went below.' Then with a wink like he was going to try something, he added, 'And between you and me, madam, that's where I'd rather he stayed for now.'

'I'll say' - just as long as he didn't come knocking on my door, I wanted to add, the way I was feeling right then.

As it was, the rolling didn't make for any more sleep than the pitching had, and it was just as I was finally nodding off that I heard the racket of the anchor going down. When I'd dared myself to take a look out of the window, lo and behold we were back in harbor and safely tied up against the dockside - praise be to the Lord M.

The steward came in again and confirmed it was Corunna. When he asked what I'd care for breakfast, I told him the only thing I had a chance of holding down was a pot of the strongest coffee he could produce - and even that was touch and go.

I was still on my second cup when there was another knock and who should bounce in but TLM himself, looking like the whole night had passed over him like a bad dream. We were going to have to spend a bit of time in port for repairs, he said, so he was fixing a trip to Santiago de Something to bend the knee at the tomb of Sir John Moore - 'you know, to encourage *les autres* and all that', which he said he'd just gotten out of Lord M's guidebook on Spain.

That might be fine for the rest, I told him, but no amount of encouraging was going to get me out of bed until I'd made up on all my lost sleep - not to mention the fact that I could feel my you-know-what just coming on…

So it was another week before I was fully back up on deck again, by which time we were into the Med. and tied up in Majorca.

We'd just taken an al fresco lunch at some little harbor café (and even that was my first square meal since we'd left Biarritz) when we bought a *Times* from a newstand and there on the front page was (with my additions)

PRINCE GEORGE ENGAGED
TO MARRY GREEK PRINCESS

THEIR MAJESTIES' PLEASURE

The following announcement is contained in last night's Court Circular:
It is with the greatest pleasure that the King and Queen announce the betrothal of their dearly beloved son the Prince George to the Princess Marina, daughter of the Prince and Princess Nicolas of Greece, grand-daughter of the Grand Duchess Helene of Russia and Prince William of Denmark who became King George I of The Hellenes, great-grand-daughter of King Christian IX of Denmark, great-great grand-daughter of Old King Cole…

151

The Princess, who shares Prince George's love of music (national anthems), *is a fluent linguist and speaks English well* (she'll need to). *Dancing* (ballet boys) *and shooting* (heroin) *also are among their common interests.*

Sounds like a match made in Heaven - or rather Windsor, as TLM confirmed:

'Oh yes, Pop had it fixed months ago. The only problem was whether he was going to be in a fit state to get up to the altar, but if he's still at the Fort, Cora and Jaggs will have licked him into shape, what? Ha, ha!'

'So when's it going to happen?'

'It doesn't say, but they'd better make it quick.'

'And I bet the Fat Cook won't be far behind, pushing the kids up there as bridesmaids.'

'Yep, you could be right there - I heard her talking to Fatty Archbish Temple of York about it before we left.'

As from one Yorkshire pudding to another!

TLM hired a couple of motors to take us across the island to a hotel on the other side while Walter stayed behind to top up (with drinkies, not least!) If it had been a relief to get into a room of my own on the *Rosaura*, that's nothing to what I felt now, lying out on a decent-sized bed that wasn't going to tip me out onto the floor in the middle of the night.

The Fomenter was a pretty swell joint all round in fact, and TLM let us know that he wanted us all to get up in our glad rags for dinner - I thanked my lucky stars that I'd put in the Vionnet number in malmaison red from Harvey Nicks at the last minute.

I was feeling pretty good when I went down and I could see TLM was giving it the OK, but then what did he have to do but catch the hem with his chair as he got up and rip it to pieces. I don't often blow my top, but this time I really let him have it, I was so mad. Then Gee Gee, bless him, broke the ice with a gag about his seeing red too and I was as sweet as pie for the rest of the evening, but when we got upstairs and I went along to TLM's room to kiss and make up I found he'd shut up shop. So that was another sleepless night, after all…

Friday 7 September

At breakfast TLM announced he wanted to take a look at the caves in the middle of the island some place. What the big attraction was I couldn't figure out, but I reckoned I'd better play long with the idea.

To get there we had to motor back to Palma and take a train. It may have been the Trans-Majorca, but it was no Trans-Pacific - more like some kids playground outfit with a puffing billy and a trio of toy coaches, but it went down a treat with TLM who said it was the spit image of his nursery train set.

It looked like half the people on the island - not to mention their hens and goats - were wanting to get on board, so he booked one end of the First Class. That way he was hoping would buy us some privacy, but he'd reckoned without the running boards outside of the coaches - we hadn't been going five minutes when this face showed up at the window offering us oranges for sale, followed in double-quick time by others with bags of nuts, slabs of goats cheese and a bunch of dried fish which stank to high heaven. After that little lot we all voted to put the window up and keep it there the rest of the way even if it meant getting roasted, so that by the time we got there I was ready for any place that was going to get me out of the sun.

TLM bought a map of the caves from the tourist stall and spread it out for us all 'to take a butcher's hook - that's Cockney for look, don't you know.'

'I hope you're not going to take us on another *Passage To India*,' Posey remarked.

'Passage to India? Oh no, I don't think they're that deep, ha, ha!'

'I was referring to E.M. Forster's book, actually.'

'The one who bats number four for Worcestershire, you mean? Lovely leg glide he's got (I liked the sound of that - I should meet the guy!), but I never knew he'd written about the India tour.'

'No. You know, the author.'

'Author, eh? Oh well, no wonder I've never heard of him. Come on, Wally, this one over here looks awfully interesting. Let's leave the eggheads to get on with their literature class, what?'

Should I have been insulted? Or if so, was I going to act like I was? You bet I wasn't!

Coming out of all that sunlight, it took quite a while for my eyes to adjust to see where the hell we were going. When they did, I started looking round for a chance for the usual girl's 'Help, I'm slipping, save me' dodge, but he beat me to it and took my hand to pull me across a little pool. Once over that he got straight down to business, even harder and faster than that first time in the cupboard - in fact, he set up such a racket bouncing around off the walls that it sounded like a herd of elephants were making out in there.

Then just as suddenly he left off. For a moment I wondered if the stink of the fish on my clothes - I'd been in the window seat on the train - had gotten too much for him, but I needn't have worried.

'Thank you, darling,' he panted. Thank you so much.'

'Well, you're easily pleased, that's for sure,' I was tempted to say, but instead I kept it to 'So I'm forgiven, am I?'

'Forgiven? Whatever for?'

'For snapping at you like I did last night, of course.'

'But darling, I just loved it!'

'You did?'

Yes. That's just how Nanny used to speak to me, and I loved Nanny more than anyone else in the world, don't you see?'

'But you're always complaining about how your Pop keeps ripping into you.'

'Ah, but that's different. He's the wrong gender, for a start.'

'I guess so, but -'

'And he never beat me like Nanny used to.'

'She beat you?'

'Yes, all the time.'

'Where?'

'On my bottie, of course. She made me tingle all over, it was the most wonderful feeling.'

'It was?'

'Just wonderful. And another thing - she had a mole under her lower lip, just where yours is.'

'Oh yes?'

'Yes, and I always longed to give it a kiss.'

'And did you?'

'No, no, I never dared, of course. Darling, would you mind awfully if I kissed yours?'

'No, of course not - help yourself.' And there was I doing my darndest all those years trying to cover the thing up!

He had a bit of trouble locating it in the gloom, and he was still at it when a hollering set up outside. It was Gee Gee, warning us we had to clear out as they were shutting the place down for lunch.

Just before we got out, TLM scooped some water from the pool to splash over his face, though most of it went down the front of his pants.

'Just to save myself overheating, don't you know,' he explained - as if he hadn't done that already!

We took a snack meal at the local bistro and headed back via the Toytown Express to the hotel for a second innings, but when we got there we found Walter had brought the Good Ship Venus round from Palma and wanted us all back on board for the night - he said there was another storm heading right for us and he wanted to get well clear of the island before it hit. He wasn't far wrong either, though this time we just managed to get through dinner before we had to hunker down.

So that was play closed out for today - but only today, surely??

Saturday 8 September

It took the rest of the night and most of today to ride the storm out, and Walter was just getting up steam again and TLM setting up the KTs when it suddenly came to him that he was supposed to be meeting Woodentops in his destroyer at Marseilles.

'And it'll take a couple of days at least to get there with the sort of speed this tub makes. Bloody Henry, trust him to put a spoke in the wheel. I was aiming to go ashore again tomorrow and spend the day on the fabulous beach that the chappie in the hotel told me was just round the corner. I know - Colin, you were in signals, weren't you?'

'Yes, that's right.'

'Well, just call up the Admiralty and tell them to divert the ship to meet us here, will you?'

'Are you quite sure, sir? That'll put her a good hundred nautical miles off course, you know.'

'Well, what's few tons of coal to the Navy?'

'I think you'll find she burns oil, actually.'

'Oh, really? Things must have changed since my days at Osborne - everything was coal then. I remember one day I was Duty Cadet and had to keep the fire going in the Commandant's office. He kept a dirty great Labrador in there, and he told me to make sure it didn't get out while he was taking Commandant's Parade. Well, I went in with the coal scuttle and as soon as I opened the door the animal sent me flying and was off outside before I could say knife. So I picked myself up again and went out to look for it, and I'll be jiggered if it wasn't following the Commandant right on his heels all down the ranks. He let me have quite a broadside when he got back in, I don't mind telling you. And do you know what the punishment was? Four hours in the coal bunker! Black marks all round, what? Ha, ha. And then there was the other time when -'

'So you still want me to go ahead with the signal, do you?'

'Yes, of course. And make it quick, there's a good fellow - I don't want to waste any time tomorrow hanging around waiting for him, don't you know.'

'Very good, sir.'

Tuesday 11 September

And sure enough, when I looked out of the window first thing the next morning there was this Navy ship about half a mile off and TLM heading out in a motorboat towards it.

The beach lived up to predictions too, three miles of brilliant sand and all to ourselves - but minus any caves. Not that it mattered, as it turned out, because we'd already packed up for the day and were back on board when TLM reappeared, though to give him his due he looked just as much put out as I was.

'Bloody Henry, he had this map of Australia out and wanted me to mark up every single town and even outback station I'd been to when I was out here and then tell me what they looked like, who I'd met and what I'd said, what sort of clothes I'd worn, etc, etc. As if I could remember all that after - what was it? - fifteen years or so. And even then he still hadn't got the difference between Kalgoorlie and Coolgardie, or Toowoomba and Katoomba. Talk about thick...'

By now Walter had gone down with Spanish tummy which he must have picked up in Palma and so TLM took over the wheel, rigging himself out in his Navy cap, staying up on the bridge all night and generally making out that he was the new Christopher Columbus (but maybe the fact that he'd finally finished the Folies jigsaw had something to do with it). Luckily, the sea was back to being as smooth as glass and I eventually persuaded him to hand over to Colin and go and catch up on some sleep, so we made it into Cannes safe and sound just after lunch today. There didn't seem any place to tie up, so the two of them had to row us ashore.

I'd fixed for my old Peking pals, the Rogers, to be ready to meet us and take us up to their villa in the hills in case the press had caught up with us, and there they were on the dockside - and better still, without a single snapper in sight. Katherine was as gawky as ever and looking like an average schoolma'am with a skirt right down to her ankles even in this heat, but Herman was as dashing and attractive as ever (and I should know!)

TLM went off to clock in at the Harbormaster's Office while we took a coffee or two on the promenade together and licked our lips over the five-star menus on offer, but then he came back with the bad news that there was no room for us in the harbor and so we'd have to put back to sea again and park about half a mile out. So it was back to the usual corn-beef hash again for dinner - though at least TLM had gotten some decent French wine on board instead of the Spanish gut-rot we'd been suffering for the last week - followed by another jigsaw session with a new one he'd brought back of some sun flowers in a jar 'knocked up by one of those pavement artist johnnies, I suppose.'

Most of us were ready to turn in for the night, but TLM was still firing on all eight cylinders and said why didn't we call up the Rogers and go ashore again for a spot of dancing, and when Herman suggested the Palm Beach Club where they had a South American band that clinched it. Poor old Walter was pulled off his sickbed to take us in again close enough to reach the pier in the rowboat, but as it was going to be our last night on board I guess he didn't mind too much.

After an hour of non-stop rumbas and tangos I was practically dead on my feet, but TLM was still well away and roped in a couple of broads from the cabaret to keep going with. They turned out to be from the States and I could see they were starting to get fresh with him, so when he suggested bringing them over to join us I told him they could easily be acting as stringers for an East Coast agency and did he really want to blow his cover again? That did the trick, though how we ever made it back on The Good Ship Venus I'll never know...

Wednesday 12 September

Today was supposed to be the end of the chapter, when we'd all split up and go our separate ways - TLM + Gee-Gee to Marseilles to take the Royal Plane back to London which the Big Chief had laid on to make sure they were back in good time for the launch of the Squaw's new liner, and the rest of us to take the train to Como and collect Big Bucks for the return trip, but now suddenly it was all change.

He'd hired a launch and taken off into town first thing with Walter, and by the time (mid-siesta) they got back again they'd hatched a new deal: Big Chief's pilot had been told to turn round and fly back again, while Walter had agreed to hang around for another week and then take us all (plus the Rogers) on to Genoa, where we'd hire a couple of motors and drive up to Como. That was pretty much OK by me (unless we were going to be caught out at sea in another hurricane, that is), but the others didn't seem too pleased and Posey announced she'd take the train back to London tomorrow.

'And what about Bessie?' I reminded TLM. 'She'll be jumping up and down wondering what's happened to us.'

'With all those gigolos pinching her bottom, don't you mean? You bet she will be, ha, ha! But don't worry, I've left a message at the Villa explaining everything.'

'But what is she going to do with herself for another week?'

'Oh, well, there's rather a good course just down the road at Montorforno, don't you know, even if most of the tees are off sisal mats. I remember there's one frightfully tricky hole - the fifth, I think it is - where there's a dog's leg to the left around the corner of a vineyard, but you wouldn't mind hooking into that at this time of year, what? The sixth's no piece of cake either, I can tell you - I got quite a decent drive away, but then…'

Herman had fixed for us to have dinner on the yacht of a pal of his, Dwight Branson or some such, the boss of St. Louis Rubber Manufacturing Inc, which was tied up in the harbor. It may have been the biggest boat there, but it didn't even run to a gramophone - let alone a piano - and I could see that TLM was pretty soon getting itchy feet. Eventually he made some excuse about needing some fresh air and signalled me to go up with him.

'Darling, we're going ashore,' he announced as soon as we got out on deck.

'Who is?'

'Just you and me.'

'But what about the others?'

'Oh, they're so busy talking rubbers or whatever, they'll never notice we're gone. I'll call up Walter in the morning to come and pick us up.'

'In the morning?'

'Yes, I've booked the top suite at the Miramar just across the road, don't you know.'

'Oh, no!' I let out - nothing to do with the gangplank swaying like crazy because he was taking it on the run, but all down to this being the very same place that Connie and I had such a ball (so to speak) in a couple of years ago. It would be just my luck that the same sourpuss of a maid who I hadn't tipped would still be there too, and what she might do to get

158

her own back didn't bear thinking about. Still, I might as well hang for a sheep as for a lamb, I reckoned - and this was no lamb...

'Anything wrong, sweetheart?'

'No, it's - I just caught sight of the water below, that's all.'

'What, frightened of getting out of your depth, are you? I'll soon take care of that, don't you worry.'

Soon was the operative word - it was all over in two minutes flat, in fact. The next thing I knew he was in the lounge calling up the night manager and telling him to get the Cartier staff out of bed and open up their store in the lobby. '*Toute de suite, mon homme, toute de suite,*' he kept saying over and over.

'I'm just going to spend a penny,' he told me as he passed through again - as if I didn't know it's not pennies you spend in Cartier's!

He must have had them turning out the whole store because I was well asleep by the time he got back again, even though I'd kept pinching myself to make sure it really was all happening and stay awake to see what he was going to come up with. I was going to have to sweat - literally - on that, however, because it was straight back to business again. The Little Man he may be, but what he lacks in inches he sure makes up for in pep. Shooting from the hip was his only problem, but the Chinese Grip soon took care of that...

'And here's a little thingie I'd like you to have, sweetheart,' he whispered when he'd finally had his (or rather my!) fill, taking the Cartier's case out from under the pillow.

Inside was a diamond and emerald charm in the shape of a frog to go on my bracelet.

'Why, it's just beautiful, David.' If I sounded disappointed, maybe, it was because I was expecting something more, well, circular - but at least it was a whole jump up on Ernest's souvenir pendant of the Eiffel Tower.

'It's just a very small thank-you for my best time ever, don't you see.'

'It was?'

'Yes, it was just the most wizard, the longest, hottest, well, you know -'

'Hotter even than the Fiery Furness?'

'Hotter even than the Fiery Furness, yes.'

Well, compliments don't come much bigger than that, I guess... 'And the frog - that's to remind me it all happened in France, is it?'

'Oh Good Lord no, that's got nothing to do with it.'

'So what has?'

'Well, it's all to do with what a frog does when he's in love, don't you see?'

'No, I don't think I do.'

'Why, he hops into bed, of course! Ha, ha…'

Thursday 13 September

And he kept on hopping, all the next day and night until breakfast, when I asked him if he'd made that call to Walter.

'Oh no, I forgot.'

'Well, hadn't you better do something about it? They might all be worrying that something's happened to you.'

'I don't see why they should - Gee-Gee's been with me long enough to know that I go over the wall now and then. Besides, they'll all be too busy with the new jigsaw to be thinking about us. Come on, darling, just let's -'

Just then there was a knock on the door, and who should put her head round it but Maid Sourpuss! I couldn't be sure that I'd got down under the sheet in time and I made it plain that I wasn't going to stay in the place one minute longer than it took me to get dressed and down in the elevator.

'Oh, okey-dokey then, you may be right,' he eventually conceded. 'I know, I'll drop in on the rubber people and get them to take us back in their launch - that'll save Walter the bore of having to come and fetch us.'

I kept my distance behind him, just in case there was a snapper hanging around. There wasn't - but instead there was a posse of cops right there on the dockside by the Branson yacht, and in the middle of them I could make out Walter looking like he was blowing his top.

I couldn't hear what TLM said as he strolled up, but I heard what Walter came back with right enough: 'I'll say there's a problem! Do you realise every gendarme in the town has been scouring the countryside for you for miles around? And now the press are going to be here any minute for a photo I said I'd give them to go in tonight's paper, so if you don't want that to happen you'd better get into the launch and make yourself scarce pretty damn quick.'

Which he did - so quick, in fact, that he almost left me behind. We'd just got back on board The Good Ship Venus and started up when we saw a great fleet of motorboats heading towards us. Walter ordered full steam ahead and made straight out to sea, but it was mid-afternoon before he dropped the last of them, and that was only thanks to quite a wind getting up. They'd all know he was making for Italy, he reckoned, so to throw them off for good he decided to head west instead. He was going to have to top up with gas again some place, so he'd put into a fishing village called Saint Tropay where we'd be out again before anyone could catch up with us again - with luck…

Thursday 27 September

The last couple of weeks are all still a bit of a blur, I have to say.

After finally making it ashore again at Genoa, we drove like crazy to Como in the two hire motors - TLM being desperate to get away from Walter and his monkey (which had spoilt the new jigsaw by running off with a handful of pieces and ditching them over the side), and Hughie ditto to see what damage Big Bucks had done to his jalopy.

As it turned out, there was nothing worse than a scrape on the front fender where she'd had an argument with a French tractor, and in Italy she'd only had the usual adventures: 1) she'd been in a traffic jam in Milan when the hooting got so bad that she'd reckoned she must have punctured a tire and got out to have a look, but by the time the guy behind had got through to her that every Italian driver sounds his horn every ten seconds for no reason and got back in she found all her travelers cheques were gone. 2) She'd been sitting around the Trevi Fountain in Rome after dinner admiring the statuary when a bunch of student drunks from Oxford had bumped her into the water, but when the cops had fished her out they'd accused her of being after the coins in the bottom and marched her off to the slammer for the night! So that had cost her a few more bucks to get out again, naturally…

Then it was back to the Biarritz routine - golf in the morning, (sun) bathing in the afternoon, KTs and jigsaw after dinner in the evening, and no go at night (maybe Big Bucks wasn't in the next bed, but she was in the next room through an open door)

After a few days of this we shifted across to another Villa something on the Borromeo islands in Lake Majore, but because we hadn't booked it was right back to double rooms. Next morning TLM took me out in a rowboat to try and find a place on one of the smaller islands where we could get together on our own for a change.

It was well into the afternoon before we did. We could see there was some fancy pile in the middle through the trees, but nobody seemed to be around so we decided to chance it. We found the perfect spot on the edge

161

of the wood and got out the picnic lunch we'd brought (including a bottle or two).

We were just clearing it away again and getting ready for action when there was a sudden crashing of undergrowth and some huge hound jumped out and grabbed TLM by his Bermudas which he had just gotten down to his knees. He was still trying to beat the brute off with a bottle when some wizened little peasant native came running and called it off, but not before it had made a pretty good meal of them.

'*Stranieri!*' he yelled at us as we got to our feet, then beckoned us to follow him across a big stretch of lawn towards the house. '*Ho preso stranieri! Ho preso stranieri!*' he kept hollering louder and louder.

We'd just got to the bottom of a flight of massive steps leading up to it when a pair of doors opened and out came a dude dressed in a morning coat and suit as if he was just stepping out for the first day at Ascot.

'*Qui e -*' he began when he was half way down the steps, then stopped dead in his tracks. '*O mio Dio, e mi'amico Edouardo, il Principe di Gallo!*'

He took the rest of the steps at the double and flung his arms round TLM, hugging and kissing him all over while the poor guy was still wondering what had hit him.

'You remember me, Prince Borromeo?'

'Oh, rather,' TLM replied, still looking a total blank.

'We have met at the funeral of the King Leopold in Brussels just this year, have we not?'

'Ah yes, that's it, of course.'

'And how are you, *mi'amico caro*?'

'I'm fine, thanks, but -'

'And who is the beautiful lady here?'

'Oh, this is just a friend of mine, Wallis Simpson - I mean, Mrs. Wallis Simpson.'

'Enchanted, signora, enchanted,' he said, taking my hand and giving it another working over with his lips. 'I am so honored that you visit me at my humble home here. But tell me, why did you not inform me in advance? Then I could have made ready a formal reception for you.'

'Oh no, we wouldn't have wanted to put you to that.'

'No?'

'No. We're not really supposed to be here, don't you see? We're traveling - oh, what's the word...

'Incognito, yes?'

'Yes, that's it.'

'Ah, we understand that very well here in Italy. Even the princes must

162

have their privacy at times, yes?' - this with a hammy wink at the two of us. 'But at least you will do my family the honor of joining us for tea, will you not?'

'Well, that's awfully nice of you, but I really didn't mean to intrude on you like this.'

'No, no, it is not an intrusion, it is a great honor for us, I must tell you.'

'And besides, we're hardly dressed for the occasion, I'm afraid. I mean... ' TLM added, pointing to the rip in his pants.

'Ah, I see. You have had an accident, yes?'

'Yes. We'd just finished our picnic when your dog - well, you see...'

'The dog has done that? *Luigi, veni, veni!*' he called to the minder.

After a lot of jabbering and arm waving, our host turned back to us and said to TLM, 'Please accept my deepest apologies, Edouardo, and of course my wife will find you some new trousers. And now please come this way...'

The guy was clearly never going to take no for an answer, so there was nothing for it but to follow him in.

The rest of the family turned out to consist of granny, wife and five kids, and even the four-year-old was dressed up to the nines. TLM was taken off to try some new pants for size, but the best they could do was a pair of Scotch tweeds which reached down to the floor on him, even when they sat him up in a throne that the King of Italy might have been crowned in five hundred years back.

Nothing appeared in the way of food and drink for well over an hour, then a fleet of maids brought in silver salvers of cucumber sandwiches and scones with cream and strawberry jam, plus Grade 1 China tea and porcelain - I even began to wonder if it hadn't all just been flown in from Fortnum's. Aside from our host, none of the others had a word of English between them except the old crone, and wherever she'd picked it up certainly wasn't in England - she had some idea that the country was about half the size of Rome and joined together by the Forth Bridge, while she refused to believe that anything grew there bar potatos. Alice and her Mad Hatters Tea Party had nothing on this lot!

I was just about falling into my cup like the dormouse by the time it was all over and we were outside again doing our addios.

'And hail to Our Great Leader!' the Prince fareweled us with a Fascist salute, and TLM shot him one straight back.

'Just as well there wasn't a snapper around to shoot that,' I told him when we'd finally got clear of them.

'Oh, absolutely - Pop would have my guts for garters if he saw me in a pair of old bags like these,' he replied.

Every day telegrams had been flying in from Buck House reminding him that the big launch was this Wednesday, then on Sunday another came with news of a Welsh mining disaster in Wrexham with some 250 dead and demanding that he put in an appearance.

'Only two-fifty? That's nothing - I can remember when the *Titanic* went down there were thousands of people lost, and I never knew that Wrexham was in Wales anyway. Oh, what a bore - I was hoping to stop off at Troon on the way up and have another crack at the Postage Stamp. Still, I'd better keep the peace, I suppose...'

We (aside from Hughie, who headed off home in the jalopy - he'd had no takers as passengers) caught the Orient Express at Arona and arrived Paris early Tuesday in time for TLM to catch his plane to London and for me to give Big Bucks (plus checkbook!) a tour of the fashion houses in Rue Rivoli before going on to board the *Manhattan* at Le Havre - me to come off again at Southampton, she to go all the way back to Monica County, thank the Lord.

Over dinner, just when I thought I was getting away without her dragging up THE subject, out it came.

'Wallis, isn't the Prince getting rather sweet on you?'

'Why ever should you think that, darling?'

'Well, these old eyes of mine have seen enough of life to know a man when he's keen.'

'And so? He may be a bit fond of me, but that's all. What's wrong with that?'

'Nothing at the moment, my dear, but there's a danger you could get so used to his style of life that you begin to expect it of everyone else.'

'Oh, hooey! I'm just having a great time while it lasts. Isn't a girl allowed to do that?'

'Yes, but how do you know when it ends? That's the problem.'

'Look, Bessie darling, you don't have to worry about me. I think I'm old enough now to now what I'm doing.'

'Very well, have it your own way, Wallis, but I've known smarter people than you get swept off their feet and live to regret it.'

OK, the deal wasn't in the bag yet, but it was looking pretty good - and it wasn't as if she hadn't done pretty well out of it herself so far, I wanted to tell her. And if it was Ernest she was thinking of, he wouldn't be doing too badly either if he was getting hooked into Mary and her millions, as I was hoping to find...

OCTOBER
Into The Straight

Monday 1 October

If there's something on your mind that you feel intensely about, sooner or later you are going to have to disclose it to the person closest to you. It will take courage, but there's no escaping it and now that Mars is moving into your inner orbit, this is the time to do it. If you're worried that you may risk over-dramatising it, remember that he or she will appreciate your honesty and react accordingly. In these situations, there's nothing to beat speaking from the heart. I'm sure you're right, Madame Claire, but maybe I'll make it later rather than sooner…

It was back to earth even before I'd stepped off the gangway - the sight of Ernest waiting on the dockside with a king-size bunch of chrysanthenums, then the rail trip back up to town jam-packed in Third (of course), the flat as sun-less and gloomy as ever, a new cook (though Mrs. Ralph promises to be back at the end of the month), Mr. Loo still set in his charming ways and Cain in hospital with her bronchials yet again (but maybe I shouldn't be too hard on her - the cook takes the *Sketch*) In spite of all that Ernest made it plain he's still expecting a full (and I mean full) service - or should I be grateful and take it as a sign that Mary's given him back the taste??

I couldn't get much out of him on that score except that he'd stayed over an extra week 'for a bit of rest and relaxation', but that didn't stop him from wanting a blow-by-blow (did I really say that?!) account of my little jaunt, and in the end I just had to say 'I really can't describe it any better. Wallis in Wonderland, you could call it.'

'Sounds more like a trip behind the Looking Glass,' he cracked.

Was that a two-way job he was meaning? Then he'd really be laughing on the other side of his face!

'Oh, and by the way honeybunch, I'm going to be in Paris myself for the week at the end of the month for the World Shipping Convention to sort out the whole question of government subsidies. Strictly business, of course.'

And having it out with the oily little Greek? That sounds more like it…

Tuesday 2 October

TLM still up in Scotland with the rest of the Woebegones - he's due back tonight, I think he said - so spend the day catching up with back numbers of the papers.

I skipped all the bull on the launch - one look from the Squaw would surely have been enough to send it down the slipway, whatever size it was - but this one in the *Times* of a week or so back caught my eye:

PRINCESS MARINA AT BALMORAL

—

AN ENTHUSIASTIC WELCOME

—

FAMILY GREETINGS

Aberdeen, Monday. Thousands thronged the railway station early this morning and gave a hearty welcome to Prince George and Princess Marina.

When the train reached the platform several minutes late, having been delayed by the enthusiastic scenes at King's Cross last night, there was a rush to get near the Royal coaches. The crowd had not far to go, for the first three were reserved for the Royal party. When Prince George and Princess Marina came to the door of one of them, there was instantly a great cheer.

The Duke and Duchess of York had earlier driven from Birkhall with Princess Elizabeth to welcome them. As soon as the door opened the Duke of York stepped forward to congratulate his brother (now in Highland dress) and gave Princess Marina a kiss of greeting. The Duchess's welcome was particularly

*cordial. She gave the Princess an
affectionate kiss, which was returned
with warmth.*

*But most charming of all was the
greeting of little Princess Elizabeth. A
little shy, she stepped forward and stood
on tiptoes to kiss the Princess, who bent
down and gave her an affectionate hug.
It has already been announced that she
is to be one of the bridesmaids at the
Royal couple's wedding on November
29th...*

I didn't bother with the *Sketch* after that - it didn't need Madame Claire to tell me that the Fat Cook would get her snout in there first.

Emerald called and of course wants to know the full story - she'll be lucky, but as she was going to pay I fixed for lunch on Friday at the Ritz.

Wednesday 3 October

Ernest was hardly out of the door before TLM was on the blower, booking himself in for 'pot luck' tonight. Is he talking billiards now? If so, he'll have better luck in a couple of weeks.

Along with the action, the temperature's cooled right down and I told the new maid to make up a fire in the drawing room. Dumb bunny that she is, she laid it practically on the rug and would have sent the whole block up in smoke if Mr. Loo hadn't happened to have peed on it minutes before. Even worse, she'd used cook's *Sketch* for the kindling and so I've had to make do without Madame Claire's thoughts for the day.

Called Mary to try and gauge how hot things were at that end, and she claimed she'd only met Ernest once for a couple of KTs - but that's what she would say if there'd been anything between them, wouldn't she? And when I began talking about Paris, she said that even when she'd been with Jacques she'd never been there before... She was pretty cool on the business front too - Chuck reckoned the Picture Book would only go for peanuts, but one of the others - LITTLE DORRIT which she'd found had written it *'David, With hopes that this is more your size and best love, Freda'* - could have more going for it.

It had better, that's for sure - Big Bucks was so wrapped up in giving me the Third Degree on that last night together that the checkbook stayed in her bag, and Ernest called from the office to say that Mr. Tightwad had turned him down flat when he tried to touch him for a $1000 loan. But maybe if I play my cards right with TLM tonight…

He came bouncing in with his face lit up like a pinball machine hitting the jackpot.

'I made it! I made it!' he kept yelling over and over, and even Ernest looked as if he couldn't believe what he was hearing.

'Oh, yes?' I said, catching hold of Mr. Loo before he got over-excited too.

'Yes. The wind had gone round to the south, so I thought I'd never have a better chance of hitting The Postage Stamp in one, don't you see.'

'But I thought you were giving the golf a miss.'

'Oh, that was on the way up - I'm talking about yesterday on the way down. The railway passes right by it, so I got them to stop the train and have some clubs sent across and plenty of balls. I normally take a niblick to try and beat the wind, but there didn't seem to be one in the bag and so I had to make do with a mashie, and what do you know? My very first shot caught the top lip of the front bunker and just rolled on! Mind you, it still took me another four to get down. The first putt was -'

'I think I'll just go and check on the casserole, if you, don't mind, David…'

Well, even Ernest's loyalty to the Crown must have its limits, because when I got back they'd moved on to the jump in the price of cigars, which didn't exactly help to put over the idea that we're on the breadline.

He had to hang on in there to the death as usual, and the only thing I got from TLM was the promise 'of a nice surprise' if we'd care to come down to the Fort for the weekend…

Friday 5 October

People with your warmth and outgoing personality often don't find it easy to pick and choose their words or to keep your thoughts to yourself, but sometimes it can pay to curb your instincts. You also run the danger of being misconstrued, particularly just at this time when Mercury is entering its own sign of Gemini and even the most innocent statements tend to be taken the wrong way. By taking a back seat, you'll also become a better listener, and who knows what fascinating information you might pick up! - which is exactly why I'm lunching with Emerald …

Took in the Debenhams fur sale on the way down for a little window shopping only (I hope your ears are burning, Big Bucks) - they had a full-length Canadian mink reduced to 98gns, but maybe the Harrods sale next week will have some better deals (their ad. in the paper today has one in Persian lamb with a silver fox collar reduced by half)

She'd booked an alcove table to block any snoopers, and I'd hardly sat down before she was putting me through the Third Degree (or Fourth, if there is one) - who was in the chateau/boat/villa, who said what to who, who danced/swam/slept (in so many words) with who...

'And your aunt was there the whole time, was she?'

'Yes, that's right. And sharing a room with me, if you really want to know,' I added for good measure, reckoning that it was high time now to put the shutters up.

'Oh, I'm so sorry, I didn't mean to be nosy, darling.'

'No, no, that's OK.' (as if I'd ever dream of you being that, darling...)

'And actually I owe you another apology - remember how I had a little laugh on you last time for confusing the two Guinness girls?'

'Posey and Diana, you mean?'

'That's right. Well, there's not such a big difference between them after all, so I gather - in fact, they're like two peas from the same pod.'

'Oh, yes?'

'Yes. She - Posey, I mean - well, let's just say she enjoys her abdominal merriment. (that's a new one on me! I must remember to save it for Big Bucks) So she must have had some fun with all those men, I imagine.'

'You bet she did!' said I - if I'm actually asked to lay a smokescreen, I'm not going to say no, now am I? It was only when I had her off with Gee-Gee that I could see maybe I was overstepping it, so I shifted onto the other foot with 'And what's Thelma been up to recently? Still with her Black Prince?'

'Thelma? Oh, they had a few months in Spain together, but now they've gone their own ways, so I've heard. Right now she's back in New York, of course, since Gloria's custody case reopened.'

'It has?'

'Yes, just last week. I've brought along a clipping from the *New York Times* on the first day when the old mother was on the stand, in case you hadn't seen it...'

MOTHER OPPOSES MRS. VANDERBILT
AS ADJOURNED CUSTODY CASE REOPENS
Swears She Neglected Ten-Year-Old Gloria
And Is Not a Fit Person to Have Custody

MRS. GERTRUDE WHITNEY ALSO IN COURT
Says Girl's Visit to Parent Made Her Hysterical

Mrs. Laura Kilpatrick Morgan, mother of Mrs. Gloria Morgan Vanderbilt, widow of the late Reginald C. Vanderbilt, joined Mrs. Harry Payne Whitney, the latter's sister, in opposing the proceedings brought by Mrs. Vanderbilt to regain her ten-year-old daughter Gloria from Mrs. Whitney. She agreed with assertions by Mrs. Whitney and others that her daughter was not a fit person to have custody of the child, and asked Justice Carew to give the little girl to the care of Mrs. Whitney.

Mrs. Whitney arrived with the child, who appeared pale and frightened and clung to the hand of her aunt. On entering the court and seeing her mother sitting opposite, she didn't greet her or even glance at her. On her side, Mrs. Vanderbilt was supported by her two sisters, Lady Thelma Furness, wife of the British shipping magnate Lord Furness, and Mrs. Consuelo Thaw, wife of Mr. Benjamin D. Thaw, First Secretary at the US Embassy in Oslo, Norway.

'We lived in Paris for four and a half years, and during that time my daughter paid absolutely no attention to the little girl,' Mrs. Morgan stated. 'She devoted herself exclusively to her own pleasures. She usually slept until one or two in the afternoon, and from that time until the early hours of the following morning she was at cocktail parties, dinners and night clubs. Her constant companions were people who led very gay lives. Frequently she took long trips to Germany without leaving any forwarding address, and she seldom wrote to me or enquired about the baby. Little Gloria was like a poor orphan. She was not wanted.'

Mrs. Morgan told of several alleged instances when Mrs. Vanderbilt pushed the child away when the latter came near her. She said that on one occasion' the child screamed and cried and pleaded with me not to let my daughter hurt her, whereupon Mrs. Vanderbilt replied, "I don't care if she cries, and for all I care she can bawl until her eyes bulge and drop out of their sockets".'

'In 1931 I returned to New York with my grand-daughter, whom I placed in the care of her aunt, Mrs. Whitney. She lived there very happily, and when she was told that her mother

By which time I'll have things sown up in the Court of St. James, with any
luck…

Sunday 7 October

Fruit-Face drove us down in the Rolls, with Baba sounding off beside him
like some volcano that was going to turn us all to cinders any minute -
according to Emerald, she'd taken up with Grandi again when she'd got
back from her month in France with Tom Mosley and had one terrific bust-
up with her sister Irene for trying to pinch him (Grandi) in her absence - she
(Baba) having pinched him (Tom) from the other sister Cimmie in the first
place! And they say the Brits are cold-blooded…

Brer George was there of course, along with Gee-Gee, and, according
to TLM, still on the straight. He was a bag of fun as usual - I could really
go for him if ever I wanted a second Windsor Lad in my stable - and he has
to be several sizes up from TLM when it comes to mounting!

The chain gang had just got its marching orders after lunch when the
rain arrived and set in for the afternoon, so it was all hands again to the
latest jigsaw - The Rape of The Sabine Women which he'd just brought
back from the National Gallery after the last Trustees meeting.

'As you can see, Ernest, George has broken all your rules about doing
the edges first and gone straight for all the Bristols, the devil! Wasn't there
some novel called THE RAPE OF THE LOCK? I suppose he'll be going
for that next - I'd better tell Osborne to put the library under lock and key,
what? Ha, ha!'

Just as well he didn't mean it seriously, what?

The Ogre was all bowing and scraping as if he had something over me,
and when I handed him five shillings for looking after Mr. Loo for the month
until Ernest got back he refused to take it - 'You look as if you need it more
than I do, if I may say so, madam,' and for once I had to admit he was
dead right.

Dinner, and no sign yet of 'the little surprise'. I was put between the
two Brers, and we were on the sweets when George started talking about

173

a wealthy pal of his who was picking his brains about a wedding present for Marina.

'How about a fur coat?' I suggested.

'Oh yes, that sounds like a good idea. Where would he find one?'

'Harrods are having a sale this week - he might be able to pick up something there.'

'Oh no, he wouldn't want anything on the cheap - he'd want the finest that money can buy.'

'Well, there's nothing to beat Bond Street for the real class usually, I find.'

'You've hit the nail on the head there, Wally,' TLM cut in. 'That's why I've booked up Ma Feathers for your stag night, I might as well tell you now, bro, if that's not giving away any state secrets, what? Don't look so worried, old girl, you're not invited, ha, ha... I say, people, how about raising a glass to the lucky couple? Here's to -'

He'd already done his toastmaster turn about five times over, so I decided it was time to take him in hand. Luckily he was back up on his feet, so it only needed to put an arm round him and point him in the right direction for the bathroom.

I wasn't surprised to hear some pretty sick-making (literally) noises coming from down the passage, but then they were followed by a long silence - so long, in fact, that I was beginning to worry that I'd lost him (and my little surprise) for the night. Just as I was thinking I ought to get up and check what had happened to him, all of a sudden he came marching back in again followed by a regular Scotchman, both of them dolled up in bonnets, kilts, sporrans, dicks, etc and blowing on a set of bagpipes like they were fit to bust.

Even with my hands over my ears I couldn't begin to describe the racket - two hundred hell-cats tied up in a sack doesn't even get close. Then just when I felt I hadn't a brain cell left in my skull they stopped and made us a little bow.

The gallant general was the first to recover, and even he took some time. 'I thought I knew my pipe tunes, sir, but I can't place this one. I don't know where you found it, but I must say it's quite, er, quite - memorable.'

'Glad you think so, Gee-Gee. As a matter of fact, I wrote it myself. It's called Majorca - after the wizard time we had there, don't you see? (giving me the eye) I had the tune buzzing round in my head all the way up to Balmoral, and then as soon as I got there I roped in Forsyth here to get it down on paper for me. We really sweated blood over it, didn't we, Forsyth?'

'Ay, that we did, sir. You had me marching up and doon the terrace with you in the rain all one afternoon, up and doon, up and doon, until the window flies open and His Majesty yells out -'

Pause, then TLM took over. ' - yelled out, "For fuck's sake, David, stop that infernal noise, will you! I've been listening to the pipes for sixty years and I've never heard such a fucking horrible din in all my life."

"No, you wouldn't have, Papa. I've just made it up myself, you see."

"Oh, well, that explains it, then. If you must have a new tune, just leave it to the Highlanders - they know what they're doing. I never want to hear that again, do you hear?"

Poor old Pop - always did have a tin ear, what?'

Maybe, but if ever you spoke for your loyal subjects, Big Chief, you did then, I wanted to say.

Woke to rain and yet more rain, so that ruled out going down to the woods today for my surprise, big or little.

The Sabine Women were knocked off some time after lunch, and then TLM suggested a game of Sardines, with himself as the bunny. I hardly needed telling what the real game was, of course, and when I got to the cupboard there he was all ready to pounce (now I realised too why he was so keen on fitting these new zip fasteners to his pants instead of buttons)

'So this was my little surprise, was it?' I said when he was through.

'This? Oh no, darling, that was last night.'

'Last night?'

'Yes - you know, the Majorca. My pipe tune.'

'Oh.'

'You didn't like it?'

'No, no, I thought it was just - just gorgeous.'

'Oh, good. And now I've got Forsyth working on another one which you'll like even better.'

'To be called the Cannes, I suppose. Or the Cannes-Cannes.'

'Can-Can?'

'Yes - after the wizard two days we had there too.'

'Oh, I get you now. Yes, we certainly knocked the Folies Bergeres into a cocked hat, what? Ha, ha, ha…'

'Sh, not so loud!'

'Oh, sorry. Anyway, I wanted to tell you I've got another surprise for you, only this is going to be a really big one.'

'It is?'

'Yes - a really, really big one, I promise you. You're not going away at all, are you, darl -'

Next thing the door was pulled open and who should be standing there? Yes, you've guessed it, Ernest.

How he squeezed his great butt inside I'll never know, but anyhow squeeze it he did. Did that make the game a three-ball or a four-ball, I almost got to ask!

We were all in the lobby on our way out when Osborne came creeping up to TLM.

'Beg pardon, Your Royal Highness, but can I have a quick word?'

'What, right now?'

'Yes, if I may. It's rather urgent, you see.'

'Oh, all right, then.'

'I thought I heard you say something yesterday about needing to keep a close eye on the library.'

'Oh, did I?'

'Or words to that effect, Your Royal Highness. So I took leave to make a quick check, and I found there were a few books missing.'

'Well, so what? I mean, a book or two is neither here nor there, is it?'

'Oh, quite so, Your Royal Highness, quite so. Normally I wouldn't have troubled you about it, of course, but I just happened to notice that one of them was the copy of LITTLE DORRIT that Mrs. Dudley Ward gave you. By Mister Dickens, it was.'

'Oh yes, she was always bombarding me with those sort of books. I really can't say I'm going to miss it that much, Osborne, don't you know.'

'That's as maybe, but the point I'm making is that it could make rather a lot of money if it ends up in the wrong hands - particularly American hands.'

'Good Lord, Osborne, you're not accusing Mrs. Simpson here of running off with it, are you?'

'Oh no, no, no, Your Royal Highness, I wouldn't dream of that.'

'I should think not.'

''I'm merely suggesting that it might be worth keeping a watch on the catalogues of sales coming up in the near future.'

'Well, I can't say I'm all that bothered myself, Osborne. But if you want to pursue it, then that's your affair, I suppose.'

As I supposed too. As soon as I got back I called Mary, and she said yes, Chuck would be putting LITTLE DORRIT and the others into the upcoming sale in early November, so I told her to pull it for the time being. And she was coming over to Paris in two weeks, to sell off Jacques' flat that was hers as part of the divorce deal - that was her story, at least…

I also called the Rogers to put them in the picture and ask them to keep an eye on Ernest if by any chance they were going to be in Paris too that week. Oh yes, Herman said, he'd be delighted to do that for me. Just a thought - is he still hoping to get back in where we left off in Peking together?

Friday 19 October

Given your get-up-and-go character, when someone makes you a commitment, you naturally expect them to fulfil it at the earliest opportunity - and no more so than at this juncture, when the Sun is about traverse the dynamic sign of Aries. However, you should recognise that this person may not share your own decisive instincts, and that by putting pressure on them he or she may begin to resent you and be tempted to downgrade their obligation. Besides, there is always the chance of an unexpected event causing even the most conscientious of us to rearrange our priorities. However much it goes against the grain, you will learn that patience sometimes has its own reward.

And so I stayed in waiting for the big surprise - and waited some more, hardly even daring to move out of the door in case I missed it. I didn't accept for the weekend at the Fort either, though that had more to do with waiting to find out exactly what game Osborne was playing at.

I have to admit though that I snapped when TLM called and announced that he'd persuaded some Yankee to take him along as co-pilot on this air race to Australia.

'It ends in Sydney just the day before Henry gets there in his cruiser, and I can't wait to see his face when he comes down the gangway and finds that I've beaten him to it. And not only that - Pop is going to be starting the whole thingie and his face is going to be a sight worth seeing too when he spots me climbing into the cockpit, what?'

'But David, that's plain crazy!'

'Oh, I don't see why - Jack's done plenty of this long-distance stuff before.'

'Yes, but he isn't going to be at the controls all that way himself, is he?'

'No, but I've got a pilot's licence too, don't you know.'

'And how many times have you even been across the Channel?'

'Oh, I've been over to Paris three or four times solo. Then I hopped

177

over to Le Touquet last summer for the Stableford Bowl, and do you know, if I hadn't shanked my approach to the -'

'David, let me tell you something: if you go ahead on this, then I'm going to head off the other way back to the States - and stay there.'

'But you can't do that to me, Wally!'

'I not only can, but I will. OK?'

That shook him out of it - and when one of the planes ran into the side of a mountain in Italy he wasn't arguing any more.

Monday 22 October

Mrs. Ralph back again at last, and with Cain out of hospital everything's back to normal - except that Cain was relying on the temp. cook's *Daily Sketch* and didn't bring one in, so no Madame Claire today.

Saw Ernest off to Paris last night, but can't very well tell Mrs. R to make up supper for two, so I said not to bother, I'd be cooking for myself in the evening till he got back.

Then it came to me that of course this is what TLM had been waiting for, and that he was going to be the big surprise! Only he wasn't...

He called first thing to confirm for tonight, and it was about eleven - just after I'd got my war paint on for the day - that the bell rang. I did reckon it a little odd, I have to say, as he'd always made such a point of not coming during the day while the staff were still around, but then I guessed it was all part of the surprise.

'Darling, aren't you so glad now I - ' I began and was about to throw myself into his arms when I suddenly thought 'That's funny, I've never seen him in a trilby before', and a split second later the trilby came off and I saw it wasn't TLM but the guy/Guy from the Ford garage!

'Good morning, Mrs. Simpson, it's Guy Trundle from Excelsior Motors. So you remember me, do you?'

That threw me even more off course, and when he offered me his hand I must have held it for full minute or so before letting go.

'Why, yes. Yes, of course,' I finally managed. 'It's - it's swell to see you again.'

'That's my pleasure, madam,' he replied, putting the trilby back on again.

'I'm sorry if I seem a little confused, but I was expecting it to be someone else.'

'Oh, don't worry, that's quite all right.'

'Well, won't you come in? For some coffee, or something?'

'That's very kind of you to offer, madam, but I won't, if you'll excuse me this time. You see, I've got a bit of a surprise packet for you down in the square.'

'Can't you bring it up?'

'No, that'd be a bit tricky, I'm afraid. If you'd care to follow me downstairs, you'll see why…'

And there it was, parked right by the entrance - WE 1.

'We did suggest to His Royal Highness that he went for a rather less conspicuous number, but he wouldn't hear of it and so there you are. It's the very first model in our new Prince range, you see. His Royal Highness drove it off the production line himself when he visited the factory in July, but then we had to make a few, well, adjustments to it. He's put it in your name, of course - you'll find all the registration bumf and the owner's manual in the glove-box. I'd just like to point out all the latest fashion accessories on it - you know, the white-walled tires, the vanity mirror on the passenger's sun visor and the seat covers in real leopard skin which he provided himself. And as for the mechanical specifications, there's the new syncromesh gearbox with automatic transmission, which cuts out all the business of double declutching…'

Also in the glovebox was one of TLM's crested envelopes with a note - 'To my beloved sweetheart Wallis, with all my love and hopes of miles and miles of happy motoring together for WE, plus a little something for the running expenses, from your adoring (and other-top-of-the-range Prince!) David' - and more to the point, a cheque for £200.

Mr. Trundle/Trilby told me to take it easy on the accelerator for the first thousand miles, but I had my foot flat to the floor the whole way down to Harrods in the hope that there was still something on offer in the fur sale. The half-price Canadians had all gone, but they had a ¾ length in chinchilla with a matching wrap reduced from 240 to 170 gns, which will be just perfect for the ski slopes (and last time at the Fort TLM had given a little hint about taking a party to Austria in the New Year).

That left plenty over for an American-style thank-you dinner à deux with the biggest lobster in the store for the main dish. I didn't let Mrs. Ralph have a sight of it, of course, but put her onto preparing the rest - black bean soup and pumpkin pie. She did wonder why I needed such a big pumpkin just for myself, but I said I took the first one I could find as I wanted to make sure of getting one, and didn't she know Halloween was coming up? (most Brits don't in fact, believe it or not)

The bell went sharp at six and this time it was him for real - BUT I was still getting him inside when a guy came out of the fire exit and popped a flash-bulb off at us.

'Lovely job. And now another one a bit closer together. That's right!' Another pop.

'Who the devil are you?'

'Andy Oxtail of the *Daily Express*, squire. Here's my card, see.'

'Now, look here, my man -'

'David, get inside, for God's sake!'

'Sorry, madam, I don't do God.'

So that was the end of our happy little reunion before it had even begun. TLM tried to say we should just ignore the guy and carry on as planned, but I said he'd probably hang around all night for us to show again and so the quicker we got out again, the better - and then better still, dive into a cinema.

We had a quick KT while we went down the flick reviews in the *Times*. TLM went for *Now And Forever* with Gary Cooper until he saw that Shirley Temple was playing opposite, and I passed on Douglas Montgomery in *Little Man, What Now?* as being too near the bone. *One Night Of Love* seemed like too much of a let-down (even when described as 'the story of a modern-day Trilby'!) and I'd already seen Harold Lloyd in *Cat's Paw*, so we finally fixed on James Cagney in *He Was Her Man* at the Regal.

There was no sign of the snapper on our way out, but we decided to play safe on WE 1 and took separate cabs down to Leicester Square, then ditto after the show in our separate directions - sadly...

I came up the stairs instead of the elevator, but he must have heard me coming and got his foot in the door before I could get it closed, though I did just manage to get the chain on.

'May I have just a few words, Mrs. Simpson? Just a few, there's a good sport...'

There seemed to be no way I was going to get rid of him, even when Mr. Loo started to take an interest and bare his fangs. Then the pooch gave me an idea...

I backed off into the kitchen and of course it had done itself proud on the lobster which I'd had out on the table all ready to serve, so I scooped the end products into some paper, went back to the door and let him have it full in the face - which was plenty enough to get his foot out of the way.

I could hear him dancing around and carrying on a treat outside, but then he must gotten down on his hands and knees because next thing he was hollering through the letter box.

'You fucking bitch, I'll fucking get you for that, don't you fucking worry, you're a fucking great faceful of shit (as if that wasn't exactly what he was just then!), do you fucking hear me, just you fucking wait, I'll screw the fucking daylights out of you, you fucking great cunt, do you fucking hear me…'

There was only one way of dealing with this, I decided, just like I used to deal with Win when he came back hammering on the door high as a kite after dinner in the mess. Luckily the soda siphon was pretty much full, and after a couple of good squirts between the eyes that was the end of Mr. Nosey-Parker Oxtail for the night.

Sunday 28 October

'Don't worry, I'll have a word with Beaverbrook and that'll be the end of it. There's nothing like a Dominions press wallah when you need the keep things out of the papers, don't you know,' TLM said when I gave him the story the next morning.

I wasn't so sure myself, so I told him I'd give it another day before I dared show my face again (which meant having to cancel Emerald - thankfully).

'Okey-dokey, sweetheart - I'm off to Brummie-ham anyhow today to open some new hospital and do my usual for the local layabouts,' he agreed. 'And if you're still worried, I've got just the place for the rest of the week. It's a little hideaway in Sussex that my pal George Chumley keeps for me in his place down near Wadhurst. Nobody'll ever find We there, I promise you…'

We fixed for Ladbrook to drop him off at Excelsior Motors - making out that he wanted to check on the service warranty - and I'd pick him up there in WE 1. Nice Mr. Trilby was around to go through it with him, giving me a 'I've heard this one before' sort of look while TLM was on the small print.

He'd brought along his ten-gallon Alberta cowboy hat to hide himself under, so the driving was down to me.

Everything went fine until we were sitting at the lights on the Croydon by-pass, when some guy came up alongside and yelled across 'We won, get lost.' Which in fact was just about exactly what happened. We were coming out of Wadhurst when we hit fog and TLM took over the wheel because he said he knew the road backwards - and that's just how we ended up, in a ditch.

At the first house we knocked up (Caplin Cottage was the name on it,

I seem to recall) some hideous old witch appeared in a white nightdress with tennis shoes on her feet. 'Hen's teeth, it was your lucky stars that brought you to me, and that's a fact,' she cackled when I told her the problem. 'Just you see, with one click of my little finger I'll have every man jack in the village come running to help you out, just you see, just you see…'

And lo and behold, we were out of the ditch and back on the (yellow brick?) road before we could say abracadabra.

After that, it was all plain motoring - three days of uninterrupted automatic transmission, never mind the double declutching…

Got back in just before Ernest showed, and in time to call Herman - yes, he'd tracked him down to a dive of a hotel in the Rue St. Denis and taken up station in the café opposite, but there'd been no sign of Mary and Ernest hadn't even tipped his hat to any of the ladies of the street outside. He'd finally given him a call yesterday and suggested a boys night out on the Pigalle, but Ernest said no thanks, he'd been in the Louvre all day staring at the Mona Lisa and that was the only memory of Paris he wanted to take back home with him.

Par for the course, as TLM would say.

NOVEMBER
The Final Hurdle

Thursday 1 November

Today's mail brought

    1)   from the *Baltimore Post News* of 20 September, courtesy (if that's the word) of Big Bucks:

BRITISH PRINCE IN MED CRUISE WITH BALTIMORE BELLE

Prince Edward, 40-year-old heir to the British Throne, arrived in the French port of Cannes this week on his luxury yacht after a month-long vacation in the fairy-tale medieval Castle Metermont in nearby Biarritz.

Also on board was 39-year-old Wallis Simpson, daughter of Mr and Mrs Teackle Warfield of Baltimore. First married at 18 to US Navy air ace Win Spencer of Chicago, she left him for UK-based shipping broker Ernie Simpson. Since 1926 she has lived in London, where she first met up with the dashing Prince.

Once ashore, they booked into the 5-star Miramar, and at midnight he roused the staff at the luxury Cartier store to purchase her a $500 diamond and emerald encrusted ring.

They had reboarded the yacht two days later when your correspondent arrived, but pretty 22-year-old hotel maid Josephine Villepin told me, 'They never left the suite the whole time they were here.'

Where they are heading next is not yet known, but it doesn't take Admiral Nelson's telescope to see that a major romance is under way.

Plus a note - 'Wallis, I found this on returning here via a few days with Cousin Lelia in Trenton. It seems that you have been less than candid with me, Bessie.'

And, I don't have to say, minus a check.

2) From the *New York Times* of 3 October, courtesy of Emerald who's off to Paris to check on Nancy and her nigger again.

MRS. VANDERBILT ACCUSED BY MAIDS
'She Gave All-Night Parties And Slept Up to 6 PM, exposed child to pornography,' says one 'I SAW HER IN BED WITH WOMAN FRIEND during stay in Cannes hotel,' alleges another

———

Maria Caillot told of five years in Mrs. Vanderbilt's service, during which she observed that her mistress either stayed out late at night or gave all-night parties at home, after which she slept late next day and left her child entirely to her nurse.

She recalled Mrs. Vanderbilt rising on one occasion at 6pm and having champagne served in her bedroom, where she shared it occasionally 'with a man'. She could tell nothing more because it was the butler who poured the champagne.

In her judgement, a few of the books in the room were 'dirty', and she considered them unfit for a child to see. When questioned, she assured the court that she had seen Mrs. Vanderbilt intoxicated. Gloria Vanderbilt then rose from her seat and shouted across the court, 'Just you wait until I get my day on the stand.'

The next witness, Josephine Villepin, a maid at the Miramar Hotel in Cannes, then gave evidence on the week that Mrs. Vanderbilt had stayed there in 1931. 'She was running about with people there, was she?' Justice Carew asked. 'Yes. She shared a suite with Lady Milford-Haven in one room, and her sister Mrs. Thaw and a Mrs. Wallis Simpson were in the one next door.'

'And did you see anything improper take place?'
'Once when I took the breakfast in they were in the same beds.' 'And what were Mrs. Vanderbilt and Lady Milford-

Sorry, Madame Claire, but I've had enough of the papers for one day.

Sunday 4 November

Motored down yesterday to the Fort under our own steam for once.

'I really don't think we ought to accept it, you know,' Ernest had said when he first set eyes on WE 1.

'Why's that? Because of the little accident David had with it driving it off the production line, you mean? The factory fixed it up good as new.'

'No, no, it's not that.'

'Or do you reckon we're so grand now we'll have to take on a chauffeur again, which we can't run to right now?' (I hadn't of course let on to the check in the glove box, making out that the fur coat was down to Big Bucks)

'No, it's not that either. It's the number plate, you see, honeybunch.'

'Oh?'

'Yes. I was thinking that it could make us look rather, well, pompous - especially if it got out that it came from David.'

'You've got it wrong, if that's why you reckon he chose it. What's his Number One interest in life?'

'Golf?'

'No, try again.'

'Dogs?'

'And again.'

'Jigsaws?'

'Oh, come on, Ernest. What does he spend half his time looking in on all over the country? Like he's going to be in Bristol next week down in the docks, then in Durham a couple of weeks later up in the minefields.'

'You mean unemployment centers?'

'You've got it. So that's what it stands for - I'm the Number One guy for Workers Employment. Get it?'

'Oh, I see. Well, that's all right, then.'

'I should just hope so' - only my hopes are some way else, honeybunch!

Arrived to find the place stiff - and I mean stiff - with royalty of one place or another, as Brer Henry had brought down the lucky bride and assorted sisters/cousins/uncles for a getting-to-know-you session. Plus, as if I didn't know all I needed about them already, thanks very much, Mr. & Mrs. Temple - though at least we were spared the kids (but not the corgis - just as well we hadn't brought Mr. Loo or they'd have wiped the floor with him. In fact, the wiping was down to Osborne and do you know, I almost felt sorry for the guy) It only needed Woodentops to fly back from Australia and it would have been a case of death by a thousand yawns. Even Ernest had had enough by breakfast today and announced that he was taking off to Salisbury in WE 1 to have a look at the brasses and gargoyles or whatever it is he rubs.

Marina herself may have been quite easy on the eye facewise, but that was about as far as she went. Her clothes made even The Fat Cook like a mannequin hot off the Chanel catwalk, and the only bit of jewelry she had to her name was a string of pearls the size of pinheads. I know mine is all costume (bar TLM's frog), but at least I look a million dollars. 'A girl can't be too rich or too bitch,' as they say, but she doesn't seem to have heard yet. And as for any box of tricks upstairs, a Chinese Grip looked like it would mean to her something in amber to keep her hair in place (on her head, that is) Still, George won't be too worried if he's got a rent boy on tap, I guess...

Most of the talk at lunch was about the program lined up for The Big Day - who was going to be invited to this, who was going to be sitting next to who at that, who was going to be wearing what, etc, etc. I had TLM to myself for precisely two minutes all day to ask him where I came in.

'Of course I've got you seats in the Abbey on the day itself, my sweetheart. I'm afraid there's no way I can get you an invite for the dinner on the Monday which is for Royals only, but I'm trying to get you in on my party for the ball on the Tuesday.'

'I should just hope so!'

'But it's not going to be so easy, I have to say.'

'Why, what's the problem?'

'Well, Pop is cutting up rough, don't you know. I had you down on my list, but then he crossed you off when I put it into HQ.'

'He did that?'

'Yes. He seems to know rather a lot about us, I'm afraid - almost more than we know ourselves, in fact.'

'So where does that leave us?'

'Well, I think we'll just have to keep ourselves apart for the moment. I know that's awfully tough on We, sweetheart, but that's the only way I'm going to be able to swing it, don't you see?'

'Yes, maybe I do…'

Sometimes if a girl's got to wait for the main chance, she's got to wait. But that's not to say she can't play other strings on her bow, is it?

Wednesday 7 November

The Times

THE PRINCE AT BRISTOL

——

A CROWDED TOUR

——

INTEREST IN WELFARE WORK

Bristol, Tuesday. The Prince of Wales today visited Bristol, devoting his time almost entirely to unemployed welfare centres and a new housing estate. The city has just over 21,000 unemployed, for whom there are 12 welfare centres and 3,048 new houses and flats built after a major slum clearance. These facts were brought to his attention in a special souvenir programme.

Arriving at the Docklands Settlement, he was received by the Lord Mayor, the Duke of Beaufort and Lord Dulverton. He witnessed various activities of the members, including a boxing match. On inquiring how many of them played golf and being informed that there was no golf course in the area, he repeated 'Something must be done,' several times.

He next visited the university centre at Barton Hill, where he saw a number of unemployed men engaged in handicrafts and accidentally left a highly treasured souvenir. This was a tray which he had picked up to examine the workmanship. However, it had been freshly enamelled, and he found, to his own amusement, that it now bore his fingerprints. On being informed that the newly-built library was appealing for books, he said, 'I've got hundreds at the Fort that I don't want, so I'll get my man Osborne to send them down.' (that sounds like the end of that nice little racket, then)

The Prince lunched at Red Lodge, the sixteenth-century home of 'The Bristol Savages' group of artists. 'This must be the Wattle-and-Daub School,' he observed while touring an exhibition of their work afterwards.

Nowhere did he get a more enthusiastic welcome than the Dings area, where he inspected the new council housing estate. At one point he asked his entourage to stay behind while he stopped to speak to some of the residents 'as a man of the people', and at one house he was presented with a bunch of leeks dug from the garden.

For his final visit, he took tea at the Imperial Tobacco factory and toured the production lines. In the cigar section he was shown some being made from Costa

Rican leaf. Lord Dulverton told him that they cost barely a quarter of the price of Havanas, but were otherwise indistinguishable. 'You can put me down for a standing order, then. That'll save me a pretty packet, especially if you can leave off the labels!' the Prince joked to hearty laughter from all those present.

'You poor darling,' I sympathized when he called. 'You must have been worn out.'

'Jeez, it was the most awful grind, don't you know. There was one story they didn't print, though.'

'Oh, yes?'

'Yes. I took Cora and Jaggs along with me to that housing estate in Dings - just to give me the common touch, what? Well, the first door I knocked on was opened by this great battleaxe of a woman, and the next thing I knew was that Cora was doing the honours on her doorstep. After that the conversation was a bit sort of sticky, so I took my chance and hopped it at the first opportunity. I tried a few more, but then I must have got a bit lost - the streets all look the same in these estates, don't you know - because when I tried the first door in what I thought was the next one, who should appear again but The Battleaxe - and not only that, but Jaggs cocked his leg right on her foot! 'Ere, Bert,' she called inside, 'this carpet salesman's back again with his dogs doing their business all over me. Come and sort 'im out, quick!' I didn't even stop to say sorry this time, and I was half way back to the gate when a dirty great leek came flying over my head. Just as well I didn't have Mister Loo with me too or I'd have been really in the shit, what? Ha, ha!'

He had no news either on what I was really wanting to hear about - ie, The Great Ball Invitation Question. Emerald's asked me to put a word in for her too - fat chance!

Sunday 11 November

TLM on parade for Armistice Day, Emerald down with the Astors at Cliveden and Ernest off for the weekend in WE 1 to Ely (wherever that is) and Lincoln for some more rubbing, leaving poor little ME all alone.

But not for long.

I'd just put the kettle on for elevenses when the bell rang. I could only think that TLM had cried off the parade because I knew they'd all be standing there saluting on the stroke of eleven, but then I realised that was about the worst move he could make with Big Chief if he was still aiming to get me into the Ball - so who the hell…

Mr. Loo seemed just as interested as I was to find out, and was out of the door almost before I'd opened it.

'Ah, someone knows his friends when he sees them, eh? Been behaving yourself lately and not going absent without leave again, have you, young fellow?'

'Why, Mister Tril - Trundle!'

'Good morning, madam. I do hope I'm not disturbing you.'

'No, not at all. Do come in.'

'Thank you. Mister Simpson's in, is he?'

'No, I'm afraid he's up in Lincoln, poking around the cathedral there.'

'I see. I just happened to be passing and saw the car wasn't there, so I rather assumed you were both out but popped up just in case you were having any problems with it.'

'No, it seems to be going fine, except the engine makes a sort of knocking noise.'

'I say, I don't like the sound of that - it usually means there's a problem with the big end. I'd better call back another time when your husband's in to book it into the garage.'

'No, no, do stay. I've just got some coffee going, if you fancy a cup.'

'Well, yes please, that'd be very nice.'

'That's my pleasure…'

And it was - there was no problem with his big end, that's for sure!

Wednesday 14 November

You may be approaching a major watershed in your life, but at times it feels as if you're hardly making any progress to speak of, or worse still, that you're drifting at the mercy of events over which you have no control at all. However, you must try and be patient, and remember that no one's life can be in a state of perpetual motion. Above all, don't be tempted into doing something just for the sake of it, which is almost always counter productive. With the Full Moon approaching, you won't have to wait long for things to pick up speed again.

Still no word from TLM on the TGBI?, but I took Madame Claire to heart and when I heard someone at the door I told Beckham, the new terror of a maid - after a week of waiting for her to get out of hospital, I'd given up on Cain - to tell Mr. Trundle I was out (there was always his 'little pad' in Bruton St. to fall back on).

'It's a Mister Ladbrook, mam. Say's 'e's something for you and must hand it to you personal, like.'

And there it was:

THEIR MAJESTIES KING GEORGE AND QUEEN MARY
REQUEST THE PLEASURE OF THE COMPANY

OF MR. & MRS. ERNEST SIMPSON

TO A BALL TO MARK THE OCCASION OF THE MARRIAGE
OF THEIR BELOVED SON, PRINCE GEORGE EDWARD
ALEXANDER (etc, etc)
plus a letter -

'My darling sweetheart,
So you see your eanum boy has been very very clever,
don't you think? I never thougt I'd manage to talk
the Old Brute round, but then I hit on the wheeze of
saying that the Americans would take it as a terific
insult if you weren't invited and did he really want to
give the pip to our galant allies in the trenches and
all that rot, and that did the trick!! This was just after
wed all got back from the armistice day thingie, so I
thougt I'd strike wile the iron was hot, don't you
see. Mind you I had to swear on scouts honour that
there was nothing going on between WE, but WE
know better, don't WE?!!
I feel so eanum not having seen you for all this time,
my sweetheart, and by the time WE take the floor
together do you realise it'll have been one whole
month apart, but when WE do a boy will be holding
a girl so very tight she litrally won't be able to
breathe! I wish I could make a drowsy to last the
next two weeks and wake up in your arms, but at
least I have my two eanum babies here to remind me
every minute of you and Mr. Loo, and after that a

girl knows that not anybody or anything can separate
WE not even the stars - and that WE belong to each
other for ever and that your David will love you and
look after you so long as he has breth in his eanum
body.
God bless WE Wallis.
David
Here's a little something for a gown to dazzle them
all with - though even if you were dressed like
Cinderella you'd still be the bell of the ball.

£300 - that should leave enough left over for some REAL rocks, even without the loot from the books. Must give Mary a call to see how they went.

Saturday 17 November

When you're working on a project that requires flair, you must expect any others involved to be looking to you to supply your own special brand of magic and so you shouldn't let yourself be restricted by any feelings of false modesty. In fact, you can afford to be even more imaginative and daring than usual, because they would rather that you went too far than inhibit yourself in any way. And if you do look like spiralling out of control, you can be sure that they - or he or she - will be there to save you. Go for broke, in other words, girl…

Fog that you could cut with a knife, but the thought of a day inside with Ernest and Beckham had me downstairs and out on the street by half nine.

After three days scouring the West End I'd picked up a floral-pattern diamond brooch at Ogdens (for 105gns, so I had to tell them to reserve it until I saw how the rest of the budget was going to work out) and a couple of wedding outfits at Harvey Nicks - one in crimson velvet and another in mid-blue satin, both with silver fox fur collars and matching hats - but drawn a complete blank on something for the ball, so there was nothing for it but to head out to Ken High and would you believe, I found the perfect number in Barkers of all places! It just happened they were having an anniversary show of ballroom designer models, and the minute I saw this Eva Lutyens gown in violet lamé with a vivid green full-length sash I just knew I had to have it even at double the £40 price-tag - if that doesn't hit Big Chief and the Squaw between the eyes nothing will!

That still left nearly £50 in the kitty, so I looked in next door on the Derry & Toms mid-season coat sale and picked up (for £18) one in a novelty woollen material with an arctic fox collar dyed in 'Hollywood' - ie, brown with surface highlights - and then just had time to get back to Ogden's before they closed. I passed it off as paste to Ernest of course when I got back in, and all he could find to say about the rest was some crack about having so many coats now that I must be going into hibernation. Little does he know yet about TLM's skiing idea, and anyhow he's hardly one to talk as he's having himself kitted out in a new Grenadier Guards mess uniform. As for Beckham's comment on the gown - 'Gor blimey, mam, you'll look all got out like one of them fancy Easter eggs, I'll say' - the less said the better. She won't be staying here one minute longer than it takes me to find a substitute, that's for sure - even one of those Spanish maids without a word of English to their name will do. Cain was Cockney down to her fingertips, but at least she tried to hide the fact.

Called Mary: the books only made $415 - call that £100 - so it's all down to LITTLE DORRIT now. She's already mailed me a cheque, she said, plus the final news clip on Gloria's case.

Wednesday 21 November

Which arrived today -

> MRS. WHITNEY WINS CUSTODY OF GIRL, COURT HOLDS MRS. VANDERBILT UNFIT *Latter to see daughter only at weekends, the month of July and Christmas Day, Carew rules* GLORIA TO BE BROUGHT UP AS CATHOLIC *by governess of that faith. Mother plans appeal.*
>
> ———
>
> *Judge Carew today handed down his decision at the end of the two-month hearing based on his conclusion that 'Mrs. Vanderbilt, traveling constantly between London, Paris, New York and other places where she enjoyed a round of parties with persons of her own age and, on at least one occasion, sex while the child followed in the care of a nurse, has provided a life for the child which was in every way unfit, destructive of health, neglectful of her*

moral, spiritual and mental education...'

    Mrs.Vanderbilt's lawyers stated that she would lodge an appeal with a higher court. On hearing of the decision at her home she immediately collapsed, while her sister, Lady Thelma Furness, had to compose herself before she could be photographed. 'This is a travesty of justice,' she told reporters, 'and we'll fight it to the bitter end.'

And if I know Thelma, when she says bitter, boy, she means bitter...

Sunday 25 November

    All thoughts now on the ball, both waking and sleeping - eg, this funny (funny = peculiar, that is) dream I had last night.

    Getting to the head of the line to be presented to 'Their Majesties', I was surprised to see they had pumpkin cut-out crowns on their heads while everyone else was got up in sheets and Halloween masks.

Queen	'Who is this?'
Me	'My name is Wallis, so it please Your Majesty.'
Q	'Wallis? There's no such name.'
King	'Yes there is, dear. Let's see... Oh yes, Wallace & Arnold - you know, the haberdashers in Bayswater.'
Q	'Bayswater? I've never been to Bayswater.'
K	'No, but you send out for your brasseries there.'
Q	'Brasseries? Whatever are those?'
K	'You know, those French thingies you wear.'
Q	'I wear them? Where?'
K	'Around your, well, you know -'
Me	'I think he means brassieres, Your Majesty.'
Q	'Speak when you're spoken to, child!'
K	'I don't think she's a child, dear.'
Q	'Not a child?'
K	'No, I'd call her a woman myself.'
Q	'A woman? Are you sure?'
K	'Well, that's my impression.'
Q	'Yes, perhaps you're right, now that I look at her properly.'
Me	'And my name is Wallis, Your Majesty.'
Q	'That doesn't prove it, one way or the other.'
Me	'And I'm married to Mister Simpson.'

196

K	'Oh, she comes from Piccadilly, then.'
Q	'And not from Bayswater?'
Me	'No. And before that I was married to Captain Spencer.'
Q	'Good gracious, you sound like a walking stores directory. I suppose you'll be marrying a Mister Marks next.'
Me	'No, I'm going to marry Peter Pan, Your Majesty.'
K	'Peter Pan? Never heard of him.'
Q	'I think she means Peter Pansy, dear.'
K	'Oh, the queen.'
Me	'And then I'll be the queen.'
K	'But two queens can't mate!'
Me	'Yes, they can, when it's stalemate.'
Q	'Fiddlesticks!'
K	'And you haven't passed the proper examination.'
Me	'Well, I've studied for it long enough.'
Q	'That doesn't mean to say you'll pass. What's your handicap at croquet?'
Me	'Croquet? I've never played the game.'
Q	'Did you hear that, George? The woman says she's never played.'
K	'Oh, I say - '
Q	'Off with her head!'
Me	'Then I would have a handicap, wouldn't I? I mean, playing without my head.'
K	'She has a point there, dear, don't you think?'
Q	'Very well, I'll let you off this time. Trick or treat?'

She suddenly clenched both her fists and held them out for me to choose. I pointed to the left one, she turned it over and opened the palm. At first sight it seemed quite empty, but then a small cat began to materialise - first its face with a grin from ear to ear, then the rest of its body right down to its supersized tail. As I looked at it in fascination it continued to grow - either that, or I began to shrink - until without warning it leapt at me and pinned me to the ground. I tried all I could to free myself, but its great tongue was pressed right into my face and I felt as if I was being smothered to death...

But of course it was only Mr. Loo wanting to be let out.

Tuesday 27 November

And that was pretty much how it turned out in fact - the main difference being that instead of us lining up for the Royal Presence, they broke ranks and came to us.

The first to head over was a guy who introduced himself as Prince Paul of Yugo-slavia (or was it Checko-slovakia? One of those places right off the map of Europe, anyhow)

'I knew immediately when I saw you that it was you, Mrs. Simpson.'

'You did?'

'Yes. You see, my friend David told me to look for the woman with the most flashy dress in the whole room, and so of course I -'

Just then David came up behind and tapped him on the shoulder.

'Ah, so you've found my American I was telling you about, what?'

'Without any difficulty, yes.'

'And isn't she the most wonderful woman you've ever met, don't you agree, Paul?'

'Yes. Very wonderful, I am sure.'

'There you are, I told you so. Oh, excuse me, I must introduce her to Mom and Pop while I've got the chance. I'll be back in two ticks.'

When we got to them, I did the little curtsy I'd been practicing over and over while Ernest just about hit his head on his knees, he was bowing so low.

K 'Simpson, eh? You don't own the restaurant in the Strand by any chance, do you?'

E 'No, I don't actually. I'm awfully sorry, Your Majesty.'

K 'Pity. I'm told they do the best roast beef in town.'

E 'Oh, I agree absolutely, Your Majesty.'

K 'Mind you, I don't know about their Yorkshire Pudding.'

Me 'They do a great Brown Windsor Soup, though.'

K 'Do they? Perhaps you ought to get their recipe, dear.'

Q 'Yes, I should. And where do you come from, Mrs. Simpson?'

Me 'From Baltimore, Marm.'

K 'Ireland, eh?'

Me 'No, Maryland, United States of America.'

K 'Is that so?'

Q 'Perhaps you're confusing it with Ballymore, dear.'

K 'Yes, I daresay you're right. Awfully big place, America. Never been there, of course. Prefer Bognor myself.'

Me 'Well, there's always a first time, sir.'

K Yes. Come to think of it, there are one or two gaps in my collection I could fill.'

Me 'Collection?'

K 'Stamps, you know. I'm still looking for the Civil War fifty cents magenta overprinted in red and -'

Q 'Excuse me interrupting, dear, but I think Birt's signalling for dinner.'

K 'Oh yes, so he is. Well, awfully glad to have met you, what?'

Well, it was a start, I guess - at least I still had my head on my neck.

Wednesday 28 November

If you discover something about somebody close to you which could threaten the bond between you, your forthright, no-nonsense nature will spur a temptation to confront him or her with it at the first opportunity. If so, you should resist it, because words spoken in the heat of the moment can often destroy a relationship for good. Remember, we all make mistakes and that includes even you, and would you want it thrown in your teeth every time? No, and that goes for everyone else.

I reckoned I had the answer when the bell rang just as I was on my way out to lunch with Emerald (TLM had managed to get her a last-minute ticket to the wedding reception - nothing to do of course with the £50 she'd sent me 'as an early Christmas present, darling') Mrs. Ralph was still out shopping and Beckham had just left for her afternoon off, so I had to take it myself and was greeted by this apparition - I really could hardly believe my eyes - of a chinless wonder of a youth got up in a top hat, frock coat, wing collar, floral waistcoat, spats and, to round it all off, a pink carnation between his teeth.

At first I reckoned he must be a flunky from the Palace round with some plan for the Wedding, but he didn't seem to be offering anything and anyhow we'd already had all the directions we needed twice over.

'Ggggggood mmmmmorning, mmmmmmisssssus SSSSS -'

All this was even after he'd taken the carnation out of his mouth, so I felt I had to help the poor guy out.

'Simpson.'

'SSSSSimpson. Awfffffly sssss -'

'And how can I help you?'

'I've ccccccome fffffor JJJJJ -'

'Joan?' (Mrs. Ralph)

'Nnnnno, JJJJJean.'

'Are you sure you've got the right address, young man?'

'Yyyyyes. JJJJJean BBBBBeckham.'

'Oh, I see. Well, in that case you need the servants' quarters. You'll have to down again and round to -'

Just then - when I was reckoning this conversation was going to go on all day and night - Beckham herself appeared out of the elevator, dolled up to the nines in a straw hat, print dress, shawl and heels so high she could hardly put one foot in front of the other.

'Algie, you daft twat, I told you to take the back stairs.'

'Oh, ddddd -'

'E's my bloke, you sees, mam. Tell her who your dad is, Algie.'

'Oh, hhhhhhe'sssss the CCCCC -'

'Controller of the Royal Household. (not for long when I get there, I thought!) Does all the accounts, 'e does.'

'Yyyyyesssss, that'sssss -'

'Been walking out six weeks now, 'aven't we, Algie? Ever since we met when I was behind the bar in the Cadogan Arms. And next week - tell 'er, Algie.'

'Wwwwwe're gggggetting enggggg -'

'- aged. And you'll be buying me a ring, won't you? Sparklers an' all. Come on, we'd better be going or we'll be late for the party. That's the staff party at the Palace, in case you're wondering, mam. See you later, then.'

'Yyyyyesssss. Ggggggoodbbbbb -'

'Algie, come ON!' she hissed at him and took hold of his arm - which was probably just as well, or she'd never have made it back to the elevator.

Well, if tomorrow's is rated the Wedding of the Decade, this one should be the Wedding of the Century, I'd say...

Friday 30 November

Up at 7am as we had to be in the Abbey by 10. Mrs. Ralph and Beckham didn't show of course, as it had been declared a national holiday, so breakfast was down to me - toast and coffee, and if he wanted his usual fry-up the pan was right there beside the stove, I told Ernest.

As it was, I had my work cut out pouring him into his new mess kit - I reckon he must have just given his tailor a repeat order of his measurements of 15+ years ago when he'd signed up at the end of the war, and I said he'd better not go in for any more bowing and scraping or the buttons would come off him like dried peas out of a popgun. When it came to myself, I couldn't decide between the crimson and the mid-blue, but then I thought why shouldn't it be my red letter day too and so I went for the crimson.

We made it on time - just about, as there wasn't a cab to be had for love or money (well, you can't have them both, can you?) till we'd gotten more than half way there on our own four feet and I was telling Ernest to go back and fetch the motor - which gave us an hour's rubber-necking before the show began.

Our seats were on the end of a row in a side aisle, so we had a terrific view of the whole Woebegone tribe arriving in all its war-paint. The Fat Cook appeared half way through with Meg, and guess what she was in? Crimson velvet!! I could have died - or more likely done her to death if there hadn't been a couple of thousand others on hand to witness me at it... At least the little kid was in cream (and the other kid in white like all the other bridesmaids, of course.)

TLM came in with together with Brer George, and they only beat the curtain-up by a matter of seconds. If anything, he looked the jumpier of the two and most people would have guessed he was the groom rather than the other way round. 'Always the best man and never the bridegroom'? Not for much longer! All the way through, I couldn't help rehearsing to myself the words of our service: 'Wilt thou, Edward Albert Christian George Andrew Patrick David Windsor, take this woman, Wallis Simpson, to be thy wedded wife, wilt thou love her and look after her so long as thou has breath in thy eanum body...'

It was another hour before it was all over, another before we were out and on our way, another before we reached Buck House, and yet one more before I got my hands on the first tray of haddock boats on offer.

'You should count yourselves lucky, 'TLM greeted us with. 'You didn't have to sit through the Greek Orthodox jamboree.'

'So how did it go?'

'Well, it was all Greek to me, don't you know? And there was a bit of a stink when I lit up my cigar on one of the candles - and I'm not talking about all the incense wafting around, what? Ha, ha...'

Next up was Fruit-Face, who looked as if he'd been in the wars again. I'd seen something in the paper a couple of weeks back about Tom Mosley and some of his buddies being charged with causing a riot some place, but according to Emerald it was just as likely that he'd been caught in the middle of cat fight between Baba and Diana Guinness - apparently there's a showdown going on about who he - Tom - is spending Christmas with. Whatever, I wasn't going to hang around for the answer - especially when I caught sight of Baba in full sail on the horizon.

Emerald had homed in as soon as we'd gotten there, of course, and for some reason all the Yanks - the Bates, Nancy Astor, Laura Corrigan, Betty Lawson-Johnston, Foxy Gwynne & Co. - made a beeline for me too. Quite why, I didn't discover until we were back out on the street again and Ernest was trying to hail a cab when she slipped a bit of paper to me - she'd been in the embassy yesterday renewing her passport when she'd happened on this piece on the *New York Post*'s ticker-tape and taken it home with her:

Baltimore Belle To Be Queen of England?

London, November 27 39-year-old Wallis Simpson, born Wallis Treacle Warfield of Baltimore, Maryland, was the belle of the grand ball held last night at Buckingham Palace ahead of tomorrow's wedding of Prince George of Kent to Greek Princess Marina.

Wallis stole the show with a dazzling violet gown tied with a brilliant green sash, an outfit put together by famous designer Eva Lutyens.

She then danced the night away on the arm of her new beau, the dashing 40-year-old heir to the throne and the groom's brother, Prince Edward of Wales.

Rumors of a romance first spread this fall after a two-month tour together of France and the Swiss islands. These were dismissed at the time on the basis that they were 'just good friends', but now all of London society is openly talking of marriage.

Though already twice-wed, divorce

from her present husband, 37-year-old Anglo - American shipbroker Ernest Simpson, would not be a problem for Wallis. As a US citizen, she would be free to obtain a 'quickie' in Arizona in a matter of weeks, while the Prince is unmarried.

Nor is her husband thought likely to oppose such a move. He hasn't drawn a salary for more than two years from his New York-based firm which has been hit by the worldwide recession in shipping, and he would probably settle for a generous pay-off.

America awaits!

So it was to be my red-letter day after all! Or so I fancied until I got back home and found this telegram from New York on the mat:

JUST IN CASE YOU'RE GETTING IDEAS, WALLIS, THE GUY'S ALREADY MARRIED

DECEMBER
Wallis The Winner!

Monday 3 December

Court Circ, Forthcoming Marriages

The Hon. A.P.M. McCartney-
Ferguson and Miss J.D. Beckham

The engagement is announced between The Hon. Algernon Peregrine Murdoch, younger son of Sir Gervaise McCartney-Ferguson, The Comptroller of The King's Household, and Lady McCartney-Ferguson of 2, Buckingham Palace Mews, SW1, and Jean Dolly, daughter of Mr. & Mrs. Tony Beckham, of 58 Porter Street, E16.

After that I hardly needed Madame Claire to set my imagination alight.

'So when's the grand wedding going to be?' I asked the lucky bride.

'I dunno yet - soon as Algie's finished 'is exams, I expect. And we're going to Spain for our 'oneymoon.'

'You don't say. To Madrid, that is?'

'Yes. My dad was there when 'e was in the Merchant Navy before 'e went into the docks, and 'e says there are ever so many lovely beaches there like.'

'Don't you mean Majorca, then?'

'Well, one of them places. And Algie's taking me shooting grouses in Scotland next week, so I'll be leaving Sunday.'

I've seen some shotgun weddings in my time, but this is...

Luckily Mrs. Ralph has kept in touch with Cain and is going to see if she's still free - though I'll have to make it clear to her I can't be paying for any more time off sick.

Wednesday, 5 December

I'd almost given up on Madame Claire's bit about lying doggo (well, there's no such word as bitcho, is there?) after 4 days of silence from TLM and was even beginning to think that maybe Frederika - the Boche princess that according to Emerald friend Adolf had lined up for him - had given him the hots, when he called at last - awfully sorry and all that, he said, but he'd only seen the back of the last of Marina's hangers-on late on Monday and yesterday he'd been on parade at Windsor for the staff party there and they'd hung on too for ever, so now he just couldn't wait for his little treat one minute longer...

'But you're not thinking of coming here, are you? That snapper could still be nosing around, for all I know.'

'No, no, you needn't worry about him - Beaverbrook's seen to that OK, like I said.'

'And I've got the staff here all day.'

'Sweetheart, don't worry, I tell you - your eanum boy has got it all fixed, don't you see.'

'You have?'

'Yes. You know Dickie and Edwina's place in Park Lane, don't you? Well, he's just sailed off to Malta and she's making herself scarce with one of her darky fancies, so they've let me have the run of it for the rest of the month. Isn't that the best thingie ever for WE, what? So all a girl has to do is get down there as soon as she can and she'll find a boy all ready for her...'

I actually walked to give myself time to sort out my game plan, but I'd still have been there in twenty minutes flat if I hadn't bumped into Posey racing into the Grosvenor and looking like she had some more 'abdominal merriment' on the menu (join the club!). By that time I'd decided that the best option was to go fishing - tickle him up with the 'Prince To Wed' clip till he was ready to surrender, then haul him in with the telegram and 'now let's see if you really mean it.'

Well, it didn't quite work out like that...

First, he jumped on me practically before I was through the door, so that was goodbye to any tickling and it wasn't until they brought round the picnic lunch he'd ordered from the Dorch that I could even get my line out.

'Well, I don't know about any wedding, I'm sure,' he said over the foi gras and fizz.

'Why not?'

'Trouble is, I can see some people making a bit of a stink if we went ahead now, I'm afraid.'

'Such as?'

'All those ghastly colonials in the Dominions with their hairy knees and knicker-bockers, for a start. You only have to mention the word divorce to them and they look at you as if you'd gone native - do you know, I had a letter from Henry in Melbourne only yesterday saying how they wouldn't let one of his chaps into the golf club because he was divorced, what? Then there's our home-grown pollies - Old Farmer Macdonald's a decent enough stick, but he's talking to Pop about chucking it all in and then we'll have that Birmingham Bible-Basher Baldwin, who's bound to try and put the kibosh on it. And then to cap them all is Pop himself, of course, who'll do anything just to spite me.'

'Are you sure you're not being a bit hard on him?'

'Oh, absolutely not, sweetheart - not hard enough, in fact, seeing the old sod's been doing his best to do me down ever since I can remember, don't you know. For instance, there was that time I was having such fun in Kenya when I had to drop it all and race home just because they said he was on his deathbed, and what d'you think he said to me when I got there? "Oh, for God's sake, what the hell are you doing here?"'

'No kidding?'

'Those were his very words, I promise you. And those people in Kenya really know how to enjoy themselves, I can tell you - if it was down to them, we wouldn't have any problem at all, that's for sure. So we'll just have to wait till he kicks the bucket, I'm afraid, my darling, and then once I'm King I can do what I jolly well like - and if anyone still wants to make trouble, I'll just tell them to go hang and get on with their bally old coronation without me, what?'

'But don't you think it'd be better just to get on and do it? We could be waiting for ever, otherwise.'

'No, no, he's on his last legs, scout's honor - it was touch and go last time whether he'd pull through, and that was three years ago now. Anyhow, let's forget about all that now. I'll crack open another bottle and then maybe we'll have a little drowsy - I've got the Scots Guards dinner tonight at the Savoy before I catch the train for my wretched Durham jamboree, don't you see…'

Two hours later he was still out for the count, so there was nothing for it but to put the telegram back in my bag and leave him to it - Ernest getting back earlier and earlier with the lack of action in the office. I seem to recall some poet saying something about the best laid plans of minx and men coming unstuck…

It was still daylight - just - when I got out onto the street, and there was a guy in a trilby hanging around on the sidewalk opposite who had a familiar look about him - surely it wasn't… Then I realized it couldn't be, because he headed off towards Park Lane and Bruton Street of course was the other way.

Friday 7 December

He didn't catch up on too much 'drowsy' on the train by the look of it -

DURHAM'S DELIGHT
—
PRINCE VISITS UNEMPLOYED
—
'OURS THE BIGGEST PORKIES'
SAYS LOCAL M.P.
(photo of bleary-eyed TLM at train window)

His Royal Highness, The Prince of Wales, was warmly received on his lightning tour of Durham's coalfields yesterday. He covered 120 miles, visiting unemployment centres and some self-supporting schemes for raising pigs. 'We produce the biggest porkies in the country here,' Charles Lynton, the M.P. for Sedgefield, proudly told the Prince.

Leaving London overnight on the Royal Train, he had arrived at Sunderland station at 7am. Alighting three hours later, he caused considerable amusement both to himself and to the Lord Mayor's party waiting to greet him by declaring how delighted he was to be back in Newcastle…

He must have made it all back again on the way down again though, because he was obviously raring to go again when he called just after I'd got back in from lunch with Gladys Beast (I'd told him that Ernest was taking off today for a conference in Hamburg)

'Fancy a little show tonight, my sweetheart? Nothing too heavy, of course, but I happened to see in the paper coming down that something called *The Dominant Sex* opened at the Embassy this week starring Diana Churchill who's always such a sweetie, don't you know. It said it was all about how men think they're boss but it's the women who really wear the trousers. Awful rot, of course, but it should be good for a few laughs, what?'

'Sounds hilarious.'

'Okey-dokey, then, I'll book the tickets. Why don't we meet up at Dickie's place for a KT or two and we'll go on from there??'

'Yes, all right...'

When he opened the door, I was a bit surprised to find him still in his dressing gown because I'd reckoned I was cutting it a bit fine myself - Beckham had made a scene because I'd docked her wages a pound for 'borrowing' one of my head bands.

However, that was nothing to what I was when he stripped off to show what he had on underneath - sweet fanny all except a baby's diaper!!!

'Caught you out there, my sweetheart, what? Ha, ha...'

'What the hell's going on?'

'Well, I said I wanted to see a show of the dominant sex, don't you see? And here's my favorite slipper with the raised heel.'

So there you are - I never could figure out why a pooch should be called Slipper before.

'And so how am I meant to go through with this?'

'Bend me over the end of the bed, of course, just like Nanny did. "You've been a very, very naughty little boy, David," she used to say, "and now I'm going to give you six of the best on your little bottie so you'll learn to be good." Come on, hurry up, or I'll start wetting myself.'

'Well, if you say so...'

The first strike was pretty much in the target zone and quite hard enough to satisfy him - or so I reckoned.

'Call that a stroke? Just a tickle that was. Try again.'

So I did.

'Harder! And tell me I've been a naughty boy, Nanny.'

And again, plus 'You've been a naughty boy, David.'

'Haven't! Harder!'

And again. 'You'll be good now, won't you?'

'Shan't! Harder!'

'And you've been telling Nanny fibs, haven't you?'

'Haven't! Harder!'

'Don't lie, David.'

'I'm not! Harder!'

It was time for the big hit.

'You've been married before, haven't you?'

'Not true!'

'Oh yes, it is, and I can prove it. Look,' I told him, laying out the telegram on the bed right in front of his eyes.

'What's that?'

'Something I got last week. From New York.'

'Oh, Lordie,' he said, straightening up.

'So it is true?'

'Yes.'

'In that case I reckon we ought to just sit down and talk it through, David.'

'Okey-dokey, but I'll do it standing up, if that's all right with you, sweetheart. And I wouldn't mind getting my trousers back on.'

'Go ahead. I'll be in the drawing room.'

I helped myself to the stiffest bourbon I've ever had in my life while I waited. When he appeared again, he was just about fully dressed except for a tie but still went over to the fireplace to warm his ass - as if it wasn't warm enough already! - after pouring himself a KT.

'And so who's the lucky lady?'

'Oh, just some little floosie who threw herself at me, don't you know.'

'Where?'

'In Canada.'

'Alberta?'

'No, no, it was somewhere near Toronto.'

'But that's why you have that place in Alberta, is it?'

'Well, sort of.'

'Sort of?'

'Yes. The boys were adopted there, you see.'

'Boys? How many are we talking about?'

'Oh, just the two.'

'Just the two. So it was a bit more than a passing fling, then.' Silence. 'And when did all this happen?'

'The year after the war, I think it was.'

'And you went back again, obviously.'

'Oh, I go over off and on to see the boys, don't you know, but I haven't seen Millie - that's Millicent, not Camilla - for ages now. Not since the second one was born, in fact - or it may even have been before.'

'But you still tied the knot, yes?'

'Yes. She insisted, don't you see? Said she'd go public otherwise.'

'Yes, I do see. So that makes the kids heirs to the British throne, is that right?'

'Oh, no, no - the marriage was one of those morgy thingies.'

'Morganatic, you mean?'

'Yes, that's right, That was her part of the deal, what?'

'But you're still married in the eyes of the law, and now you want to marry me, you say.'

'Yes, of course I do, my darling - like I said, as soon as Pop kicks the bucket.'

'Well, I've got news for you, David - I'm not going to hang around that long. Either you get a divorce or anulment or whatever by the end of the year or you'll never see me again once I'm out of that door, OK?'

'Oh, you don't have to worry your little head about that - it'll be no problem at all, I promise you.'

'No?'

'No - all I'll have to do is have a word with Bob Bennett - he's the PM over there, don't you know - and Bob's your uncle, so to speak, what? Ha, ha!'

'Oh, yes?'

'Yes. Awfully good chap, he is - plays off scratch, or as near as dammit. We had a day at the Berkshire together when he was over here in October, and you know that terribly long hole on the Blue? The eleventh, I think it is. Well, he had a terrific drive right down the middle, then he took out his spoon and -'

'You'll have to tell me another time, David, because I'm off - if there is another time, that is.'

'You're not going, are you, sweetheart?'

'I most certainly am - and I'm not coming back either till you produce the goods, like I said.'

'But Wally -'

'You've got three weeks, remember.'

'Three weeks! A boy'll never survive that long without his eanum girl, don't you know.'

'Well, the ball's in your field. Bye, bye.'

'Aren't I even going to get a little kiss - just for Nanny's sake?'

'For Nanny's sake?'

'You know, on your mole.'

'Well, OK then - just for Nanny...'

If I was back on the poker table, I'd say it looked like I was facing a Royal Straight Flush...

Saturday 8 December

Seeing the back of Beckham has to make my day, but even better, Mrs. Ralph tells me that Cain is ready and able to start again on Monday - whoopee! With Ernest not due back till Tuesday, I gave her the weekend off on the strength of it.

Then just when I was reckoning that my Christmas had already been, the postman came with Chuck Spencer's catalogue from Mary, which had LITTLE DORRIT estimated at $1200-1400, a bit up on his first quote. And not only that - she'd also put in the one for Parke Burnet's upcoming furniture sale 'as Lot 121 might be of interest to you.'

It sure was -

121 ***A late Victorian Folding Stand*** *in traditional style, comprising a tray and collapsible stand, supplied by Army & Navy Stores, London to the late Lord Curzon, the celebrated British Imperial Viceroy of colonial India, and still carrying its original label dated June 1898 and addressed to The Viceregal Lodge, Simla. $650-750*

Of all the brass-faced, two-timing shysters, that has to beat the lot of them!! Well, buster, you can bet your life that's the last punch you'll ever throw.

Just after Ernest had headed off to the office TLM had to call, of course, saying he'd forgotten to mention it yesterday but was I still sticking to my offer to see to all the staff's Xmas gifts, and if so, could I take them down to the Fort to be wrapped? Twenty minutes earlier I'd have told him that he had to be kidding, but now…

That was surely all the bonanzas that one morning could bring, I was telling myself when I heard the doorbell - and guess who? there was that guy/Guy again.

'Terribly sorry to be troubling you again, Mrs. Simpson, but you know that knocking noise you mentioned the Prince was making the last time we spoke? Well, I just happened to be passing again, so I took the liberty of having a look under the bonnet and I could see in a jiffy that it was nothing to do with the big end.'

'No?'

'No - it's just the belt that needs a little tweaking, that's all. Also, it must be about ready for its free 1000-mile service, isn't it? I could run it into the garage tomorrow if that's -'

'It's OK, honey, you can cut all that - there's no one else here. Come on in.'

'Don't mind if I do, I'm sure. So how are tricks, Wally? Still sweet as pie, eh?'

Well, he was as good as his word on the tweaking - and it wasn't any chastity belt either! And talking of tricks, it came out that he'd also been out in Hong Kong on an Air Force posting back in his service days and obviously hadn't wasted any time picking up a few there too...

'So I'll run her in tomorrow and get come back Wednesday afternoon, if that suits you, sweetie,' he said on his way out again

'Yes, OK.'

'Or if the staff's a problem, you could always pick her up from my little place, couldn't you?'

'Well, I'll see how I'm going on the day... By the way, you didn't happen to be in Curzon Street this Wednesday afternoon, were you?'

'This last Wednesday that's ever been, you mean?'

'Yes. I just thought I might have seen you, but it was getting dark so I couldn't be sure.'

'Wednesday. Hm, just a tick... Oh no, it couldn't have been me - I was out at Biggin Hill for an Old Comrades fly-past and lunch. Hell of a shindy it was too - old Squiffy Dunkers-Smythe in the chair gassed away half the afternoon, and by the time it was all over we were crawling out on our hands and knees. How I ever got back to base again I haven't foggiest, but it was Squiffy himself who tucked me up in bed, I do know that.'

'Sorry, I must have got the wrong man, then.'

'Not for 'abdominal merriment', I haven't!'

Sunday 16 December

Spent the whole week searching the town high and low for the best buys for the staff's gifts - all 94 of them - and ended up round the corner in Oxford Street cutting a discount deal with a sidewalk trader. Clockwork mice, bouncing monkeys, crawling dolls - all that sort of crap. TLM had sent me a cheque for £300 to cover it and when it was all over I still had £110 left, which can't be bad. As for Osborne's, I went for a wind-up pooch that cocked its leg - I'd just love to be there to see him open it, but even that wasn't going to beat the look on his face when he sees what else I've got in store for him.

Motored down today with them because TLM said he'd be up in the Midlands hunting with the Beaver.

The Ogre himself came down the steps to meet me, taking my case out of the trunk for the first time ever and grinning his head off like it was him who was going to land the KO.

I decided I might as well pull the wool off his eyes straight away, so as soon I'd touched myself up in the mirror, I came down again with the Parke Burnet catalogue and cornered him in his pantry.

'Mister Osborne, I'd like a word with you, if I may. Take a look at this, please.'

I wasn't exactly expecting him to drop to the floor and stretch out at my feet - just some sort of admission that he'd been caught with his pants down - but after reading it for a few seconds, all he did was pick up what looked like a magazine lying open on the sideboard and pushed it into my face.

'And you can take a butchers at this, you thieving bitch.'

'Osborne, how dare you speak to me like -'

And then I saw what it was - Chuck Spencer's catalogue, with LITTLE DORRIT ringed in red ink!!!

We must have stood there eyeballing each other for a good couple of minutes, then he suddenly started shaking all over with laughter.

'Well, stone the crows, that's a fair cop if ever I saw one, innit, duckie? Blimey, just wait till I tell my mates down at the Star and Garter - they'll heave their guts out, I'll bet yer!'

'But you won't be telling them, surely? Because if -'

'Don't yer worry, duckie, they're in it too. They all work out of the Castle, see.'

'And how long has this been going on?'

'Oh, I dunno - five years? Ever since Fingers Byers 'opped it over the water with some gold model of a ship and sets up shop, anyways. Sells it to some Greek who's running drugs in his tankers who introduces 'im to the Mob, but then they gets 'eavy so 'e goes independent like and starts selling through Burnets. Then this Spencer charlie opens up and 'e decides to 'ave a butchers at 'im too.'

'I see.'

'An' how long 'as you been at it, if I may make so bold?'

'Oh, just this year. And just with a few books, that's all.'

'More than a few, I'd say. That's when I starts smelling a rat, see? I says to myself, she's never going to be reading all that lot 'erself, so she must be passing 'em on some place else. And yer knows what gives yer away, don't yer? LITTLE DORRIT.'

216

'Why's that?'

'Cos that was one of Mrs. Ward's, an' it's Mrs. Ward what's set me up 'ere, see? She an' 'er Feathers Club - that's where all the villains meets up when they've done their bird. That's where I first comes across Slimboy Jaggs - remember when one of them dogs go missing this summer?'

'Yes, very well.'

'Well, we worked that one together. I collars the little bastard one night and 'ands it over to Slimboy at the gates, and 'e gets clean away of course to Southampton and lies low till 'is Nibs comes up with the asking price. Ten ponies we clears on that, we did. I 'ad to wait till Slimboy gets back from his cruise for my 'alf, mind.'

'That's honour among thieves for you, I guess.'

'Oh, Slimboy's no thief.'

'No?'

'Nah. You really wants to know what 'is line is? Buggery, that's what it is - with a spot of blackmail thrown in. 'E got the taste when 'e was a beak at Eton, then when they cottoned on to 'im he jumps on the first ship 'e sees an' that's where 'e's been ever since - barring one little stretch on His Majesty, that is. Says 'e gets it all on a plate on them liners, 'e does.'

'What, with the passengers?'

'Nah, with the other stewards, mostly. The 'ole lot of 'em are bent as boomerangs, so 'e says, so you'd best watch your backside next time yer goes back 'ome.'

'If there is a next time.'

'So yer's aiming to move in with 'is Nibs, eh?'

'"No comment" is the answer to that one, I think.'

'Please yourself, duckie, it's no skin off my nose - I mean, now as us is on the same side, like. Yer scratch my back an' I'll scratch yours, that's the name of the game, innit?'

'If you say so.'

"Poverty has strange bedfellows," Mom kept quoting at me as a kid (especially after she remarried to Mr. Raisin), and they don't get much stranger than this, I'd say! Even if I don't have to take it literally…

Monday 17 December

Cain back, plus Madame Claire

With Mercury causing some confusion in your chart, you will probably be going through some rough water at the moment. As any seafarer will tell you, your best option is to set aside your chosen course and sail with the wind until it blows itself out. In these circumstances you will doubtless come across others who have thrown the usual rules overboard, and you may be tempted to take advantage of the protection that they offer. But remember: ships that pass in the night seldom turn out to be reliable companions in the longer run.

A call from the garage - 'Mrs. Simpson? I'm awfully sorry, but Mr. Trundle has rung in to say that he's gone down with flu and regrets that he won't be able to collect your car for a service this week. '

Well, that's one boat off the high seas....

And from TLM - another idiot girl had knocked him off his horse out hunting with the Beavers and he was resting up with a sprained ankle, so I wouldn't be seeing him tonight at the Italian Embassy KTs.

That didn't stop Baba acting like she owned the place; I guess she was cashing in her chips, because there was no sign of Tom Mosley either.

I was just deciding I'd had enough when I felt a hand running over my butt and up my back, and it didn't take me more than a split second to figure out it was an Italian - and one particular Italian.

'Galeazzo!'

'Why are you so surprised, mia cara? Did I not write to you that I was coming to London?'

'Yes, but that was back in the summer sometime.'

'Ah, but then my father-in-law - excuse me, Our Great Leader - has decided to invade - excuse me, to liberate - Abyssinia, and so I have come now to talk to the Disarmament Conference with my honorable friend here from Germany and Special Adviser on Foreign Affairs. Please allow me to introduce Herr Joachim von Ribbentrop.'

There was a loud snapping of heels and I clung on to my glass in case a Nazi salute came flying up, but instead he grabbed hold of my hand and gave it such a mighty squeeze that I almost dropped the glass anyhow. It gave my memory a jog too, and I recalled where I'd seen him before - it was at Emerald's Anglo-German Fellowship do last year when I hadn't gotten to speak to him, but I had registered a divine dimple on his left cheek. Now I saw it close to, I reckoned that we had to be made for each other because if we got into a clinch, my mole would fit into it exactly!

'Ah, yes, I remember seeing you also. You were wearing your ostrich feathers, were you not?'

'Yes, that's right.' (Well, Thelma's)

'And do you know why I was there? Because I was selling the

champagne to Lady Cunard! German champagne, of course.'

'German champagne?'

'Yes - made in Alsace-Lorraine. That was part of the First Reich, as you know, and the Fuehrer is sure that one day it will belong to the Greater Germany again.'

'So that's why you're rearming, I guess.'

'No, that is not correct at all. It will only become ours by the will of the people, and if Germany is rearming it is only because we see other nations building weapons of massive destruction and so naturally we must prepare ourselves also.'

'What sort of weapons?'

'Ah, of course I cannot tell you precisely, but Herr Goebbels has made a dossier of them. For instance, we know that you have very many chemical and biological weapons remaining from the English War, and Herr Goebbels says that in forty-five minutes the Englanders can be dropping them on Berlin.'

'You know this for sure?'

'Yes, yes. At least, we know that they have the programs for making them.'

'But you can't prove that any of them actually exist, is that it?'

'No, I do not say that - absolutely not. And the Fuerher has promised to search for them in all the places and show the evidence to the whole world.'

'Don't look so worried, mia cara - he is only talking about English champagne,' Galleazzo cracked, pinching my butt. 'You know that the Germans have a so strong sense of humor, don't you?'

'Oh, that's OK, then. I was beginning to reckon that I should be hiding my new Elizabeth Arden face cleanser under the bed in case Adolf came hunting for it.'

'No, no, please, this is no joking, I assure you. The Fuerher has said that -'

We never did get to hear Adolf's latest wisecrack because just at that moment his other half marched up and put him under close arrest. I'd heard that her family were the Heinkels who apparently turn out the biggest bombers in Germany, and with her at the controls it didn't take much to see London being blasted to bits in two minutes flat.

'What have you been saying, Joachim?'

'Nothing important, *mein liebe* - just little talk, you understand.'

'And who is that woman?' (by this time I was beating it to the nearest air-raid shelter)

'Frau Simpson - Frau Wallis Simpson.'

'Ah! The mattress of the Prince Edward, I am told so. Remember, Joachim, what the Fuehrer has said - "Keep mum, she is not so dumb." Come with me, please - and you also, Conte.'

From the way that Galleazzo jumped to it too it didn't take much to see whose side he'd be on when the balloon goes up, though he managed to slip it to me as he went past that he'd booked a table for two at the Kit-Kat and he'd be there just as soon as he could bunk off parade.

There weren't too many others around that I wanted to see (and for all I knew, Thelma could have been back from New York by now and there somewhere making more trouble), so I sneaked off back to the flat and rested up for an hour or so before heading back out again.

I had a surprise waiting for me - not that there was no sign of him when I got there (he'd stood me up often enough at the Shanghai Lotus, after all), but that when he did eventually show he still had his Boche pal in tow! But at least they'd somehow managed to shake off the Heinkel - looping the loop? They certainly weren't flying too straight by then, and the Boche looked as if he'd taken more dud fizz on board than he'd ever sold in his life.

When it came to the dance floor, it was all I could do to keep either of them vertical, so there was nothing for it but to head back to the flat again with them and go horizontal…

Well, a girl's got to do what she can for her country to keep it out of any more foreign wars, hasn't she?

Wednesday 19 December

A dog's breakfast of a day if ever there was one, even without Mr. Loo's usual contribution (and Cain taking the day off for her Christmas shopping)

1) Ernest back from his conference last night and expecting an on-the-spot - or rather, in-the-tub - resumption of normal service.

2) A delivery of seventeen carnations from Harrods, plus a tag saying *'My dear Wallis, Please accept these as a token for my gratitude. Always I will remember the 17th day as the most exciting in my whole life. With my eternal love, Joachim.'* So love's labour isn't lost after all, whatever Shakespeare might say (though I haven't heard another word from Galleazzo, but then every Italian in the world takes his women for granted - bar his mother, that is).

3) A signing-off letter from TLM before he takes off for the Woebegones' Sandringham pow-pow -

My sweetheart,

A boy will be holding a pillow very tight in his arms at night for the next ten days thinking of an eanum girl. How he will get through them he doesnt know, and he is so weak and drowsy from being a week without her already that the golf wont be good, but I spoke with Bennett again today and he is doing everything he can he says, so I'm sure everything will be alright. Oh! To be alone together for ages and ages, and then some more ages and ages. God bless WE sweetheart but I'm sure he does - he must.

Your everloving David.

4) A call from Mary - LITTLE DORRIT never made its reserve! Apparently Freda's old hat now since I've been hitting the headlines, so I'm to let her know whenever TLM starts signing books to me or vice versa. Well, at least that solves the problem of what to get him for a present - and as for a title, how about GREAT EXPECTATIONS??

Tuesday 25 December

Ditto - just a pack of Selfridges soap from Ernest and half bottle of schnapps passed on from one of his Norwegian clients, a box of liqueur chocs from his snot-nosed sister and the usual Virginia ham from his Pop. Sweet Fanny Adams from Big Bucks bar a charity card, which I guess is about as much as I can expect there from hereon in - or pending further developments, anyhow…

Friday 27 December

Nothing more in the mail, except -

Good night and good morning, my sweetheart - as I won't be able to say either by 'phone from this prison. I'm longing for an eanum letter - this one has to be eanum as the post leaves in a few minutes. I just can't wait to see you for your party on the 31ˢᵗ - WE all say more and more and more. David

Hugs and kisses to Slipper - my babies have new ribunds and say hello to "Eanum Mister Loo"

- and not a word on what I really wanted to hear about, and with the papers saying Canada's under a couple of feet of new snow I'd guess the whole place has seized up.

Four days to go. With all that time on the poker tables under my belt, I'm never usually the one who blinks first - but then I've never played for stakes like this before...

Monday 30 December

The crack-up. For the first time since I hooked Ernest I went through three packets of Camel non-stop and got so snappy with the staff that Cain took off in tears and Mrs. Ralph followed her out with 'I haven't put the carrots in, milady, but you can lump it or leave it.' I couldn't even bring myself to read what Madame Claire had in store for me, so I dug out my Evangeline Adams horoscope and spent the rest of the day going through it again over and over: *'You will lead a woman's life, Wallis - marrying, divorcing and marrying again, with several emotional crises. Between the ages of 40 and 50 you will win fame and exercise considerable power of some kind relating to a man.'*

Then -

ENTER STAGE LEFT, TLM
Ernest was right beside me when I answered the door and there was no way TLM could get any sort of message across on why he'd shown a day early, so we had to sit there playing dumb for the best part of three hours while we knocked off the carrot-less casserole with the end of the ham, the last of the Christmas pudding and the bottle of cherry brandy Ernest had won in the office draw.

It was TLM who finally broke through the ice.

'Oh, by the way, I've booked a suite at the Kaiserhof in Kitzbuhel for a couple of weeks at the beginning of February, and then I thought it'd be awfully jolly to go on to Budapest for another fortnight - those Magyars really know how to whoop it up on the dance floor, what? So I can count you people in, can I?'

'Oh, David, what a wonderful -'

'I'm very sorry, sir, but it would be quite impossible for me to come as I'm already booked for some very urgent business meetings in New York in February - and even if I wasn't, I could think of better ways of spending my time than fooling around on a couple of wooden planks. But I suppose you're dead set on going, are you, Wallis?'

'Yes, of course - I wouldn't dream of missing such a trip.'

'I see,' he snapped, getting to his feet. 'I was rather hoping that we might have gone to New York together, but obviously I was wrong.'

EXIT ERNEST (with a slam of the door that must have shaken the whole block)

'Did I say something I oughtn't have, darling? Ha, ha! Well, that's one less to take up space on the slopes, what?'

'I guess so.'

'And here's your prezzie.' He felt around in his pocket and handed over a small Cartier jewelry case. Well, the case may have been small, but inside, fixed on a hair clip, was the biggest rock I reckoned I'd ever seen. 'Awfully sorry it's so late, sweetheart, but I didn't really think I should put it in the post, you see.'

'Oh, sure. It's so kind of you, David - it's so beautiful...'

'It's to keep a girl's hair out of her face while she gives a boy an eanum kiss, don't you know? Put it on now.'

'... but I don't really think I can accept it.'

'Not accept it?'

'No, not until, well, you know...'

'Oh, of course, I know what you mean. Silly me, I almost forgot it. Here you are.'

He reached inside his jacket and brought out a wad of paper.

IN THE DIVORCE REGISTRY
IN THE HIGH COURT OF OTTAWA, IN THE STATE
OF ONTARIO
BETWEEN
HIS ROYAL HIGHNESS, EDWARD ALBERT
CHRISTIAN GEORGE ANDREW
PATRICK DAVID PRINCE OF WALES Petitioner

and

MILLICENT MILROY Respondent

223

PETITION FOR ANNULMENT
OF MARRIAGE

ON THE GROUNDS OF PERMANENT SEPARATION

GRANTED

'So that's it, is it?'
'That's it, my sweetheart.'

ADVANCE CENTER STAGE, WALLIS BESSIE WARFIELD-SPENCER-SIMPSON-WINDSOR of Baltimore, USA, future Queen of England, Empress of India and the whole darn'd shooting match - just like the gipsy said!

EDITOR'S POSTCRIPT

20.1.36   King George V dies, succeeded by the Prince of Wales
           as Edward VIII

7.1936   Ribbentrop appointed German Ambassador,
           sends Wallis 17 carnations daily

11.12.36   Edward abdicates the Throne

3.6.37   Entitled now as the Duke of Windsor,
           he marries Wallis Simpson

30.5.38   Ernest Simpson marries Mary Raffray

31.1.03   Newly-released Abdication papers do not include
           'The China File' reputedly compiled by
           Guy Trundle for MI5